Amber's Pony Tales
Books 1 - 3

Little Pearl

The Second Best Pony

Trusting Molly

Amber's Pony Tales Books 1-3 Collection

Little Pearl

The Second Best Pony

Trusting Molly

Print ISBN: 978-1-913953-05-8

eBook ISBN: 978-1-913953-06-5

Contents

Little Pearl

Amber's Pony Tales

Book 1

Author's Note

"Remember me when you ride those 17hh warmbloods and sports horses. Remember me when you are grown and competing in earnest. I may not be the fanciest horse you will ever ride, but I was the best horse I could be when you needed me. Remember me."

~ The first pony's plea, author unknown

Little Pearl (aged 14) and Helen in 1992

This book was written in memory of Little Pearl, my first pony, and to recognise all the other first horses and ponies out there. Those wonderful animals that are quiet, safe and forgiving enough to be our firsts deserve a very special place in our hearts. They put up with the mistakes we make through lack of experience and knowledge and help us to learn. We owe them so much and must always appreciate and honour them.

I have very fond memories of Pearl. She was a stubborn wotsit and had very firm ideas about what she thought was worth doing and what was a waste of time, but she was a good teacher and taught me a lot about *a lot*. Pearl never did anything unless she could see a good reason for it and, like Amber, at first, I felt out of place at shows with the other riders on 'proper' show ponies.

I soon learnt, however, that a pony's value is not really measured by how high it can jump or how fast it can go. A pony's value is measured by the trust placed in it by its rider, by the bond of unspoken communication they share, the feeling of oneness and complete confidence in each other. I was lucky enough to experience this wonderful relationship with Pearl and I will never forget what she gave me.

She wasn't the fastest or the boldest, but she took care of me and became my best friend.

Our ponies are always trying to tell us something if we would only listen. If I had listened sooner, I would have heard Pearl say, "Don't worry. I'll look after you."

Always listen. You don't know what you could be missing.

Little Pearl (aged 27) and Helen in 2005

For my parents who bought Little Pearl
for me and started me on the path
towards sharing my life with the most
wonderful friends anyone could wish
for

– THE HORSES

- One -

Make Believe

"Are you ready Dad? Hurry up or we'll be late!"

"I can't find the car keys!" called the harassed voice of Mr Anderson from the kitchen, where he could be heard rummaging through coat pockets and searching under newspapers and piles of junk mail for the missing keys. Amber flicked her long blonde plait back over her shoulder and checked her watch impatiently. If he didn't find them soon, they would be late for their ride.

Amber Anderson was eleven years old and an only child. She lived with her parents and her pet dog and cat – plus the goldfish Freddy and Felix. The whole family were animal mad, but horses were everyone's favourite. Amber couldn't remember a time when she hadn't been passionate about horses. When she was in infant school, she recalled painting crude pictures of a blob with four legs and proudly telling the teacher it was her pony. She didn't have a pony though, except for the one in her imagination, which wasn't that bad because an imaginary pony can be a perfect pony.

Her imaginary pony had been a gleaming grey mare called Sapphire, inspired by pictures she had seen in a book about Pegasus. They always won show jumping competitions in Amber's garden, where she pretended she was riding to glory against a field of famous competitors she'd seen jumping huge fences at Hickstead and Olympia. What's more, her imaginary pony didn't need to be groomed, mucked out or ridden on cold, rainy days. But even though Sapphire was the perfect pony and provided her with hours of daydreaming fun, Amber always longed for the real thing.

Eventually, on her tenth birthday, her parents decided to grant her wish. The memory of that day still made her smile. She had come down to breakfast in her pyjamas to find her parents sitting at the kitchen table, looking at her over the top of a mound of presents. Often, presents can be more exciting when they are wrapped up than when the contents are revealed, but not these presents. She tore the wrapping off the first gift to reveal a deep blue sweatshirt with a pretty palomino pony emblazoned on the front. The next parcel held a pair of jodhpurs. Amber had started to feel a swell of excitement as she continued unwrapping presents to find a hat covered in a brightly coloured silk, a pair of gloves and some shiny black riding boots. Alight with happiness she had looked hopefully at her parents.

"Your last present couldn't be wrapped," her mother explained. "We've booked you a course of five group and five individual riding lessons at a riding school half an hour from here." She paused to smile at Amber's glowing face. "You'd better get dressed. Your first one is today."

Pine Tree Riding School was set out in the countryside amidst the fells and forestry. As soon as she stepped out of the car and smelled the intoxicating aroma of sweet hay, leather, and horse, Amber knew she was going to love it there. She felt as if she had returned to some long-lost favourite place she hadn't been to for a long time.

Claire – the owner and instructor – led a small, grey pony that reminded her of Sapphire into the yard. He was called Blaze, and according to Claire, was "a nice schoolmaster."

Amber hadn't heard the term 'schoolmaster' before, so Claire explained that the word is used to describe safe, experienced ponies. Amber could only think of old-fashioned school teachers she had seen on TV who threw board rubbers at naughty children or gave them the cane. She was a bit worried about Blaze 'The Schoolmaster'. *"What if I do something wrong?"* she thought. *"Will he buck me off to teach me a lesson?"*

Amber needn't have worried. After being shown how to mount and hold the reins properly, a stable girl led her into an outdoor arena where three other children were waiting on ponies. Next to each pony was a helper who had the pony on a lead rein just like Blaze. Claire explained how to use their legs and hands to encourage the ponies to move forward, change direction and stop.

Amber felt extremely precarious on Blaze's back. He was only twelve hands high, but she felt a long way from the ground. She was glad she had someone there to help her while she got used to the sensation of Blaze's body swaying underneath her as he walked. It was a strange feeling; powerful and helpless at the same time. Amber marvelled at the way Blaze turned when she asked him. She could get him to stop from a very gentle squeeze on the reins and move forward with a little wiggle of her legs. He was very responsive, and she knew that he was reacting to her commands rather than the helper who was really only there for support and encouragement.

Gradually, as the riders became more confident, the helpers unclipped the lead ropes and let them carry on by themselves. Amber was delighted that she managed to get Blaze to walk in a figure of eight all by herself. She became lost in the moment. It was just her and Blaze working together. Amber was so focussed on communicating with the pony, she forgot about everything and everyone else. All too soon the lesson was over, but Amber knew she was hooked.

"I hope you enjoyed it everyone," Claire said cheerfully. She was answered with four nodding heads and lots of "yeah, great," and "brilliant," from the young riders.

"Good," she replied, "next time you'll be having a go at trotting."

Amber had enjoyed her lessons on Blaze, and when she had had all ten, Claire thought she was competent enough to go for a hack out.

Amber enjoyed hacking out much more than the lessons. It was lovely riding through the forest, breathing in the smell of fresh pine, or being blasted by invigorating winds on the open fells. As time went by and she became more experienced, she was able to try different ponies and enjoy canters and gallops with the others, instead of having to go on ahead with the ride leader while the others cantered up behind.

On seeing her joy after every hack, her parents, who had both ridden when they were young, decided to join her every Sunday.

***

"I've found them!" Mr Anderson cheered, running from the kitchen clutching the elusive keys tightly in one hand, as if he feared they might escape and get lost again. "Let's go."

Amber rolled her eyes and chuckled as they dashed down the drive to the car.

"We'll be just in time." She thought to herself, fastening the seatbelt across her chest.

"I wonder who I'll be riding. I know who I want it to be."

With that the car rolled onto the road, heading in the direction of Pine Tree Riding School.

– Two –

Pearl

"Phew! Just in time," Amber sighed in relief. They had arrived at the stables just as the horses and ponies were being led out into the yard, while riders stood around waiting to find out who they were riding. Amber spotted Claire, who was leading a piebald cob out of the barn, and ran straight to her. Claire saw her coming and gave her a knowing smile.

"I know who you're after," she said.

"*Please*," Amber pleaded, her hands meeting in prayer.

"Oh alright, but you really should try other ponies you know. It will help you to improve as a rider."

Amber shrugged, "I know, but I just love her."

"I don't know what it is about that pony that's got you so smitten. No-one else ever asks for her." Claire shook her head and stroked the piebald's nose. "Lisa is holding her and Polly over by the water trough. Tell your dad he can ride Polly today."

Amber told her dad what Claire had said, and they walked together to where Lisa was standing with the ponies. Pine Tree had sixteen horses and ponies; mostly natives and cobs, as they were hardy, sensible and able to carry riders of all shapes and sizes.

Ever since the first time she'd ridden her, Amber's favourite was a black Fell x Welsh pony called Pearl. She was a little under 13 hands high, with a long, flowing mane and tail. Amber adored Pearl's cheeky face and the mischievous eyes that peeped out from under her long forelock. Whenever Amber rode Pearl, the two seemed to click. She didn't understand why, but they seemed to have a special bond that she hadn't felt with the other ponies.

It was a blustery day. The ponies' manes whipped about, and sharp blasts of cold air caused Amber's eyes to water. They walked in single file up to the gate before entering the forest. Tall pine trees stood in neat rows like silent sentinels, guarding the paths and keeping the forest's secrets. As soon as the ponies' feet touched the soft dirt track, they were on their toes, champing on the bits. Amber noticed that her dad had to work hard to keep Polly under control as she side-stepped and tossed her head, trying to get free of his grip on the reins. Polly was a pure Fell pony. She was short legged and stocky but incredibly strong and fast, with amazing stamina. Claire only let experienced riders on Polly. Amber patted Pearl, who was always steady and safe and felt glad she was riding her and not getting her shoulders yanked out of their sockets.

By the time the ride was over and they traipsed back into the yard, Amber's face was numb with cold and spattered with mud from being at the back of the galloping horses. She ran her stirrups up and led Pearl into her stall in the barn. She took off Pearl's saddle and bridle and gave her a good brush all over to remove the sweat and dirt.

"Good girl," she whispered as she brushed. "I hope Claire lets me ride you next week. I don't want to ride any of the others. You're the best, aren't you girl?"

Pearl gave her a little nudge as if to say, "I agree."

Amber dug deep into her pocket and pulled out a carrot she had brought for her favourite companion.

As she closed the stall door behind her, Amber wished for the week to pass quickly so that she could be back riding Pearl again.

***

The following Saturday morning Amber dragged herself out of bed and pulled on her jeans and her favourite green t-shirt, grumpy at the thought of having to go shopping with her mum. She trudged down the stairs and into the kitchen.

Mrs Anderson looked up from the book she was reading and said nonchalantly, "You'll have to get changed dear. You can't go in those good clothes."

"What?" Said Amber, creasing her brow in confusion, "I'm not going to go shopping in my old clothes, am I? I'd look a right sight."

"Ah, but we're not going shopping today," her mother replied, closing her book and standing up, "we're going for a little surprise. Put on your riding clothes."

Amber didn't need telling twice. She'd much rather go riding than shopping any day, but they'd never been on a Saturday before. Wondering what was going on, she changed into her jodhpurs and flew down the stairs, where her parents were both waiting by the door, whispering to each other. As soon as Amber appeared, they abruptly stopped and smiled warmly at her.

"Ready love?" her dad asked. She nodded and followed them out to the car.

"Where are we going?" Amber asked, although she thought she already knew the answer.

"You'll see," replied her mum, tapping her nose with a finger. "Like I said, it's a surprise."

"Well it's obviously a surprise involving ponies," thought Amber to herself, *"and anything to do with ponies is ok with me."*

She settled back in the car watching houses and other cars whiz by in a haze of colour, while butterflies formed in her tummy, tickling her with their delicate wings making her feel both nervous and excited. Oh, what was the surprise going to be? She couldn't wait to find out.

– Three –

Surprise

Finally, they pulled into Pine Tree's car park. Walking into the barn, Amber could see there were only two ponies in the stalls. One was Pearl, and the other was a Fell pony called Honey that her mother liked to ride. This had happened before. One time, her dad had brought her to the stables on a Monday during a school holiday. That was strange as Monday was the ponies' day off – when they all got a day's relaxation in the fields. But on that Monday, there had been two ponies in the barn and Amber had been worried, wondering why things were different. Mr Anderson had laughed and told her that the other horses and ponies were out in the fields, but he had hired two so they could go out together on their own.

It had been great, just the two of them; they'd been able to decide when to trot or canter and could choose where to go instead of having to follow the ride leader. It looked like he'd done the same thing again, but she was wondering why he'd only hired two ponies when all three of them were there.

"Who are you going to ride, Dad?" she asked.

Mr and Mrs Anderson exchanged a knowing look before Mr Anderson answered.

"Well, actually, we haven't hired them... we've *bought* them. Pearl is for you and Honey is for Mum and me so that we can take turns to ride out with you."

Amber didn't quite know what to feel, say or do after that bombshell. She blinked hard, feeling positively queasy. "*Pearl is mine? Pearl is my pony? Is this a dream?"* She couldn't believe it.

"But...it's not even my birthday," she exclaimed weakly, leaning against the wall as if she needed its support to stop her from toppling to the ground.

"Oh, well if you want to wait until your birthday we can tell Claire–"

"*NO!* Of course I don't want to wait," Amber interrupted her mother, "I definitely want her now! Thank you, thank you, thank you. It's just such a surprise and so unexpected and for no reason and…" She had to stop to get her breath back.

"We just thought the time was right. You've proved you're serious by not chickening out on cold, wet days, and it's a good, healthy hobby we can all enjoy," her mum explained.

The three of them stood looking at the ponies – who were happily munching on their hay, completely oblivious to three people standing staring at them – while the idea that they owned these beautiful animals sunk in. After a few moments of thoughtful silence, Mrs Anderson suggested that Amber should go and say hello to her new pony. Amber snapped out of her reverie and practically skipped over to Pearl's stall, marvelling at the fact that she hadn't thought of doing so herself.

A thought suddenly occurred to Amber while she lovingly pulled her fingers through Pearl's long mane, gently easing out tangles and pieces of hay.

"Where are we going to keep them, Dad?" she asked, "Here?"

Mr Anderson, who had been looking at Honey with his wife, came over to Pearl's stall.

"No, not here love. There's a farm just up the road. The farmer's daughter has a horse, and he's agreed to let us have DIY livery. It'll mean we have to come through every day after school to see to them."

"That's okay," Amber replied brightly, "Maybe I'll be able to make friends with the farmer's daughter, and she could come for rides with us."

Her father chuckled, "Maybe dear, but I think it's unlikely. The farmer's daughter is twenty-three, and her horse is a 16.2hh Irish Draught. These two of ours could practically walk under its tummy."

"Oh," said Amber, slightly crestfallen. "Well, never mind."

That night Amber's sleep was brimming with dreams. As her mind sifted and sorted through the day's information, storing it as life-long memories, she relived everything that had happened; from arriving at the farm to meeting Jerry the farmer and turning the ponies out into their new field. When her alarm clock went off, she was smiling in her sleep, leaning on the field gate watching the ponies grazing contentedly with the sun warming their coal black coats. She awoke with a start, feeling irritated that her wonderful dream had been disturbed. It took her a moment to remember that finally, her dream had become a reality. Happiness coursed through her like an electric current and made her feel wide awake. She dressed hurriedly and raced downstairs to see if anyone else was up yet.

***

Amber looked out of the window as they drove past Pine Tree. She could see the girls pushing wheelbarrows or carrying hay nets across the yard. It was strange to pass the car park and carry on up the bumpy track that led to the farm. As their car trundled into the farm yard, the front door of the house opened and a boy of about fourteen emerged, wearing green overalls and eating a slice of toast. He quickly climbed into a tractor and started it up. As he drove past them, he waved. He had the same friendly face, soft blue eyes and wide, smiling mouth as Jerry the farmer.

"He must be the farmer's son," thought Amber to herself, blushing as she waved back at him.

Two black and white collies bounded towards them, wagging their plumy tails and grinning broadly. Amber bent down and stroked their smiling faces. Amber's dog, a golden cocker spaniel called Kasper, viewed the farm dogs suspiciously. She was just about to speak to the dogs when a loud whistle pierced the air and they shot off after the retreating tractor like twin missiles. Kasper jumped and looked after them in surprise. His interest didn't last long though, as usual, and he soon had his nose to the ground again following all the interesting new smells.

With no more distractions, Amber and Mrs Anderson caught the ponies with ease and brought them in from the field.

After Mrs Anderson saddled Honey and Pearl, she checked that all the tack fitted comfortably, then they led the ponies into the yard and mounted. Amber buzzed with excitement. Although she had ridden Pearl many times, this was to be her first ride on her as her own pony.

She looked between Pearl's neat, pricked ears and felt her heart swell. She gave the pony a gentle nudge to walk on. Pearl didn't move a muscle except to sweep her ears back and lay them flat against her head. Amber looked at her mum, who seemed to be having the same trouble with Honey.

"What's wrong with them?" Amber moaned. "Why won't they go?"

"Because…" Mrs Anderson puffed, "neither of these two are used to leading. They're so used to following other horses they don't know how to think for themselves." She dismounted and took the reins over Honey's head. "We're going to have to show them what we want them to do."

With that, she began to lead Honey down the track. As soon as Pearl saw another pony in front of her that she could follow, she flicked her ears forward and sauntered after it as if nothing had happened.

Amber got the feeling that owning a pony would be a little harder than she first thought.

- Four -

An Unexpected Meeting

It had taken them several weeks to be able to get out for a decent ride. Neither pony was willing to lead, nor would they walk side by side. One was always trying to slip in and hide behind the other.

"We must teach them to think for themselves," became Mrs Anderson's motto. "They've got to stop being so dependent on each other."

At first, the rides were terribly hard work. The ponies would stop regularly and refuse to walk past any rock, gate or dandelion for fear that some great monster was lurking behind it, waiting to pounce on them. There was lots of dismounting and dragging as well as sitting, patiently waiting for the stubbornness to pass and for the ponies to give in. They would never let the ponies turn around when they tried or allow them to hide behind each other. Riding out became more of a battle than a pleasure and progress was painfully slow. Amber began to wonder if she had imagined the bond she had with Pearl as the pony tested her patience to the limit.

"This is ridiculous," she whined one day when both ponies had planted themselves at the end of the farm lane and refused to turn right towards the forestry, trying instead to turn left and head back to their former home at Pine Tree.

"They're not getting any better." Amber pulled on her right rein to try and encourage Pearl to turn in the direction they wanted to go, but the pony was having none of it. She shook her head but didn't move. If Pearl couldn't go where she wanted, she wasn't going anywhere at all.

"We have to stick at it and persevere." Mrs Anderson puffed, allowing herself a short rest from encouraging Honey to move forward. "If we are firm and consistent, we will get through to them…at some point."

Eventually, after lots of hard work, Honey and Pearl became a little more confident and would walk alongside each other without seeing monsters in every hedgerow, though Honey still wouldn't put her head past Pearl's shoulder. She remained too nervous to take the lead.

The experience had helped Amber immensely. She had grown into a stronger rider in her battles with Pearl, and she had learnt the art of quiet perseverance, of insisting on obedience and cooperation without losing her temper or using violence. Now, when she asked Pearl to do something, there was no resistance. They were a team who respected each other and could face anything together. It felt good.

**

One day Amber and her mother decided on a ride through the forest. The two ambled along silently, enjoying the cold, fresh air.

Suddenly, they heard the pounding of hooves and a shrill, "look out!" from behind them. Before they had time to turn and see what the fuss was about, a small pony thundered past. It was ridden by a young girl who was frantically tearing at her reins trying to stop her pony's headlong gallop. She disappeared around the corner in a cloud of dust, and the rapid hoof beats receded. Amber and Mrs Anderson exchanged looks of surprise and the ponies snorted to show their displeasure at the sudden shock of the disturbance.

"Phew. I wonder who that was?" Amber exclaimed. "Her pony looked like a *maniac*."

"Yes," agreed Mrs Anderson, "and it looks like she's out on her own. I wouldn't be happy about you riding a loony like that at all, never mind on your own."

They hadn't gone much further when they heard hoof beats again, this time coming towards them. It was the same girl that had just charged past. She trotted back to join them, her chestnut pony tossing its head, and curling its upper lip to reveal long, yellow teeth.

"Hi," the girl said cheerfully. She looked about Amber's age, but she was taller with long legs that hung well below her pony's sides. "I just came back to say sorry for charging past you like that. I didn't mean to, but Flash had taken off and when he goes – I can't stop him, he's so str–"

The last word was lost as Flash snatched the reins and jumped forward, nearly dragging his rider over his head. She quickly recovered and reined him in as he continued to bob about restlessly.

"Sorry," she said.

"He seems a bit of a handful," observed Mrs Anderson, eyeing Flash disdainfully.

"Yes," agreed the girl brightly as she was pulled forward again, "he's a total nutter."

"Don't your parents mind you riding out on such a...er...*lively* pony?" Mrs Anderson chose her words carefully.

"Oh no," the girl replied, "I've been riding since I was three," she beamed with pride.

"Oh," said Mrs Anderson, simply. She didn't think having ridden since the age of three was enough to mean the girl was safe on this pony, but she decided to change the subject.

"Well, this is Amber," she said, indicating her daughter, "and I'm Carol, Amber's mum. We've not had our ponies long. They're kept at Shaw Farm in the village."

"I'm Joanne, and I live on the track just before the farm. You'll ride past my house."

"Oh yes," piped Amber, "we saw the stables and wondered who lived there. We've never seen you about before."

"Well, I don't hack out much," explained Joanne. "I practice jumping in the field most of the time. Obviously they've been too wet to ride on over winter, so we've just gone to a few indoor jumping competitions and Flash has had a bit of a rest. I've got to start doing something with him now though to get him fit again."

Amber thought Flash looked fit enough. He was revving himself up again, grabbing the reins and threatening to leap forward.

"I'll have to go now. The big hill is coming up and Flash will take off again. Maybe we could ride out together sometime? I don't do it much 'cause there's no-one to go with. It would be better to have some company." Joanne just about got her sentence finished before their track reached the bottom of the forestry hill. Flash gave a mighty fly buck and launched himself into the air as if he was clearing an imaginary jump. He used the force of the leap to propel himself into a powerful gallop and was away up the hill like a streak of lightning, his hoofbeats reverberating through the valley.

Honey and Pearl tossed their heads and quickened their step, but made no attempt to go after him.

"Well, there's one thing for certain," said Mrs Anderson, "if Joanne wants to ride with us, she'll have to learn to slow that lunatic down. These two will never keep up with him."

- Five -

♞

An Unusual Invitation

After their brief meeting, whenever the Andersons drove past Joanne's house on their way to the farm, Amber would call in and ask if she was riding with them. At first, they didn't get to talk with Joanne much as she was always fighting to hang on to Flash as he jogged, snatched, bucked and leapt, or galloped off, leaving them behind.

Flash would wind himself up like a tightly coiled spring until eventually he would just explode from walk into a flat-out gallop. There was nothing Joanne could do to stop him except wait until he decided he wanted to be stopped, and then she would trot back and re-join them until the next time. Amber couldn't believe how Flash could go from nothing to full-speed in the blink of an eye. She decided that Joanne's pony could be compared to a Ferrari, while Honey and Pearl were more like Ford Fiestas.

Gradually, after a number of hair-raising rides for Joanne, Flash began to calm down slightly. He would still champ on his bit and toss his head around, and when they started to trot, he would crab step sideways and get upset because he couldn't keep up with the Fell ponies' smart trotting pace. But the bolting eventually decreased until it stopped almost completely. After a couple of weeks of being exposed to the Fells' calming influence, he finally managed to walk up the forestry hill.

"It's much better now Flash doesn't take off all the time, isn't it?" remarked Amber as she and Joanne were out on their own one day, and finally able to have a conversation.

"He's probably just worked out that there's no point rushing 'cause your ponies are so slow," Joanne laughed.

Amber wasn't sure if she was joking or if she was having a subtle dig at the Fellies. She scrutinised Joanne's face for clues to reveal what she was thinking, but Joanne quickly changed the subject.

"The season will be starting soon," she said, "I can't wait. I really want to do well this year as it will be my last year on Flash."

Amber was puzzled, "What's the season?" she asked, "And what do you mean, it's your last year on Flash?"

Joanne explained that 'the season' referred to the season of outdoor competitions which started on Easter Monday and finished at the end of September.

"I'm getting taller, and soon I'll be too big to ride him. I'll need a 14.2hh next year," she beamed, excited at the thought of a new pony.

"What will happen to Flash then?" Asked Amber, feeling quite alarmed. She had never thought of 'growing out' of a pony like you do with clothes and shoes. After all, her dad wasn't short, and he rode

Honey, who was nearly 14hh, without looking particularly under-horsed.

"Oh, he'll go to Matthew, so he can start competing properly. He'll never win anything on Sam."

Matthew was Joanne's eight-year-old brother. Amber had seen him in the yard sitting on a bucket, looking gloomy while his mother brushed a small, hairy bay cob-type pony. She couldn't imagine Matthew riding Flash in a million years.

"What sort of things do you do at shows?" Amber enquired.

"Oh, there's all sorts," Joanne replied enthusiastically. "There's gymkhanas where you can do show jumping, games and handy pony...oh, and equitation if you want. Then there's hunter trials, horse trials, tetrathlons, camp and Member's Cup. I like hunter trials best."

Amber's head was reeling. *What on earth was a 'handy pony'? What's equitation and what was it... trakalons?*

41

She asked Joanne, who then went into tremendous detail describing the difference between show jumping and cross-country, what Pony Club games were and what you did at Member's Cup.

"I just tend to do jumping and games. I only do dressage at Member's Cup 'cause you have to. It's so boring, trotting around in circles, and Flash is useless at it – he usually ends up jumping out of the arena."

"Er…what's dressage?" Asked Amber, whose head continued to swim with information.

"It's supposed to be a test of the horse's obedience to the rider," sighed Joanne, sounding suddenly bored, "and you have to plait up and learn a sequence of movements that you remember and perform inside a rectangle on the ground. It's dead boring, so I don't do it."

Amber was just about to ask why it was boring to have an obedient pony, when Joanne had an idea and exclaimed, "Hey, we'll be putting our jumps out soon now the fields are drying up again. Why don't you come and have a go?"

"Yeah…sure," Amber agreed politely, but inside she felt nervous. She'd never jumped before and didn't know the first thing about it.

And neither did Pearl.

- Six -

Jumping

Amber had had an awful day at school. First, she hadn't brought her science homework in because she couldn't find it. Stig had been asleep on top of it and she hadn't thought to look under the cat.

Stig was so called because a lady had found him and another young kitten inside a cardboard box on a rubbish dump. She had heard them mewing and opened the box to investigate. One of the kittens was a small tabby female that she decided to keep for herself. The other kitten was a black and white male, and the lady – although desperately sorry for both of them – knew she could only keep one. She had taken the male kitten into the Post Office where Mrs Anderson had worked at the time and asked if anyone was interested in him. Mrs Anderson took one look at the tiny, helpless creature and agreed to take him there and then. When she brought him home and explained the situation, there had only been one name for him: Stig, after the book, *Stig of the Dump*, as Carol Anderson was a bit of a bookworm.

That tiny, half-starved kitten had grown into a large, sleek adult cat. He was now so enormous that it was quite possible for him to lie on a sheet of paper and completely hide it from view.

After getting in trouble for her lack of homework, her mind was too busy fretting about it to concentrate during the mental maths test, and she'd only got 9 out of 15. To top it all off, Miss Burton had given them maths homework.

Maths was Amber's most dreaded lesson, and she was quite convinced that she was subjected to enough of it at school without having to do it at home as well. Teachers were evil, she decided.

Now that home time was approaching, the knot that had been growing inside her all day began to twist and coil, feeling like it was both crushing and tickling her insides at the same time. In less than two hours she would be having her first attempt at jumping in front of her parents and Joanne, and probably Joanne's parents too. Amber clutched her stomach as a sudden wave of nausea washed over her.

***

At the farm she brushed Pearl half-heartedly as the knot in her stomach continued to tighten. Mr Anderson had brought her a sandwich as usual, to keep her hunger at bay until tea-time, but she had been unable to eat it, feeling that the knot had extended to her throat.

Mrs Anderson laughed at her daughter, "Amber, you look white. You don't have to do this you know, nobody's forcing you." She placed a reassuring hand on her daughter's shoulder.

But Amber felt that she did have to do it. She didn't want Joanne thinking she was afraid, and her new friend's remark about the Fell ponies being slow still rankled her. She wanted to prove that Pearl could jump. And so, with grim determination, she saddled up, mounted, and rode down the lane to Joanne's house.

Flash and Sam were tied outside the stables. Joanne was fiddling with Flash's bridle which jingled and jangled like Santa's sleigh, while her mum was extracting twigs and leaves from Sam's bushy black mane. Joanne's curly-haired brother Matthew sat on a low wall examining an ant that was scurrying across his hand. He and Sam seemed to be a well-matched pair, as they both looked rather shaggy and a bit grubby. Joanne noticed Mrs Anderson opening the gate into the yard and ran over to greet them.

"Hi," she called out cheerfully. "We're nearly ready. Mum's just finishing de-tangling Sam."

She pointed to a small gate beyond the stables. "The jumps are just in there. Go in and warm-up. We won't be a minute."

On the other side of the gate was a small paddock; 'the jumping field' as Joanne called it. A number of jumps were spread around. Some were brightly coloured with white wings like those on TV, while others were made from old oil drums or lemonade crates.

Amber was quietly trotting Pearl around the perimeter of the field when Joanne and Matthew appeared through the gate. Flash practically exploded into the field despite all the straps and chains he had around his face and neck, while Sam plodded in sensibly behind.

Mrs Jones, Joanne's mum, introduced herself to Amber's parents and explained that her husband was at work. Then she addressed Joanne, who was explaining to Amber that Flash was wearing a martingale, grackle noseband, pelham and curb chain because he was even stronger at jumping than he was at hacking out.

"Right, Jo, take Flash round so Amber can see how it's done."

Joanne started to gather up her reins and Flash jumped as if he'd been electrocuted.

"And remember to take it *easy*. He isn't fully fit yet," Mrs Jones called out.

Flash side-stepped around the field in what Amber thought was supposed to be a trot, crunching his bit and foaming at the mouth. Then Joanne turned him towards a low cross pole.

Flash tossed his head back showing his wild white eyes. Then he rocked back on his haunches, grabbed the bit from Joanne's hands and raced madly towards the tiny jump.

When he got there, he devoured the jump in one massive stride then careered around the field for a few laps before he settled back to an uneasy, eye-rolling jog.

Amber looked at her parents, who appeared to be quite unnerved by Flash's unconventional approach to jumping. Mrs Jones had also noticed their worried expression.

"Perhaps Flash isn't the best example to watch," she offered. "He's much better over bigger jumps – he has to think about them, so it slows him down a bit. *You* go around Matthew and let Amber see how Sam does it."

Matthew flapped his short legs against Sam's sides and the pony walked obediently into the middle of the field. A little more leg flapping and they moved up to a steady trot.

Matthew trotted around the field a couple of times before giving a click with his tongue. Sam drifted easily into a slow, loping canter. As they came around the corner, Matthew pointed Sam at the same cross pole that Joanne had jumped on Flash. As Sam saw the jump his ears pricked, but he did not increase his pace. Two strides out, Matthew gathered his reins and leant forward slightly as Sam picked up his feathery feet and hopped neatly over the jump. They cantered steadily away before coming back to a walk with just a gentle feel down the reins.

Amber couldn't believe how differently the two ponies approached jumping. She much preferred Sam's way; he was steady, but he looked as if he enjoyed himself. To her, it seemed that Flash didn't really like jumping. He approached a fence as if someone was chasing him with a cattle prod and he had to escape, whereas Sam looked completely happy.

Watching Sam, Amber relaxed, forgetting why she was there. Her stomach gave a sudden lurch as Mrs Jones' voice interrupted her thoughts.

"Well done Matthew. That was lovely. Now then Amber, how do you feel about having a go?"

– Seven –

The Green-Eyed Monster

That evening Amber put her homework and P.E kit into her bag ready for school the next day. Afterwards, she had a long bubble bath and got into bed with a *PONY* magazine, but she could not concentrate. The words blurred and swam in front of her eyes as her mind went back over the events of the day. She could still feel everyone's eyes on her following Mrs Jones' invitation to try Pearl over the jumps.

She decided to follow Matthew's example by allowing Pearl to trot around the field to warm-up. She used the time to try and remember all that Claire had taught her in her lessons; keep the hands still, shoulders back, head up, heels down, seat light, correct diagonal. But with five pairs of eyes following her every move, she began to get incredibly nervous. Eventually, after several laps around the field, Amber braced herself and turned Pearl around the corner towards the jump.

She clicked her tongue, sat down and put her leg on, but Pearl did not canter. In fact, she seemed to be slowing down. Someone shouted something that she didn't hear clearly but knew instinctively that it was 'kick on', or something similar. She kicked and tried to encourage Pearl verbally, but as they reached the point in front of the jump where they should have been taking off, Pearl ground to a halt and stopped dead in front of the poles. There was a moment's silence and Amber felt the heat in her cheeks, going redder still at the thought that everyone could see her humiliation.

"Not to worry dear," came Mrs Jones' buoyant voice. "Neither of you have done it before. Don't be put off by these two," she inclined her head back towards Matthew and Joanne. "They've been doing it for years. You just need to practice."

Mrs Jones patted Amber's leg. She gave Pearl – who hadn't budged from her position in front of the jump – a rub between the eyes and smoothed her forelock over the little white star on her face. Then she showed Amber how to shorten her stirrups for better balance and how to get into the jumping position.

"This is so you don't get left behind." She explained patiently. "When the horse jumps you have to follow the movement and allow her to stretch over the jump."

She mimed pushing her hands forward and her bottom out. Amber giggled at the sight of Mrs Jones squatting in the middle of the field, looking as if she were sitting on an invisible toilet simultaneously reading an invisible newspaper.

"Watch," she said, straightening up.

Matthew leapt over the little cross pole again to demonstrate the jumping position, and once more Sam popped over the jump and cantered away happily. Amber was instructed to follow on after Sam and let him give her a lead over the jump next time around.

She nudged Pearl with her heels and the pony grudgingly moved forward.

Sam sailed easily over the poles again, but despite Amber's best attempts, Pearl stopped dead in her tracks again. Hot tears stung Amber's eyes and her cheeks burned with the shame of failure.

Why was Pearl being so difficult? It was only a tiny, stupid, insignificant jump after all. It didn't even require her to make an effort. Amber knew Pearl was just being plain stubborn as she had shown on many occasions that if she didn't want to do something, then she wouldn't... not without a fight.

Amber was filled with a mixture of embarrassment, frustration and determination. Her nerves had gone, to be replaced with a fiery resolve that Pearl would get over the jump that evening, even if she had to wait until the stars came out.

It took four more attempts, the last with Mr Anderson running behind her, waving his arms and shouting various unpleasant words at Pearl before she resigned herself to the fact that she was going to have to go over this obstacle in front of her one way or another.

At first it looked as if she was going to stick with her preferred option of refusing the jump. Amber felt her heart drop, but although she was exhausted, she summoned a growl from the pit of her stomach and so, on the sixth attempt, Pearl decided it might be easier to simply go over it.

Everyone was so pleased and fed up in equal measures that they all cheered loudly when Pearl landed over her first jump. Amber's embarrassment was replaced by a surge of adrenalin, and she was determined to have a few more goes before leaving to ensure it wasn't just a one-off.

All the other jumps in the field had been put up, and Joanne and Flash tore over them. It was true that Flash jumped better over higher fences, but his style was still rather hair-raising as he bounced sideways, holding himself stiffly erect with his head and neck bolt upright, until the last stride where he snatched the reins and hurtled at the jump. As he took off, he stretched out beautifully and flowed gracefully over the fence like molten copper. Amber watched them enviously.

Concentrating once more on the tiny cross pole, Amber made Pearl go over it another three times before she called it a night. Weary from the effort, she leaned forward and patted Pearl's sweaty neck.

"Thank you Mrs Jones," she puffed breathlessly.

"Oh, call me Lou," said Mrs Jones kindly, waving a hand in the air. "You're very welcome. You did really well for a first try. Well done."

Trudging back up the track to the farm, Mrs Anderson asked Amber if she had enjoyed her first taste of jumping.

Amber looked down into her mother's face. She didn't know what to say, so she merely shrugged her shoulders. The truth was that a silent battle of emotions was taking place within her. She remembered Sapphire, the imaginary pony, on whom she had competed and won. She thought about how thrilled she had felt when she found out that Pearl had been bought for her, and how all her dreams of winning trophies and rosettes had been forgotten in her happiness at having her own pony.

Then she pictured Flash soaring mightily over the fences in the field. Amber looked between Pearl's neat black ears and found herself wishing that she wasn't riding little, fat, stubborn Pearl, but a beautiful, athletic show jumper with spirit and elegance.

An uncomfortable lump formed in her throat as guilt swelled inside her.

"Don't think like that," she chided herself, *"give her a chance. Like Mrs Jones said; a bit of practice and she could easily improve."*

She tried to cheer up and be more hopeful, but there was another little voice in her head that kept creeping in and whispering to her in snide tones, *"Get real. Face the truth. Pearl will never be a jumper, and you know it. Best get used to it."* The voice paused. *"Maybe Pearl isn't the pony for you after all."*

- Eight -

Second Attempt

Amber did not look forward to going riding over the following few days. Usually, she was itching for school to finish so that she could get to Shaw Farm, catch the ponies, give them a brush and set off for a ride.

Now, as the bell went for home time, Amber felt her stomach twist as if a large boulder had just slipped into it and landed with a thud. The heavy weight remained as she climbed into the car next to Mr Anderson.

"Good day at school?" he enquired brightly while handing her a sandwich.

Amber nodded and muttered something incomprehensible before taking a bite of the sandwich and chewing it slowly so that she couldn't join in any conversation her dad might have been thinking of starting. They drove to the farm in silence.

Bumping over the pot-holed farm track past Joanne's house, they noticed Joanne leading Flash out of the paddock. Mr Anderson stopped the car and wound his window down. Leaning out slightly he called up to her. "Are you riding today Joanne?"

She waved and replied, "yeah, stop off for me on your way past."

Flash was his usual self on the ride. He now went slowly enough to allow the riders to have a conversation, but only because he crab-stepped and jogged on the spot, habitually wrenching the reins from his rider.

Joanne ignored him and carried on talking, despite the fact that she kept getting yanked out of the saddle and was constantly having to gather her reins.

"Don't fee- OW, FLASH. Don't feel too disappointed about the other day," she said to Amber, sensing that her friend was rather quiet and solemn-faced, "lots of ponies get confused when they're first introduced to jumping. *You* have to educate her."

Amber gave Joanne a puzzled look.

"I mean practice. I'm sure you can get her moving a bit faster than granny speed!" she laughed. "The more you do it, the better she'll get."

Amber tried to ignore the pessimistic voice inside her saying, *"No she won't,"* and agreed to have another go at jumping.

"It'll have to be Saturday though," gasped Joanne, jabbing Flash in the mouth after a particularly violent snatch, "we've got a competition on Sunday."

They were nearing the bottom of the forestry hill and Flash was prancing and head shaking with deliberate exaggeration. He no longer bolted up the hill from the very bottom, but when he was in a mood like this, he would only wait for so long before he snapped.

"I'd better let him have a gallop," shouted Joanne over her shoulder, "he's so hyped up he's going to go inside out if I don't let him go. See you at the top!" She let her reins slip fractionally and that was all Flash needed. He pounded up the hill like a rocket, sending a shower of pebbles up behind him.

Amber, who was cantering along in Flash's wake next to her dad on Honey, got hit in the face by a pebble flying up from the pony's hind feet. It struck her cheek with such force that she cried out from the sharp, sudden pain. Before she could stop it, that little voice was back again, complaining. *"Oh Pearl, why do you have to be so slow?"*

***

Saturday was pleasantly warm and sunny and Amber felt her spirits lift. Determined to shut out the negative voice in her head, she told herself that Pearl would be much better today now that she knew what to do. And, as Joanne had said, she needed to take small steps and not expect too much.

62

Mr Anderson was at work, so her mother brought her to the farm and was helping to tack Pearl up. She looked at her daughter, small worry lines creasing her brow.

"Now dear," she began quietly, "you won't get…er… *upset* if Pearl doesn't go well today will you?" She stopped adjusting the bridle and looked over Pearl's neck to see Amber, who was pulling up the girth. "Remember, horses are like people, and they have their likes and dislikes. You don't like maths, and maybe Pearl doesn't like jumping…" her voice trailed away.

"I'm glad you're being *so* encouraging," replied Amber sarcastically without looking up from the girth.

"Hey now, no need for that attitude. I'm not trying to put you off," Mrs Anderson said quickly, "I'm just trying to prepare you for…well, you know. Pearl has been a trekking pony all her life. She's not used to all this…we never bought her as a jumping pony," she trailed off, mumbling the final words to herself.

The jumps were set as cross poles or low straight poles. Matthew was warming up on Sam when Amber and Mrs Anderson arrived.   •

They noticed that Joanne was missing. Flash's eager chestnut head looked out of his stable door, his white blaze gleaming in the sunlight. His nostrils quivered, and he stood stock still, like a frozen statue before emitting an ear-splitting scream. A low answering whinny came from the jumping field which seemed to act as a key to unlock Flash from his stupor. The erratic pony began frantically weaving and banging the door with his chest and legs. Joanne came scurrying from the tack room and shut the top door of the stable so that Flash could no longer see out into the yard.

"Just keep *quiet* in there," she shouted through the door at him. "Oh hi," she said, noticing that Amber had arrived, "Matthew's practising. He's doing ten and under solo jumping tomorrow. I'm not doing anything with him today," she inclined her head towards the now quiet stable that held Flash, "he'll have his fun tomorrow."

Amber entered the jumping paddock where Matthew, watched by Mrs Jones, had begun to go over the small fences. She saw Amber and waved but did not come across to speak as she was shouting advice to Matthew. "Remember to use your legs! Don't look *at* the jump, look *beyond* it," she said while thrusting her finger in the air to indicate where Matthew should be looking.

Amber shortened her stirrups as she had been shown and let Pearl trot and canter a few circuits of the field before she began. She knew Joanne and her own mother were watching her, but this time it didn't make her feel nervous. Instead Amber was determined to prove that she and Pearl could jump.

She turned her pony towards the cross pole that had caused her so much trouble on their last attempt. Pearl broke from canter back into a trot but Amber dug her heels into Pearl's sides and gave her a smart tap on the shoulder with her riding crop. Surprised,

Pearl quickened her pace and jumped the fence from a fast trot.

"Try some others," Joanne called from where she was watching with Mrs Anderson, who was looking rather relieved.

Amber headed again for the same cross pole and jumped it easily from a steady trot. On landing, she steered Pearl round to the left, towards a low straight pole balanced on top of two lemonade crates. Again, Pearl tried to back off, but another quick dig from Amber's heels sent her up to and over the jump. She continued around the field and jumped every fence in both directions.

Pearl had never got faster than a trot, but it had been hard work keeping her going. Amber gave Pearl a hearty pat. She knew the jumps were only tiny, but still, it was progress, and she was pleased. Feelings of warmth and love towards her pony flooded back into her again, washing away every negative and nasty thought she'd recently had. She could see everyone was smiling at her as she rode towards the edge of the field.

"That was great Amber," said Mrs Jones warmly, "you rode really positively. Well done."

Amber glowed with pride at such praise.

Joanne ran ahead to open the gate, her short blonde pony-tail bouncing as she moved.

As Amber rode through the gate, an idea popped into Joanne's head. "I know," she exclaimed. "Why don't you come and watch me at the show tomorrow? You'll see what goes on and how everything works in case you ever want to have a go yourself. Will you come?"

Amber looked at her mother, who shrugged her shoulders. She knew that meant it was up to her to choose. Amber thought for a second then said, "yeah we'll come. It's the field on Watch Hill isn't it?"

Joanne nodded and grinned, "See you there then!"

- Nine -

A Decision is Made

The show field was already packed with brightly coloured horseboxes and an assortment of trailers by the time Amber and her parents arrived. Children on ponies of all shapes and sizes were milling around, from absolute tots on their little Shetlands who were being led around by harassed looking mums or dads, to children of about her own age – mostly girls – on ponies that looked lean, fit and purposeful.

Amber scanned the grounds trying to catch a glimpse of the Jones'. They walked further into the hubbub, carefully keeping out of the way of children who were cantering their ponies in all directions, apparently not looking where they were going.

Eventually, Amber spotted the Jones' bright green lorry and signalled to her parents to follow her.

Flash was tied up to the side of the lorry. The restless pony swung his body relentlessly from one side to another, trying to get a better look at Sam, who stood a little way off.

Matthew was mounted, and Mrs Jones was giving his boots a last-minute polish. Beside her stood a man that Amber had never seen before. She assumed he was Joanne's father due to him having curly brown hair like Matthew's.

Her parents shook hands with him as Mrs Jones introduced everyone.

"Jo's around somewhere dear," Mrs Jones stated, still fervently rubbing Matthew's boots, "she went to put her entries in and she's probably found someone to talk to. She'll be back soon to watch Matthew. His class starts in five minutes."

As if suddenly realising that five minutes was not a very long time, Mrs Jones stopped rubbing and started fussing about finding the practice jump and getting ready.

The show jumping arena contained ten professional looking jumps with white wings and brightly coloured poles – like the ones at Hickstead, only considerably smaller. At the moment the jumps were about 65cm and ready for Matthew's class, which was for children who were ten years or under and could ride the course without assistance.

Amber and her parents positioned themselves where they had a good view of all the jumps. She caught a glimpse of Matthew and Sam neatly jumping the practice fence amongst the other competitors in his class who were also collecting in the warm-up area. Mr and Mrs Jones were standing near the entrance and Amber could see that Joanne was with them, standing next to a girl with long dark hair.

The first competitor entered the arena. The commentator announced her and the pony's name and blew a whistle. The girl, who only looked about seven years old was riding a pretty skewbald pony. She pushed her riding hat up out of her eyes and began. She did very well, just having one pole off the second part of the double.

"That's four faults for Katie," the commentator boomed. Several more competitors had their turn and Amber watched intently, paying close attention to the commentator's scoring of each round. So far, she had learnt that a competitor got four faults for a knockdown, or if the pony refused a jump. If the pony refused twice, the competitor was eliminated, which meant they had to leave the ring without completing their round.

"Next into the arena can we have Matthew Jones riding Samurai."

Amber watched with greater interest as Matthew rode into the arena. On the other side, the Jones' watched anxiously. Matthew looked twice the size he usually did encased in his body protector, but he still sat quietly and in balance with his pony as he cantered around the jumps, waiting for the whistle to signal the start of his round.

The whistle sounded, and Matthew brought Sam round to the first jump, which was comprised of green and yellow poles. Sam hopped over happily with a swish of his tail and continued around the remaining nine jumps in the same easy, steady rhythm ensuring a nice clear round for Matthew.

At the end of the class there were five clear rounds. The commentator announced that there would now be a jump-off over a shortened course to decide the placings.

There was a pause while some other adults came into the arena and put some of the jumps up a hole. The commentator then told the competitors the jump-off course and asked the first rider, Jennifer Scott riding Oakbank Delta Dream, to come into the arena.

Amber watched as the competitors tackled the jump-off in a completely different way to the first round. In the jump-off they had to go as fast as possible, as the clear round with the fastest time won. She was amazed to see how some of the ponies were able to land after a jump and, without even taking a stride, could turn immediately to cut inside and take a shortened route to the next jump. She was in awe of the riding abilities of these young children and wondered if she would ever get to their level.

Matthew was the last competitor to go in the class. Three out of the previous four riders had gone clear so the class was going to be won on time. Would Matthew go for it she wondered? As it turned out, he did not push Sam for speed, but because his pony was so steady and balanced, he was one of the few that could turn immediately on landing and take much shorter routes around the course.

When his time was called out at the end of his round, he had come second. Everyone clapped as the five riders lined up to be presented with their rosettes and cantered away in a lap of honour around the arena. The Jones' whooped and clapped for their son as he made his way around.

The next jumping class was for ponies under 12.2hh and neither Matthew nor Joanne were in that class. The Andersons went to congratulate Matthew and find out when Joanne would be riding.

At the lorry, Sam was untacked and tucking into his hay net while Joanne was in the process of putting something into Flash's shoes. The dark-haired girl who had been with Joanne earlier was sitting on the steps into the lorry.

"Haven't you seen studs before?" she said, looking directly at Amber, who had her head on one side, trying to see what Joanne was doing.

"No, what are they for?" asked Amber.

The girl rolled her eyes and tossed her dark hair. Getting up off the step she paused to say, "See you later," to Joanne before stalking off.

Surprised by the girl's rudeness, Amber asked Joanne who she was.

"That's Elisha Templeton," replied Joanne, still fiddling with Flash's feet, "she does British Showjumping. She's got fabulous ponies."

"Oh right," replied Amber, feeling stupid for not knowing what studs or British Showjumping were, but not wanting to ask. "Are you riding soon?"

"I'm in the next class. Are you going to watch?" Joanne asked.

"Yeah, good luck,"

"Thanks."

Joanne's class was for ponies of 13.2hh or under. Flash was eligible as he was 13hh. The jumps were now higher than they had been for Matthew's class and brightly coloured fillers had been placed under some of the jumps.

As the competitors took their turn in the ring, Amber noticed that all the ponies seemed to enjoy what they were doing. They were all forward going and some of them leapt and pulled just like Flash. The riders coped expertly with their exuberant mounts.

"And the next competitor is Joanne Jones on Flash Dance."

As soon as Flash heard the whistle, he put his head down and seized the bit. Joanne managed to get him pointing at the first fence before he bolted towards it, clearing it with an unnecessarily high jump. He continued around the full course in this manner with Joanne just about managing to steer him, although there were a couple of moments where it looked like he was going to come out over the arena rope. Somehow, she managed to keep him on the correct course and they got a clear round. Fortunately, there were several clears, so she could have a rest before she had to deal with the jump-off.

Amber watched the jump-off, which was won by a pony that jumped slowly like Sam. It made the most incredible twists and turns and finished with a much faster time than the other ponies. Joanne had come fourth as Flash was just so difficult to control that she had to go wide around all the fences and lost a lot of time, even though Flash was flying.

She congratulated Joanne as she left the ring with her green rosette, but her friend seemed sullen and disappointed, and rode past without speaking, her eyes hard and her jaw set.

Amber couldn't believe that she'd been snubbed so rudely and just stared at the retreating back of Joanne as she rode moodily back to the lorry.

She felt a hand on her shoulder which gently steered her away. "Come on love, best to leave her to sulk in private." Tearing her eyes away from Joanne who had now dismounted and flung her riding hat angrily on the floor, she went with her parents to look at the other events taking place.

They saw the handy pony competition, where the riders had to manoeuvre their ponies through various scary obstacles like flapping bags and spinning windmills and were timed on how fast they completed the obstacles. They also saw some of the Pony Club games, which looked like great fun. The riders galloped through bending poles, and the ponies were clearly aware that they were racing each other.

When the time came to leave and they were walking back to the car, Amber thought back to the jumping classes she had watched that had both been won by slower, more sensible ponies. She felt hope brewing inside.

"Can I join the Pony Club?" she asked.

Her parents exchanged worried looks. "Are you sure dear? I mean, you can if you want to, certainly, but…well, Pearl is not like the ponies you've seen here today. She might do ok, but she'll never be a winner."

Amber was undeterred. "I'm sure," she said decisively. "Let's join today."

– Jen –

Pony Club Rally

The District Commissioner of the Blakefield branch of the Pony Club was a large, jolly woman with a ruddy, weather worn complexion. She was delighted to have a new member and told Amber and her parents that their next gymkhana would take place in two weeks. In the meantime, there was a rally on Thursday evening.

"We do insist that all members take part in at least two ridden rallies a year," she informed them eloquently. "We also have stable management rallies in winter. The dress code for rallies is light coloured jodhpurs, a shirt, Pony Club tie and the Pony Club sweatshirt. Obviously, we will order these for you but you won't have them by Thursday. You can come in normal riding wear, so long as it is safe, for your first rally."

"But Mrs..." Amber started but blushed and stopped as she'd forgotten her name.

"Mrs Best, dear, Mrs Best," she reminded her heartily.

"We don't have a horsebox or anything to get here," explained Amber, worrying that her failure to attend the rally would incur the wrath of this bombastic woman.

"We'll ask Lou. Their horsebox is stalled to carry three so they'll have room if they're coming," suggested Mr Anderson quickly.

"Splendid," boomed Mrs Best. "Well, I'll look forward to seeing you there then."

***

Joanne and Matthew were going to the rally and it was arranged that Pearl would be taken to the Pony Club field in their lorry while the Andersons followed in their car.

When Amber led Pearl into the Jones' yard to load her into their lorry, she noticed that Flash and Sam both wore long, padded boots on their legs. A bandage covered their tails and both ponies wore a light rug, despite the warmth of the day. Pearl was completely bare, wearing only her headcollar. Amber felt a tug of worry. She hadn't known that ponies wore such things to protect them from bumps and rubs while they were travelling.

"Not to worry," Mrs Jones reassured her when she mentioned it. "She'll be alright for this journey. We'll take it nice and steady, but you might want to think about getting her some travelling gear for future trips."

With Flash and Sam both loaded in the box, came Pearl's turn. Amber felt nervous as she stepped up the ramp in case Pearl refused to go in. Unused to being asked to walk up a steep ramp into a dark, unknown space, the pony hesitated and gave a deep uncertain snort. Amber didn't rush her. She let her sniff the ramp and patted her neck to soothe her.

Reassured, Pearl soon followed Amber like a lamb and took her place in the end stall beside Sam.

**

The rally took place at the same field as the gymkhana. As they tacked up, Amber noticed how smart everyone looked in their cream jodhpurs and the red Blakefield Pony Club sweater. She felt quite out of place in her black jodhpurs and plain green sweatshirt.

Joanne and Matthew seemed to know exactly what to do and trotted off to join the riders that were circling in different corners of the field.

There were four groups moving around; from the smallest lead rein children to the fourth group which was made up of older teenagers, who were mostly riding impressively large and powerful horses. Matthew had joined the second group that contained young riders who could ride independently, while Joanne had gone to the third group, where the riders were older and the ponies generally bigger than those in Matthew's group.

Amber noticed that Joanne was riding around next to Elisha, the girl with the 'fabulous ponies' who had been with her on Sunday. Elisha's pony was an athletic, long-legged and slender-necked mahogany bay. It was bigger than Flash and walked with a regal air, arching its neck and stepping delicately with dainty feet.

Amber mounted and rode over to join Joanne and Elisha. Everyone in that group seemed to be from about ten to thirteen years old so she assumed she would also be with them. However, when the instructor saw that Amber had joined the ride, she quietly went over to her and explained that the groups were organised by ability and experience as well as age. As Amber was not very experienced, the instructor kindly told her that she would be in the second group.

Amber turned Pearl away with her eyes to the ground and her cheeks flushing pink. As she left, Amber heard Elisha laugh and say, "As if she could be in this group on *that*."

Hurt and humiliated, Amber joined the second group, where she was by far the oldest rider. She didn't have time to feel sorry for herself for very long though as the young, enthusiastic instructor had them line up ready to go.

Amber soon found herself swinging her body around the saddle and sitting backwards so that she was looking down at Pearl's tail instead of through her ears. She practised mounting and dismounting from both sides and lying back along Pearl's spine while seated in the saddle. Next, some small jumps were put out in a line called a 'bounce'. That meant that as soon as the pony landed over one fence, it would have to jump again without taking a stride. The children rode down the line of jumps one after another with Pearl at the end so that she could follow the others.

Amber found herself laughing with joy as Pearl hopped over the jumps, one after another. At the end of the rally, she'd had so much fun that she completely forgot about Elisha's spitefulness. She couldn't wait to get to her first show.

– Eleven –

Amber's First Show

Show day arrived quickly, and Amber fizzed with excitement as they loaded the car with all the new things they had bought: a show jacket, body protector, leather jodhpur boots, gloves and a numnah and girth for Pearl.

Amber swelled with pride when she saw how smart her pony looked. She had long protective boots over her legs and a thick tail guard bulged against the bushy tail it encased.

Mr Anderson had managed to borrow a small pony sized trailer from a friend at work who only used it occasionally to move a few sheep from one field to another, so they were going by themselves to the gymkhana.

"It's no good putting on people's hospitality," Mr Anderson had said. "If we're going to do this, we'll do it ourselves instead of relying on other people."

As they drove off down the track, the trailer bumping along behind them, and Honey squealing from the field after her departed companion, Amber began to feel a strange sensation in her stomach. She definitely wanted to go but she couldn't help but worry about what was to come in the day ahead.

"I do hope Pearl behaves," she thought, silently staring out of the window.

***

The show field looked just as it had last time, with rows of stationary horseboxes and trailers. Mr Anderson found a space and parked. They unloaded Pearl and tied her to the side of the trailer while her boots were removed. Pearl had a look round as if trying to work out where she was, then with a sigh, put her head down to graze.

Leaving Mr Anderson to keep an eye on her, Amber and her mother went to find out where to place the entries.

They soon found a small caravan with a queue of people waiting outside the door and looking at a board next to the caravan. Getting nearer, they could see that the board held the schedule for the day.

Scanning the classes that were available Mrs Anderson said, "Well you might as well have a go at everything while you're here. The jumping doesn't start for a bit, and they're only doing the lead rein equitation at the moment, so you can do that while you're waiting for the jumping to start. It'll get Pearl warmed up."

Amber, who had been reading the schedule closely, said in a slightly panicked voice, "I don't think I'll be doing the jumping. The class Pearl should be in is 85cm. There's no way she'll jump that. They're the fences Joanne was doing on Flash last time."

"Oh…well, that's a shame. We'll ask about that."

They got in the queue to place their entries and when it was their turn, Mrs Anderson placed Amber's entries for equitation, handy pony and games.

"Rider's name?" asked the lady who was taking the entries.

"Amber Anderson," her mum replied.

"And what's the pony's name?"

"Pearl," Mrs Anderson replied.

"No, *wait*," Amber interrupted frantically. "People don't call the pony by its home name at shows, they have a special name for when they are competing," she cried, remembering some of the names from last week. "We need a show name for Pearl."

"How about Little Pearl?" suggested Mrs Anderson, "that's what they used to call her at the riding school remember? Claire had that old retired horse called Pearl as well. They used to call them Big Pearl and Little Pearl so that they knew which one was which. Little Pearl sounds nice don't you think?"

"Yeah, that's what she'll be called." Amber told the lady. "Put her down as Little Pearl."

Before they paid the entry fee, Mrs Anderson explained that Amber was worried about the height of the jumps in her class and asked if there was anything else she could do.

"She could go in the class before that; the 12.2hh class. The jumps will be a maximum height of 75cm but she will have to go hors concours, or non-competitively, which just means that she won't get a rosette if she gets placed," explained the entry lady.

They agreed that this was a better idea, even though 75cm was still bigger than Pearl had jumped before.

Amber's first event was equitation. There were nine riders in the class, most of whom had obviously spent a long time preparing. The ponies' coats gleamed, their manes and tails were neatly plaited and the riders themselves were immaculate. Amber had cleaned all Pearl's tack the night before, given her a thorough groom and polished her own boots until she could see her reflection in them. But Amber worried that she would be told off by the judge, who was already sweeping her critical eye over the riders as they walked around her in a circle, for not having her pony plaited.

The riders were soon asked to move up into a trot and then canter as the judge continued to scrutinise them. Presently, they were asked to line up alongside each other. The judge walked in front, examining each of them for cleanliness. This judge was very particular. She looked at the underside of the stirrups, the inside of the bridle straps and reins, under the saddle flaps and she even lifted the ponies' feet to check they were clean. Amber was glad she had picked out and oiled Pearl's hooves.

As the judge finally approached her, Amber felt that she had to apologise for not being plaited up.

"Doesn't really apply in your case though," the judge muttered absently as she ran her fingers through Pearl's mane searching for tangles. Finding none, she moved to Pearl's head to inspect her bridle, "since your pony is a native breed. Natives should always be shown in their natural state." She gave

Pearl one last look over then walked away, scribbling something on her clipboard.

Next, each rider had to perform an individual show. The judge asked them to show walk, trot and canter on both reins, and if they could manage it, a rein back or turn on the forehand. Amber was glad she was last in line as she was able to watch and see what everyone else did. She noticed how they all saluted the judge at the end of their show and made a mental note to remember to do so.

The fifth pony to come out of the line to do its show was the beautiful mahogany bay ridden by the acidic Elisha. Amber hadn't noticed that she was in the class. Her pony behaved impeccably. Just like at the rally, it stepped daintily, skimming over the ground with slender legs and an arched neck. The rein back at the end was perfect; the pony was completely obedient and didn't object once. She saluted smartly and smiled winningly at the judge before moving back into line. Elisha then looked down to where she and Pearl stood, and Amber was sure she smirked at her before disappearing back into the line of ponies.

Finally, as the penultimate pony completed its show and returned to its place beside Pearl, it was Amber's turn. Remembering everything she had watched, she nudged Pearl to move forward. Pearl, who had been standing idle for several minutes and had started to doze, moved forward sluggishly. Amber had to give her a hearty thump with the leg the judge couldn't see to wake her up. Pearl walked and trotted amiably on both reins, but she really could not be bothered to canter. Amber worked furiously to get her going, but each time she managed only a couple of strides before falling back into a trot. Out of the corner of her eye, she could make out the blurred figure of Elisha sitting pretty on her perfect pony. She could imagine the look on her face as she watched Amber's show.

Red-faced and flustered, Amber decided to give up on the canter and get out of everyone's sight. She quickly performed her rein back, which Pearl managed with only a trace of resistance, saluted and hurried back into the line feeling hot and bothered.

Amber followed on as the other riders went back into a circle and rode around while the judge looked at her clipboard then glanced up to look at the riders again. She started calling numbers out. Amber noticed that Elisha was first to be called out. She took her place at the head of the line with a smug look on her face. Other numbers were called out for second place, third, fourth, and fifth until there was only one place left with four riders still remaining.

"Eighty-Seven," called the judge.

It took Amber a moment to realise that was her number – she had been given a square of white cardboard with the number in black when she placed her entries, and was now wearing it on her back, tied around her waist with a piece of black string.

As she took her place at the end of the line, a huge grin spread over her face. She couldn't believe she had been placed. She looked at the three riders left behind. They all looked upset. Amber felt for them but at the same time was glad she wasn't amongst them. She was going to get her first rosette!

The judge moved down the line, presenting rosettes and commenting on the riders' performances. When she got to Amber, she handed her a lovely purple rosette and said, "Congratulations, you ride very well, and you have nice light hands. You could do with using more seat and leg as your pony lacks impulsion."

"Right, thanks," replied Amber, not quite sure what she meant, but sure it was about Pearl's reluctance to canter.

Everyone was delighted with Pearl's first rosette, but Amber was still worried about the challenge ahead.

Joanne congratulated Amber and offered to walk the course with her. As they walked around the fences, Amber found that she was too nervous to concentrate on the advice.

"You need to come deep into the corner for this one to get a good stride," Joanne explained while pointing to the fence. "This is a two-stride double, but if Pearl is only trotting, you'll need to kick on, so she can get out over the second part."

Amber wasn't really listening to Joanne's words of advice. She just wanted to concentrate on the order of the jumps so she didn't go the wrong way. The first two or three weren't so intimidating, but some of the others worried her a bit as they were far bigger than what they had practised in Joanne's field.

They left the arena and Amber found her father, who was holding Pearl in the collecting ring. She got on apprehensivley and began to warm-up. The practice jump was a low cross pole and other competitors were already going over it on their ponies. Amber moved in behind the others and followed them. She rode Pearl up to the jump and to her relief, she popped over it without hesitation.

"That's it, Pearl, we can do this," she laughed, giving her pony an appreciative pat on the neck.

As Amber turned and approached for another go at the practice fence, she saw that it had quickly been put up to a much higher straight pole. She kicked on and hoped for the best as they approached the jump. Pearl's ears pricked forward as if she too had noticed the new proportions of the fence in front of her. Deciding that it was far too big, Pearl dug her heels in and stopped. Time seemed to slow as she skidded slightly and knocked the pole with her chest so that it fell down on the ground in front of them.

"Oh *great*," a voice came from behind. A small boy on a bouncy bay pony had been about to follow Amber over the jump. He nearly crashed into the back of her as he struggled to pull his pony out of the way.

"Dad, come and put this jump up!" the boy demanded.

By the time the fence had been erected and people were happily flying over it once again, the commentator had announced the start of the class. Amber was mortified to discover that she was the first to go.

"And this is our first competitor," said the commentator, in his sonorous amplified voice.

"Amber Anderson riding Little Pearl. This competitor is riding hors concours."

The whistle blew. Amber gathered up her reins and gave Pearl a tap on the shoulder to show her that she meant business. Pearl cantered down the long side of the arena but upon seeing the first jump, fell back to a trot. Amber kicked hard and shouted at Pearl as they approached the jump. "Go *on*," she pleaded. Pearl slowed down and was practically ambling, but just as Amber thought that was it, Pearl managed to jump the fence from a near standstill. She jumped the next two fences in a similar fashion with Amber encouraging her in every way possible. The fourth jump was a bit bigger than the previous three and had a little spread on it. She tried hard but Pearl just seemed to run out of steam in front of it.

Amber turned, fully aware that another stop would mean elimination.

"Get over it," she commanded through gritted teeth as they came round for the second attempt.

Amber kicked madly all the way up to the fence, and sensing that her rider was feeling particularly determined, Pearl gathered herself and jumped.

Had she been going faster, everything would have been fine, but as she had taken the jump as slowly as usual, she caught the back pole of the spread with her hind feet. As she landed, the pole came down between her back legs and caused her to stumble. Amber lost her balance and was thrown forward onto Pearl's neck. She sat up quickly and tried to gather her reins back up but with the next fence so close and with her rider's reins too long, and her position out of balance, Pearl seized the opportunity to duck past the jump. The whistle blew immediately.

"I'm sorry, but that's elimination. You may jump a fence on your way out."

Feeling absolutely dismal, Amber turned Pearl towards the first fence again, which she, of course, jumped sweetly.

As she left the collecting ring, she noticed Joanne standing with Elisha. They had seen everything.

"Fancy getting eliminated over jumps as small as those. How pathetic is *that*?" Elisha laughed.

Without waiting to hear Joanne's reply, she fled back to the trailer in tears.

***

"That's it. I'm *done*. I've had enough of this lazy pony and these stuck-up girls," Amber sobbed.

But her mother was stern. "You can't just throw in the towel because your first attempt wasn't successful. You *know* Pearl has never jumped; you're expecting too much of her, and yourself." Mrs Anderson turned to Pearl and placed a comforting hand between her eyes. "If you really want to do it, you need to start having jumping lessons because you've both got a lot to learn. Neither of you can rely on the other because neither of you knows what you're doing. You can look forward to learning together. Now, you're entered for games and handy pony and I've paid, so you're going to cheer up and take part."

Amber was quite surprised that her parents weren't more sympathetic, but she knew, deep down that her mother's words of wisdom were true. It was wrong to blame Pearl. She *did* need to have lessons again if she was serious about it. Feeling slightly less despondent, they all made their way down to the next event.

***

Handy pony turned out to be Pearl's forte. While the flapping tape, large cuddly toys, plastic bags to walk over and various other frightening obstacles caused endless problems to many competitors' ponies, they were nothing to Pearl, the suddenly fearless pony. The endless hours they'd spent at home teaching the ponies to think for themselves and be more independent had clearly paid off as she didn't bat an eyelid at anything on the course and Amber finished everything easily.

"That was an excellent time," said the organiser, looking at his stopwatch. "I can't tell you what position you're in, but let's just say you're doing well." He winked and smiled. "That's a very brave pony you've got there. One of the best I've seen all day. Well done."

Amber smiled. This was one event where Pearl could shine.

Games could not begin for Amber's age group yet because the other riders entered for it were still jumping. While they were waiting, the Andersons left Pearl grazing by the trailer, took their sandwiches and went to watch the jumping.

The 13.2hh class had finished when they got there but they could see Joanne in the collecting ring. Flash was sporting a yellow rosette showing that she had come third. The jumps now looked very imposing as the 14.2hh class was about to start.

They watched in awe as the ponies thundered around the arena, soaring gracefully over the jumps. There were a few poles down and the odd refusal, but no-one was eliminated.

Amber watched with resentment as Elisha steered two ponies to clear rounds. One was the dark bay she had already seen. He was called 'North

Quest' and jumped as neatly and politely as he went on the flat. The other was a burning chestnut, much darker and brighter than Flash; like smouldering flames in a fire; and was called 'Red Revenge'. He was not as pretty as North Quest, having a sturdy, powerful body and a bigger, more robust head, but he was bold and precise and produced an energetic clear round.

The jump-off, which was very exciting, was won by Elisha on Red Revenge. He was fast and strong, but also able to make quick turns and jump from tricky angles that meant he was well in the lead. North Quest was slower but perfectly obedient, so he lost no ground and was also able to cut in and save time. He came in third. Amber didn't know any of the other riders who were placed.

The last class was Open Pony, where any size of pony could enter. But as the jumps were now over a metre, there were only five entries. Elisha was riding her two ponies, and Joanne was going in on Flash. Alongside them were two other girls; one on a 14.2hh that had been placed in the previous round and the other on a 13.2hh. As the class wasn't going to take very long, the Andersons went back to the trailer to get Pearl ready for games.

Open Pony finished with Elisha in the first two positions and Joanne third. Now that all the pony jumping had finished, the riders began to assemble for games. Joanne was there and to Amber's dismay, Elisha also turned up on the chestnut pony. There were three other riders, all of whom were riding spirited looking ponies.

The riders lined up for the first race: bending. The starter's flag went up and all eyes watched intently as riders sat poised in the saddle and ponies fidgeted with excitement. The flag fell, and five ponies spurted from the start line straight into a flat-out gallop through the line of bending poles.

Pearl did not move as the flag fell.

Amber kicked and shouted desperately, but Pearl could only be roused into her usual steady trot. By the time she reached the top bending pole, all the other ponies had finished.

The next two races, flag and mug, went just as the first had. The other ponies seemed to be watching the starter's flag and leapt off the start line as soon as it fell. Pearl, on the other hand, did everything at her own pace. She was deadly accurate and Amber never missed a flag or a mug, but she finished considerably later than everyone else. As they waited to get their rosettes, Elisha pursed her lips and gave Amber a pitying look.

"Aww, you haven't had a very good day, have you?" she mocked.

"It's only her first time," said Joanne, seeing the colour rising in Amber's face.

"It wouldn't matter if it were her hundredth time on *that* thing," she said, turning her nose up at Pearl. "She'll never do anything on that...whatever it is. I don't think it's even purebred."

A silent scream rose in Amber's throat. She tried desperately to think of something witty and cutting to say to this horrid person in front of her, but she could think of nothing. She felt the threat of tears rising in her eyes, and not wanting Elisha to see that she'd made her cry, turned and went back to the trailer without waiting for her rosette.

"Leave her alone Elisha," Joanne told her friend quietly, looking after Amber's slumped form as she rode away.

Elisha smiled to herself and said nothing.

- Twelve -

Elisha's Challenge

Amber burned with disappointment. It didn't matter that she won the handy pony; Pearl still felt like a failure. As a result, the Andersons decided that she wouldn't compete again for the rest of the season until Member's Cup. Instead, she was to attend rallies and start having regular lessons again, focusing particularly on jumping.

***

It felt strange to be back at Pine Tree now that Pearl belonged to her.

Claire was a good teacher; patient but unrelenting. Amber had expected to be jumping straight away but Claire said there was a lot to do before they could even think about jumps. Amber felt completely dispirited when, for weeks, she had to practise walking around the arena in a two-point seat. Then she had to do it in trot. At first, she couldn't hold herself in position for more than a few seconds without flopping back into the saddle but as her strength and balance improved, so did her position. Next, they worked on Pearl's canter transition and on keeping her going. Claire made Amber repeat each aspect of the lesson over and over until it was perfect. At the end of an hour, her muscles ached all over from the effort of coaxing Pearl to work hard.

Although the lessons were demanding for both girl and pony, they were beginning to pay off. Amber now had a much more secure seat and lower leg position. Pearl still had her own unique way of slowing right down in front of a fence before jumping it, but they were now managing full courses of 75cm, including doubles. Amber was delighted with Pearl and itching to get to Member's Cup and show Elisha what they could do. Mrs Best had told them the jumps for her age group at Member's Cup would be 75 to 80cm and Amber felt confident that they could now get round the course.

Member's Cup was still three weeks away, however, and was the last event of the season. For the coming weekend, a fun ride had been organised for the members in the countryside near where Mrs Best lived, and Amber was looking forward to the day.

***

Sunday arrived, dull and moody after a stormy Saturday night. The clouds were low and dark, but it was dry. Amber made sure she dressed warmly in her waterproof jacket. It looked like they might be in for some heavy downpours.

When they arrived at the venue, Amber was given a reflective tabard and a sheet of paper with the directions for the ride.

"You needn't worry too much about these," the lady flustered, trying to stop directions flying away in the wind, "everybody will go around in twos or threes, and the route is marked clearly with tape, so you can't get lost."

Amber put on her tabard, mounted and went to find Joanne. To her dismay, she found her friend sitting on Flash right next to Elisha on her chestnut pony.

"Oh no, not her again," Amber groaned inwardly. Feeling like a bucket of ice had just entered her stomach, she rode over to join them.

"Oh no, I don't *think* so," Elisha spat as Amber joined them. "You are *not* coming with us."

Amber looked at Joanne.

"I said I'd ride with her," replied Joanne meekly. "I didn't know you were coming."

"Well I'm here, and I'm *not* riding with her. She'll totally spoil the day on that tortoise." She looked down her nose at Pearl and grimaced.

Joanne looked towards Amber and shrugged her shoulders. "Sorry," she said simply, her eyes to the ground.

Amber was speechless. She couldn't believe Joanne would treat her like this; that she would bow so subserviently to malicious Elisha.

"Thanks, *friend*," Amber said coldly, emphasising the last word to let Joanne know exactly how she felt. Joanne blushed and kept her eyes down.

Amber turned Pearl, rode away and stood on her own, fighting back the tears that threatened to come once more.

Just as she was regaining her composure but wondering what she was going to do, Mrs Best bounded over.

"Now then, now then," she proclaimed cheerfully, "what's this? A rider sitting on her own, and our new girl too. Is nobody looking after you?"

"I…I thought I was riding with Joanne, but Elisha won't let me go with them." Amber sniffed, valiantly keeping the tears back.

"Oh, I say. She won't will she, little madam. I'd like to know when she became the leader of this Pony

Club." Mrs Best's ruddy face turned deep crimson as she thundered over towards Elisha.

Amber wasn't exactly sure what Mrs Best said to Elisha as she kept out of the way, but there was a lot of shouting and finger wagging going on.

Mrs Best came storming back to Amber, trembling and agitated and told her to go and join the two girls. Joanne looked sheepish and rather ashamed, while Elisha shot her a murderous glance and muttered something again about the ride being spoiled. Amber pretended not to hear – but it hurt.

The riders set out in twos and threes down a grassy track and through an open gate. Mrs Best's husband acted as the starter and was setting the riders off at five-minute intervals so that everyone didn't end up in a dangerously large clump. Amber's group ended up being the last one to start out, giving Elisha another reason to scowl.

They set off in total silence, downhill towards the woods. The track came to an end at an open field but the way was blocked by a gate. There was nobody there to open it for them.

"You can do the gate," snapped Elisha. "These two won't stand still so you might as well make yourself useful."

Without speaking, Amber steered her pony over to the gate. Pearl stood quietly while she released the catch and pushed it open. After everyone walked through, Amber closed the gate quickly and efficiently. The fact that she had managed the gate so well only seemed to antagonise Elisha more.

"Let's have a race over this field," she challenged, "to see who's fastest between Flash and Rocky. I bet Flash can't beat Rocky. I bet he doesn't even come close." She seemed to have fallen out with Joanne now and was provoking her so-called friend by insulting her pony. Amber knew exactly how that felt.

Joanne, perfectly confident in Flash's speed, accepted the challenge. Without waiting for further discussion, Elisha jabbed her pony sharply with her heels and he plunged into a gallop. Flash didn't need to be told – as soon as he saw the other chestnut pony racing away from him, he followed in hot pursuit. Amber went after them in a canter, but the field was long and also inclined steeply uphill. She knew Pearl would be tired by the time they got halfway, sooner if she pushed her too fast. She looked up to see the two battling ponies were over half way up. Amber was pleased to see that Flash was winning.

Suddenly a tremendous roar erupted from the sky as an RAF jet on a low flying exercise came streaking out from the ominously dark clouds. It thundered over them and disappeared just as quickly as it had come, an ear-splitting roar resonating in its wake. The unexpected arrival of the jet did not concern Pearl. She flicked her ears back in annoyance at the nerve-jangling sound, but that was her only reaction.

But unlike the rock steady Pearl, the two ponies still galloping up the hill were both completely terrified by the jet and bolted in panic, increasing their pace to a blistering speed. Amber watched incredulously as Flash and Rocky, racing each other and racing from their own terror, vanished from sight over the brow of the hill at breakneck speed. At that moment, the clouds burst, and a torrential downpour began.

"Well this is just great," thought Amber urging Pearl to trot faster, worried that she might become separated from her companions.

As she reached the top of the hill and found that it fell away just as steeply on the other side, Amber had to screw her eyes up against the sheet of rain to try and see into the distance. She blinked and shook her head as the image in front of her cleared. Something was lying at the bottom of the hill.

It was Flash.

There was no sign of Joanne, Elisha or Rocky.

- Thirteen -

999

For a moment Amber couldn't move. She just sat there at the top of the hill, peering through the rain in disbelief at Flash's prone form.

Then it hit her – she had to do something. She spurred Pearl on and they slithered downwards.

The hill was slippery and thick with mud, but Pearl never faltered. How many times had she scolded her pony for being lazy? At that moment, she was incredibly grateful for her slow and steady companion.

Feeling sick with shock she jumped off Pearl and ran to where Flash lay. As she got nearer, she could see there was a barbed wire fence at the bottom of the hill. The riders' route was clearly marked as turning right and following the fence along the field, but as Flash had been going so fast down the hill, he had been unable to stop or turn. He'd had no choice but to try and jump over the razor-sharp wire. Amber could see from the deep skid marks that he had tried to slow down to set himself up to jump but had slid on the rain-slicked ground as he took off. Consequently, he hadn't been able to make the height and had gone through the fence rather than over it. Now he lay tangled in wire where he had fallen.

Scrambling over the broken fence, she was repulsed to find an arm sticking out from under the pony's body. Amber gasped as she realised that Joanne was trapped. Panic rushed through her body. *"What should I do? And where on earth are Elisha and Rocky?"* Physically forcing herself to keep calm, she moved around the pony, frantically trying to work out how to save her friend.

Joanne's head and shoulders were clear of the pony, but her arms were pinned under him. Amber swooped down on her friend and shouted at her to wake up. Joanne didn't respond. Amber remembered from safety classes that she had to leave her where she was as she might have damaged her spine and it could be made worse by movement. On the other hand, if Joanne was left lying under Flash's immense weight, she could easily be crushed. Making a decision and hoping it was the right one, Amber bent down and put her hands under Joanne's shoulders. She grabbed her and pulled with all her might, but it wasn't enough. Joanne remained pinned.

She couldn't get Joanne out from under Flash and her actions had made things worse. The movement of pulling at Joanne had disturbed him.

At first it was just a gentle, testing movement, but then, as Flash realised he was caught in the wire, he started to thrash around, wildly trying to free himself. Knowing that he risked doing himself and Joanne a serious injury, Amber went to his head and tried to calm him down, but it was to no avail. Flash was in a blind panic and she could do nothing to appease him.

Hysteria threatened to take over. But then Pearl approached and rubbed her muzzle against Flash. His eyes rolled back to look at her and he stilled, though his chest was heaving and he was foaming at the mouth. Amber had never seen anything so shocking and upsetting.

She wracked her brains to think what she could do. She needed to get help, she had to find Elisha, and she had to keep Flash calm before the situation got even worse. She pushed her hand into her jacket pocket, searching frantically for her phone.

Nothing.

She checked the other pocket. "No, no, *no*," she wailed as an image of her phone lying on the back seat of the car pinged into her memory. Of all the days to forget to bring it with her!

Forcing her brain to think, she remembered that both Joanne and Elisha had their phones with them. She couldn't get at Joanne's, so she had to find Elisha and use her phone to get help. The next problem was how to go about it.

Amber knew that if she took Pearl away, Flash would be distraught, and he could tear himself badly on the wire if he continued to struggle. She knew she would have to go on foot.

With her mind made up, Amber put her plan into action immediately. Pearl was still close by, but to ensure she didn't wander off, Amber tied her reins to Flash's. She prayed that having Pearl with him would placate him until help arrived.

Amber placed a trembling hand on her pony's velvet soft nose. "Pearl, I need you to stay here and keep him calm. Can you do that for me?"

The pony stared intently into her eyes and Amber knew that she understood.

Amber hugged her tight. "I'll be back soon – I promise."

It seemed to work. Now that Flash knew that Pearl was close to him, he had quietened down. Feeling weighed down by her sodden jacket, she set off along the marked route to try and find Elisha.

As she followed the fence, all sorts of thoughts raced through her mind. *"Will I find Elisha? Is she safe? What's going to happen to Flash and Joanne?"* She couldn't believe all this was happening.

"Amber!"

She turned in all directions, sure that she had heard something.

"Amber, *help*."

This time she knew she had heard her name. She stopped and looked around but could see nothing through the rain.

"Where are you?" she called into the wind.

"Over *here*. Look right."

Amber turned and saw Elisha, bedraggled and ghostly white, crawling towards her. Without asking what had happened, she ran towards her and demanded her phone.

Elisha handed it over, all her self-assurance now gone. Amber dialled 999, her fingers trembling. "Ambulance please."

Elisha crumpled onto the floor crying and wailing, "Oh, what's happened? It's all my fault."

Amber described what had happened and where they were as best as she could from the sheet of very wet directions to the operator, while Elisha listened and snivelled even louder. Next, Amber phoned the police and told them there was a loose pony somewhere in the area and there had been an accident. Finally, she flicked through Elisha's contacts list and found her dad's number. She relayed the message to him quickly and hung up before he asked to speak to Elisha. She wanted to get back to Flash and Joanne as quickly as possible.

She positioned herself on Elisha's left side so that the injured girl could lean on her and take the weight off her injured right leg. As they hobbled back towards Joanne and the ponies, Amber found out that Elisha had been able to turn Rocky as they went careering over the top of the hill, but had been unable to stop him. They had gone some way at a mad gallop when she had grasped her right rein with both hands and proceeded to haul on it with the idea of turning the pony in circles of decreasing size until he slowed down and stopped. Unfortunately, Rocky had been going so fast that the sudden change of pressure on his mouth and the shift of his rider's weight had unbalanced him and he had fallen briefly. No harm had come to him and he got up immediately and galloped off into the distance, but as he stood up, he had stepped on Elisha's right ankle. It was now extremely painful and she was convinced it was broken.

By the time Elisha told her part of the story, they had arrived back at the broken fence where Flash still lay, with Pearl standing beside him. The stricken chestnut pony seemed to be keeping his eye on her as she stood, for all the world acting like his guardian angel. As Pearl heard the girls' voices coming towards her, she turned her head and whinnied, glad Amber had returned, but not moving from her position.

When Elisha saw the horrific sight of the tangled, bleeding pony lying upon the unconscious Joanne, she fell to the floor, sobbing uncontrollably.

"This is all my fault!" she wailed, "if we hadn't been racing this would never have happened."

"But there was the jet," Amber found herself trying to ease Elisha's guilt.

"I know, but we were already going too fast. If I hadn't suggested that we race we would probably have been able to pull them up before they got to the top of the hill."

"Maybe," sighed Amber. She left Elisha weeping on the wet grass and went to stroke her pony.

As she rubbed Pearl's nose and buried her face in her pony's long, wet mane, she considered how lucky she was. She could have been lying at the bottom of this hill with a crushing weight suffocating her, or she could have a broken ankle and a missing pony. Instead, she had steadfast, sensible Pearl. And in that moment, Amber finally realised what it was that had always made her love Pearl so much: even though she wasn't perfect, Amber could trust her.

Cold as she was, Amber's whole body flushed again with shame at the times when she had envied

Elisha and Joanne and their ponies, the times she had resented Pearl and wished she had a faster, more exciting pony.

"I'm sorry," she whispered into Pearl's ear, wrapping her arms around her neck. Pearl nuzzled her gently, silently offering her forgiveness.

Amber had never loved Pearl more than she did at that moment.

– Fourteen –

Good News

After what seemed like an age, a Land Rover rumbled over the top of the hill and bumped down to meet them. It had hardly stopped when Mrs Best, Mr Templeton, Mrs Jones and Mr Anderson flung the doors open and ran to their children.

Amber was enveloped in a tight hug from her father when she heard Mrs Jones' scream as she discovered her daughter trapped under the fallen pony.

"Joanne, oh God *Joanne!*" Mrs Best pulled the frantic mother away, telling her the ambulance was on its way and there was nothing she could do.

Elisha's dad ran to get a wire cutter from the back of the Land Rover, before leaning down to assess the damage. Flash's legs were covered in blood and parts of the wire had become embedded deep in the pony's skin as a result of his struggling. As soon as Elisha's dad attempted to remove the wire, Flash began to struggle again, his eyes widening in pain.

Mr Anderson rushed to help. He placed his hands on the pony's neck and gently stroked him. "Alright Flash, easy boy. We'll get you free."

Pearl, who had remained like a rock throughout the entire ordeal, placed her face close to Flash's. Their silent communication soothed the frightened pony. Flash placed his head back on the ground and lay still, breathing slowly.

Swearing quietly under his breath, Mr Templeton was able to slowly cut the wire before gently prising it away from the pony's legs.

The sound of sirens suddenly flooded the area and flashing lights appeared at the top of the hill. Seconds later paramedics were descending the steep slope carrying a stretcher and a large first-aid kit.

Working patiently, the two dads had managed to free Flash from the wire and were encouraging him to his feet. He stood up shakily, a mass of blood and wide-open gashes, trembling furiously with pain and shock. Mrs Best produced an old blanket from the back of the car and threw it over him.

Now that they could gain access to Joanne, the paramedics examined her quickly. Without removing her riding hat, they fitted a neck brace and swiftly got her onto the stretcher, away up the hill and into the ambulance. Mrs Jones followed alongside, holding her daughter's hand.

As the sirens blared and the ambulance sped away, Mrs Best took charge. "Right," she bellowed, "Elisha can't walk, and she seems to be in shock. I'll take her to casualty."

"No," Elisha roared. "What about Rocky? I won't leave until I know he's safe."

"Right, Mr Templeton, you come with me. I'll drop you off at my house on the way to the hospital and you can start the search for Rocky."

Mr Templeton nodded at the woman's instructions and the three of them left in the Land Rover.

Amber, Mr Anderson, and the ponies were left alone in the rain. Suddenly realising how exhausted she was, Amber began to sway against her dad. He helped her back into the saddle and tried to lead them back the way they had come. They only managed a few steps before it became clear that poor Flash couldn't be expected to walk anywhere with his injuries.

"It's not looking good Amber, I'll get your mother to bring the trailer," he said, taking out his phone and dialling first his wife's number, then the vet's office.

***

Joanne had been seriously injured. She had three broken ribs, a broken collarbone and wrist, a dislocated hip and significant muscle swelling from the overwhelming weight of the pony. The doctors said it was just as well the paramedics acted fast, or her injuries could have been life-threatening. Amber could not go and see her for two weeks as she was heavily concussed which made her very sick and confused.

After what seemed like years, the Andersons received a telephone call from Mrs Jones to say that her daughter was now up to seeing visitors, although she would have to stay in the hospital for some time yet.

Joanne was propped up in bed when Amber and her parents entered. She smiled at them and politely accepted the box of chocolates they had brought, but she looked very weak and fragile.

At first, Amber didn't know what to say to Joanne, who looked so awful and yet was being so brave about the situation. She also remembered how Joanne hadn't stuck-up for her against Elisha's taunts and wondered if they were still friends.

"How's Flash?" Amber managed to say after the pleasantries were over.

"Mum says he's pretty bad. He's cut into a tendon in one of his front legs and he's completely lame. The vet says he should come sound again but he might need at least a years' rest." She paused. "If he heals up ok and comes sound, we'll be selling him."

Amber was shocked at her matter of fact tone.

"Mum and Dad don't think he's safe for Matthew," Joanne said.

"Oh," mumbled Amber, unsure how Joanne felt about Flash being sold or whether he was safe for any child.

"But anyway," said Joanne, brightening up, "if it wasn't for you, Flash wouldn't be alive, and neither would I probably."

"What? What do you mean?" stuttered Amber in astonishment.

"Well, the vet said that if Flash hadn't lain as quietly as he did, he could easily have cut through an artery and bled to death, right there on top of me. I believe I've got you…and Pearl to thank for that."

Amber proudly remembered Pearl's untroubled steady assistance. Not only had she calmed Flash, but she'd also prevented Amber from panicking which had enabled her to compose herself and think clearly. She couldn't have done any of it without her wonderful pony's help.

"And the doctors said that if I had come into hospital much later, they might not have been able to save me. I had a lot of internal bleeding," she explained casually, "so if you hadn't got on to the ambulance so quickly…well… you know."

Amber sat in stunned silence, unable to believe what she was hearing. Joanne rambled on while Amber just sat and listened.

"Elisha broke her ankle. Just like her to get off lightly," she added testily. "The police found Rocky, heading right for the main road, thanks to you again, and he's absolutely fine, so I suppose all's well that ends well."

Amber couldn't believe she could be so positive about the accident when she could have been killed.

"No point dwelling on it I suppose," she thought.

***

Member's Cup was cancelled that year in light of the accident, and although Amber respected the decision, she was disappointed that people would not see Pearl's new and improved jumping ability.

"There's always next year," she mused, *"at least I know how wonderful Pearl is, even if nobody else does."*

The following morning, Amber sauntered wearily into the kitchen and saw a copy of the local newspaper on the table. She poured herself a glass of orange juice and pulled the paper towards her. Her eyes widened, and she slowly put her juice down before she spilled it. There on the front page was a picture of her and Pearl, taken at the farm earlier that year, under the main headline:

YOUNG GIRL'S BRAVERY SAVES FRIEND

The article chronicled all the events of the ride and the subsequent race against time to get help. The article finished with a quote that was taken from

Amber's parents. *"When have they been speaking to journalists?"* she wondered.

> 'We are very proud of our daughter. She kept cool in a very difficult situation and did extremely well to raise the alarm as quickly as she did. We would like to add that our daughter's pony, Pearl, also played a vital role in the rescue operation and it couldn't have been done without both of them. They are both heroines.'

Amber read the article with her mouth hanging open. They had done it. Her wonderful parents had ensured she had got her wish. Now, not only did they know how special Pearl was; everybody would know.

Everybody.

Acknowledgements

I want to thank my parents for introducing me to the joy of books and stories. Some of my earliest memories involve bedtime stories, with *The Velveteen Rabbit*, *Peace at Last* and *The Troublesome Pig* being some of my favourites, followed by an introduction to fairy tales. Apparently, I knew every book off-by-heart and would tell my parents off if they tried to skip a page!

Mum and Dad have been with me every step of the way with the horses. I have been blessed to have two parents who shared my hobby, and my childhood was filled with hacking out and going to shows with them. Special mention to my dad who used to stay up after a night shift to take me to shows and who, now aged 70, still rides out with me, mucks out and drives me to competitions and training events. Thanks Dad, you're one in a million!

One of the hardest things about being a writer is having the belief in yourself that your work is good enough and that people will want to read it. Thanks must go to some of the early readers of the first version of *Little Pearl*: Sophie, Amber, Georgia and Maia, for their positive feedback, and to students I have taught who have unwittingly given me encouragement and confidence through their comments on my writing and ideas.

Thanks must also go to Amanda at Let's Get Booked, who designed the front cover, creating exactly what I wanted, and also edited the book, which helped to improve the delivery of the story itself and also ensured that the message I wanted to get across was clear. I wanted to show that in reality, the world of horse ownership and equestrian sport is often tough. You can go through blood, sweat and tears with them and still not get the result you'd like. Horses aren't machines, and to work with them you have to have a lot of patience and a willingness to persevere and accept your faults as a rider. I wish I'd known what I know

now when I had Little Pearl. I wanted to put some of the lessons I've learnt into this book for the benefit of riders who are just starting out. Amanda really helped with her constructive comments and suggestions, and her input was invaluable in making the book exactly what I set out to create.

And finally, to my husband who had to put up with me being totally engrossed in writing and editing for months! Thank you for your support x

The Second Best Pony

Amber's Pony Tales

Book 2

This book is dedicated to the Fell pony; a beautiful, tough and versatile breed who was the first to introduce me to the world of ponies and horses. From their beginnings as pit ponies and packhorses, they can now be found showing, jumping, carriage driving, pleasure, and endurance riding.

As best friends go, there can be no better friend than a Fell pony.

- One -

Starting Again

Amber Anderson's stomach clenched like an angry fist. She wasn't sure whether it was nerves or excitement that was pummelling her insides as she rode her black Fell pony, Pearl, around the perimeter of the Pony Club field, waiting for the first rally of the new season to begin.

Amber had joined Blakefield Pony Club the previous year, but she'd had a disastrous time; being humiliated at her first rally; and getting eliminated from her debut round of show jumping. And of course, there was the fun ride which had ended in disaster after a terrible accident.

A sudden blast of chill April breeze sent an icy tingle down Amber's spine as she remembered that awful time.

Amber felt alone without her friend Joanne beside her. Joanne and her pony, Flash, were both still recovering from the injuries they sustained in the accident the previous summer and would probably miss the whole season. Amber yearned for a friend to ride around with as there was someone she dreaded seeing. However, glancing around the car park, she was relieved to see that Elisha Templeton's imposing blue and yellow horsebox was also missing. The problem with Elisha was that she was cruel, spoilt and nasty and was partly responsible for Joanne's accident. Last year, she had also said some very unkind things about Pearl, making Amber apprehensive about seeing her again.

She scanned the field and noticed a long-legged girl mounting a flea-bitten grey pony of about 14.2hh. The girl gathered up her reins and urged her pony into a reluctant walk. Deciding she'd had enough of being on her own, Amber took a deep breath and rode over to introduce herself.

The grey pony flicked her ears back and raised a hind leg threateningly as Pearl drew up alongside her. Fearing the pony might lash out, Amber hurriedly steered Pearl out of kicking range.

"Oh, I'm *so* sorry," gasped the girl, seeing Amber's startled reaction. "She's so unfriendly. I'm really sorry she tried to kick you," she apologised sincerely.

Amber had been about to tell her that ponies prone to kicking should wear a red ribbon in their tails to warn other riders to give them a wide berth, but seeing the girl was genuinely sorry and upset, she changed her mind.

"It's okay, don't worry. I just came over to say hello. Are you a new member?"

"Yeah, I've just joined. I'm really nervous." She smiled shyly, her round brown eyes giving her face a startled expression. "I've only been riding for a year and just got Sable at Christmas. Everyone looks so good." She looked towards the older riders who were working their horses in controlled circles of collected canter.

"I've never jumped before. I'm bound to be a total disaster and fall off in front of everyone."

Amber laughed. "That's just how I felt at my first rally, but they put you in groups, so you'll be riding with people at a similar level to yourself. I'm Amber, by the way," she added, realising she hadn't introduced herself.

"I'm Natalie," she replied.

"Oh, look, they're ready to start," said Amber, catching sight of Mrs Best, the Pony Club DC waving at them. "Let's go and see which group we're in."

- Two -

Trouble Already

Amber patted Pearl's damp, curly neck and slid gratefully from the saddle at the end of the rally. She hadn't worked so hard since her lessons last year. She had been in Geraldine's group – the young, exuberant instructor she'd had for her one and only rally last year. There were four groups; the first for very young or inexperienced riders, with the following three groups comprising of progressively older and more experienced riders. Amber remembered with a cringe how she had ridden into the third group at her first rally, assuming she would be with riders of eleven to thirteen years of age as she was eleven herself then. But because of her lack of experience and Pearl not matching up to the other ponies' abilities, she had been moved into the second group of eight to ten-year-olds, and Elisha had laughed at her.

After a lot of lessons and hard work with Pearl since last year, Amber was delighted to find that she had been promoted to the third group. As she proudly trotted towards the group, she was surprised, and a little annoyed, to see that Natalie was following her. She'd assumed the new girl would be in one of the lower groups due to her lack of experience, just as *she* had been last year.

They joined a girl called Kate on a young bay horse, and another girl with dark curly hair called Emily who rode Fudge, a chunky chestnut gelding. She looked familiar. Amber thought she recognised her from school, but she wasn't in her year group.

They had started with some flatwork that really got their muscles aching, and then Geraldine had shown them how to give the correct aids for a turn on the forehand. Amber, Emily and Kate had managed quite good turns, with Pearl being particularly co-operative for a change. Poor Natalie, on the other hand, had a terrible time. She listened carefully to

Geraldine's instructions and gave the aids clearly, but Sable seemed to be willfully disobedient. Instead of simply moving her hindquarters around her front feet in a half turn as was being asked, she laid her ears back, shook her head in annoyance, backed up and finally did a mini rear which resulted in Natalie tuning ghostly white and looking close to tears.

"Right, I think we've all had enough of that now!" Geraldine exclaimed, seeing that Natalie was shaken. "Let's have a change."

As Geraldine dragged some poles out to lie on the ground as trotting poles, Amber looked forward to showing off Pearl's improved jumping skills. Last year Pearl had been very reluctant to jump and would either just stop in front of the fence or dodge around it, rather than go over it. Mrs Anderson had endured a particularly painful experience while jumping in the field at Shaw Farm, where the ponies were kept.

Amber had been trying to get Pearl to jump some blue barrels pushed together to make a wall, but Pearl had other ideas and just kept refusing at the last minute. An exasperated Mrs Anderson had decided to take over and she mounted Pearl to 'teach her a lesson.' Feeling the increased strength and confidence of her new rider, Pearl realised she needed to employ new tactics to continue getting her own way. Mrs Anderson rode smartly around the small paddock, giving Pearl very definite aids to show her that she meant business. Sure that Pearl had got the message, Mrs Anderson turned her towards the blue barrels and coaxed her into a canter. "Come on Pearlipops," she urged the pony. Pearl cantered gaily towards the jump, ears pricked, looking for all the world like she was going to follow through, when at the very last second she simultaneously shoved her head down between her knees, dropped her left shoulder, twisted to the right and gave a little buck. Sitting on the fence, watching, Amber's hands flew to her face and she pressed them against her cheeks, almost covering her eyes as she realised, almost in slow-motion, the inevitable landing place of her mother.

Pearl careered away, and Mrs Anderson, all balance lost, flew head-first into a large patch of stinging nettles. Pearl stopped, snatched a mouthful of grass to munch, then looked up, ears pricked quizzically to admire her handiwork.

The naughty pony could not be smug about her antics for long, however, as Mrs Anderson emerged from the nettle patch like the Incredible Hulk. She hadn't turned green (apart from the fronds of nettle hanging from her hat); she was red-faced, her arms and hands covered in hot stinging pimples, her fists balled at her sides. Catching Pearl up, she remounted and booted her back towards the barrel jump. This time, the pony didn't dare resist her rider as she felt the suppressed rage travelling down the reins. So, with grass still sticking out of her mouth and her eyes wide with surprise at losing the battle, Pearl had jumped the barrels three times before Mrs Anderson flung herself out of the saddle, chucked the reins at Amber and strode away, head held high.

Then there was Amber's first show last year where she had been eliminated at the fourth fence in her first round of show jumping. After that, her parents decided she wouldn't do any more competing until she'd had some lessons.

Now, with months of lessons behind her, Amber felt much happier about jumping. Pearl had eventually realised it was easier to jump on the first attempt, as if she refused, she would only be made to keep going. So, always wanting an easy life, Pearl had become a reliable, albeit slow jumper, as long as the poles didn't get too high. Amber couldn't wait to see if Pearl would still be as good since her winter break from lessons.

"Right everyone," called Geraldine, wiping the mud off her hands, "shorten your stirrups and trot steadily down through the poles. Concentrate on keeping a steady rhythm and an even tempo. And don't look down," she added with a chuckle.

All three ponies and Kate's young horse managed the poles well, with Natalie going last so that Sable could follow the others.

Natalie's ashen face returned to its normal colour, and she smiled happily as Sable plonked over the poles.

Geraldine then raised the last pole to make a low jump and asked the riders to continue trotting down but be prepared for the fence at the end, remembering to go into jumping position over it. This task suited Pearl perfectly as she preferred to jump from trot.

"Well done Amber," nodded Geraldine as she went first down the line and over the jump perfectly. "You go next, Emily."

Emily brought Fudge round and did a good job of steadying him. As there was now a jump at the end, he tried to canter and got rather unbalanced as Emily brought him back to a trot. By the time he got to the fence, Emily had steadied him well and he produced a very neat jump.

"Well ridden, Emily," Geraldine praised, clapping her hands. "You can do it again in a minute, just to make sure he doesn't try to rush. Okay, Natalie." She signalled to the girl to come and take her turn.

Sable headed up the poles in a rather sluggish trot, but as soon as she saw the jump she quickly spun away, just like Pearl had done with Mrs Anderson, flinging Natalie up out of the saddle and on to her neck. Natalie clutched at the pony's mane tightly as she wriggled and pushed herself back into the saddle before desperately trying to recover her stirrups. Fortunately, Geraldine had sprung forward and caught Sable by the bridle to stop her from charging away. But for the instructor's quick actions, Natalie would surely have come off.

"Whoops! Nearly!" exclaimed Geraldine lightly. "I think we'll let you follow someone this time."

"Er… right," muttered Natalie, looking rather flustered.

Amber knew she was probably feeling frightened and embarrassed. After all, she'd had the same trouble with Pearl last year.

Kate had a quick turn with no trouble, then Geraldine summoned Emily to go over the poles again ahead of Natalie, to give her a lead.

"Put your leg on and really ride her forward more this time," Geraldine instructed. "Use your legs and reins to keep her straight. Wake her up out of her daydream. Be positive," she commanded encouragingly.

This time, Natalie followed closely behind Emily. Fudge, now knowing he had to trot through the poles, went perfectly. Sable followed him quite eagerly, and as she neared the jump, Natalie steeled herself and squeezed with her legs. This time, however, Sable wasn't taken by surprise and knew exactly what to expect. Just as Natalie was beginning to lean forward to adopt the jumping position, Sable put her head right down and stopped dead in her tracks. Natalie was catapulted out of the saddle, slid over Sable's withers, and crashed head-first into the jump. Finding herself free at last, the grey pony hurtled across the field, bucking madly with stirrups, reins, and clods of earth flying.

That was where the rally ended. Natalie had banged her head and hurt her neck. Her dad had left her sitting on the ramp of their trailer, wrapped in a warm horse blanket, while he and Geraldine went to try and catch Sable. This proved an impossible task, as she had no intention of going home, and trotted away as soon as they got close to her. Eventually, after causing so much chaos and disturbing the other groups so much that everyone had to give up, a whole troop of adults encircled and caught the pony.

Red-faced with embarrassment, Natalie's dad flopped wearily onto the ramp beside his daughter. Amber and Mr Anderson finished brushing Pearl, hung up her haynet, and went over to see if Natalie was okay.

Geraldine was there untacking the ungrateful pony, whose ears were flat back, her eyes rolling as she tried to fight against her short rope to bite Geraldine as she loosened the girth. Unperturbed, Geraldine ignored her and carried on, flashing Amber a smile as she walked past.

Natalie had removed her hat. Her short blonde hair was damp and tousled, plastered to her pale, clammy face.

"Uuuurgh," she groaned, rubbing the back of her neck, her eyes half-closed as she slumped against her dad on the ramp.

"Hi, Andrew Anderson," said Amber's dad, holding out his hand to the man on the ramp, "is there anything we can do to help? Could we take your pony and drop her off for you?" he offered, thinking Natalie would need a trip to the hospital to get checked out.

Natalie's dad looked up with pale blue eyes and shook his head. "Thanks for the offer," he said, standing and shaking Mr Anderson's hand, "but that devil won't travel with another pony. I think one accident is enough for today." He sighed and looked drained. "My wife is coming to take Natalie to the doctor, and I'll get that thing home." He nodded towards Sable, now booted and bandaged, ready to go, but looking as grumpy as ever. "Thanks again."

As Amber sat in the car while they drove back to the farm, she couldn't help wondering what the year would bring. Last year had ended in disaster and this year had begun with one. *Surely things will start getting better,* she hoped.

- Three -

A New Friend

It was two weeks before Amber saw Emily and Natalie again at the Easter Monday gymkhana. Blakefield Pony Club had long held the tradition of hosting the first local outdoor show of the year, and it was always well attended despite the fact that it was often plagued with April showers and cold winds – the field being situated close to the coast made it rather exposed to the weather.

The location did have its advantages to compensate; the field was large and flat with good drainage, so the going was always good and there was a magnificent view of the surrounding countryside. The field was sandwiched between the distant mountains of the Lake District, undulating valleys flecked with the purple and gold of heather and gorse, a patchwork of farmland, and the nearby coast of St Bees. It was a truly spectacular setting. But as spring was only creeping cautiously into the land with its painted fingers dabbing colour everywhere, the greys and browns of winter were not yet forgotten.

It was an unusually warm, pleasant day. Earthy smells of dewy grass, soft mud and hay were occasionally pierced by the sharper scents of hoof oil, coat gloss and boot polish as riders mounted their freshly bathed ponies for the equitation class.

Amber unloaded Pearl and was getting her ready - with some help from Mrs Anderson – for her own class of equitation, when a huge blue lorry with a striking yellow stripe like a lightning flash pulled on to the field. Amber could see Elisha Templeton's condescending face smirking down at her from the grand height of the cab as they drove by. Amber scowled and got back to brushing baby oil through Pearl's tail to make it shiny.

Although Elisha had momentarily admitted some remorse for last year's accident and had (or at least her parents had) sent a huge bouquet of flowers and

157

expensive Belgian chocolates to Joanne, she had not phoned or visited once. And now, judging by the haughty smirk she had directed at Amber, she had no intention of reforming her character.

The reason for her smugness soon became evident as the ramp of their lorry was lowered and its passenger emerged. It was not a pony, but a small black horse of about 15.2hh. He was heavily rugged to protect his clipped body, but still, his quality could not be missed. Exquisitely formed, he stopped as his feet touched the grass and lifted his head up sharply to take in his new surroundings. His nostrils quivered as he snorted and shook his head, and the muscles of his beautiful dark face twitched uneasily as he inhaled the new smells of this unfamiliar environment.

Elisha looked delighted with herself as she saw heads turn and eyes lock on to the magnificent creature by her side. Determined to show off even more, she yanked the lead-rope sharply and walked forward. Still gazing around nervously, the horse was startled by Elisha's sudden, rough movement and skittered forward, bumping into her and nearly knocking her flat. Elisha staggered and righted herself quickly, smoothing her dark hair and glancing around furtively to see if anyone had noticed. Everyone looked away politely, pretending not to have seen, while Amber giggled gleefully as she thought how Elisha had nearly swallowed and choked on her own conceited grin as the horse jolted her.

Do her good to be embarrassed for once, thought Amber.

The previous class was almost over, with the judge lining riders up to be presented with their rosettes, as Amber finished warming Pearl up. Other competitors for the class were congregating as the lap of honour cantered out of the equitation area amidst flapping rosette ribbons and beaming faces.

Amber could see other competitors riding towards her: Natalie on a neatly plaited Sable, who looked as ill-tempered as ever; a boy on a pretty dun pony; another, slightly plump boy on a piebald with blue eyes and a cute handlebar moustache; and Elisha. Amber looked around, noting Emily's absence. She'd heard her say she was coming at the rally.

The five riders followed each other around the marked area in a circle while they waited for the judge to return from collecting a score sheet and rosettes for their class. Elisha rode her mount alongside Amber who had to look up to see the girl as she was so far above her.

"What do you think?" asked Elisha, looking down at Amber with raised eyebrows.

Amber knew she was talking about the horse, but she had a sudden urge to reply with tremendous wit and sarcasm, something like, "*I think about a lot of things Elisha, could you be more specific?*" but her courage failed her under the hard expectant weight of Elisha's eyes. Knowing exactly what she'd meant, Amber replied meekly. "He's really beautiful. What's he called?"

"Thunder Cat. He's fabulously well bred. His sire, Storm Cat is North America's top stallion. He's the sire of over fifty stakes winners worldwide and his stud fee is almost half a million dollars. His dam is a Grade A show-jumper. My dad found him through some of his contacts in the States and had him imported for me for Christmas. He was *so* expensive." Elisha's eyes glistened as she uttered the word 'expensive.' "We can't turn him out – he's stabled all the time unless he's led out in hand for some grass. We're going to be aiming him at top level eventing. We'll be training with the top people and I'm hoping to get him to the BE Under Eighteen Regional Team Championships in the summer."

"Oh right," said Amber, impressed both with the horse's credentials and Elisha's ability to remember and recite it like a well-practised script. At the same time, she wondered why such a grand horse aimed at the prestigious heights of three-day eventing was entered in an insignificant equitation class at a local Pony Club gymkhana. Something of her thoughts must have shown on her face as Elisha hurriedly went on to explain her reasons for being there.

"Of course, he's *way* above these poxy little Pony Club affairs, but we thought we'd let him see things locally before he goes anywhere important. He's only five, and we wouldn't want him to show us up. Besides, it'll do him good to have some wins under his belt when people ask what he's done."

Amber wasn't shocked by Elisha's confidence or at her disdain for small, local shows. *That's what comes from having the money to buy the best and the connections to get your own way*, she thought. Last year, Amber would have envied Elisha and her super-duper new winning machine, but she had since realised how lucky she was to have Pearl, with whom she shared a special bond. Even though she knew she would never win competitions with her, she still loved her, and that made her feel richer than Elisha, who saw her ponies only as a means to success rather than as friends.

She leant forward to stroke some stray strands of mane back into place as the judge returned and Elisha rode smoothly onto the track ahead of her.

***

After completing her own individual show and watching everyone else's, Amber's prediction as to the places was confirmed by the judge. Elisha was first on Thunder Cat, who, for a young horse, was already well-schooled and performed his show with grace, athleticism and control. The boy on the dun pony, who had also given a nice performance, was second. Amber was third, the boy on the moustached piebald was fourth – he had done quite well except that he'd cantered a full circle on the wrong leg without noticing – and Natalie was fifth as Sable had been totally uncooperative, slugged around like a plank of wood then refused point-blank to canter.

As the line of riders left the equitation area, preceded by Elisha, Amber noticed Emily was standing watching them. Instantly recognisable by her thick curly dark hair, she was wearing jeans and a white t-shirt emblazoned with a jubilant Mickey Mouse. She followed Amber back to the trailer and congratulated her on her third place. Her manner was so relaxed and easy, anyone would have thought they knew each other well, not that this was the first time they'd spoken to each other.

"Aren't you riding?" asked Amber, sitting down on the ramp and loosening her tie from its strangling hold on her neck.

"No. I just came to watch. Fudge came in from the field the other day with a really hot, swollen leg. I cold hosed it and bandaged an ice pack to it, but it didn't get any better, so we got the vet out. She reckons he's twisted it while running around in the field, so he has to have box rest for a few weeks. He's not enjoying it at all. He hates being kept in. I've hung some carrots up for him to play with, but he's not interested. Every time I go in the stable, he looks at me as if it's my fault. He makes me feel so guilty," Emily laughed, sitting down next to Amber. "So, no riding for me for the next few weeks." She finished, pulling a hay stalk out of her curls, suddenly looking glum.

Amber had an idea. "You could come and ride with me," she suggested, tentatively. We've got another Fell pony called Honey. You could come with us after school. You go to Wallam Academy like

164

me, don't you? You're in Year Eight? I'll ask my dad if you want?"

"Yeah, thanks," Emily smiled, her hazel eyes twinkling, "that would be brill." Amber smiled back, pleased that Emily had agreed so enthusiastically.

The day stayed warm as the show progressed. Pearl went clear in her jumping round but then had two poles down in the jump-off when the fences were raised. She was doing so much better than last year, but she still lacked the energy and power to jump anything bigger than eighty centimetres; her absolute maximum.

She won the handy pony, which was becoming Pearl's forte as it required the pony to be steady and unfazed by the obstacles, and she had also tried games again, but Pearl totally lacked the competitive spirit required to race the other ponies, and firmly insisted on trotting all the way through the mug, flag, and ball and bucket races.

Amber and Emily had watched dismally as Mr Riley led Sable away after she was eliminated at the first jump. The pony had refused to even enter the show jumping arena, and then, after being dragged in by Mr Riley, had reared one after another until Natalie was in floods of tears. She'd spent the rest of the time before they left sitting red-eyed in the car, refusing to come out even when Emily asked if she wanted to come and walk around with her.

Elisha had cleaned up as usual. As well as winning the equitation, she also won the ninety-centimetre and one metre pony show jumping classes on North Quest (who had stood so quietly in the lorry until it was his turn that Amber had not realised he was there). Then she won the ninety-centimetre horse class on Thunder Cat and came second in the metre class after a little mistake in the jump-off. Amber couldn't believe the young horse was jumping Opens already. But what he lacked in experience and training, he made up for through sheer ability. Even Amber, with her untrained eyes and non-existent knowledge of 'good breeding,' could see he was a quality horse. He had it all: amazing presence, a huge bold jump and an impeccable temperament. Despite the racing blood coursing through his veins and his youthful energy and exuberance, he was a perfect gentleman for his slight thirteen-year-old rider.

The horse classes finished and the members who had stayed until the end helped to take the jumps down and store them away in the container.

"Do you need a lift home?" Mr Anderson asked Emily, seeing that she was alone, and everyone was leaving the field.

"Oh thanks, but my mum will be on her way now. I phoned her ten minutes ago."

"Dad," asked Amber, suddenly remembering her earlier conversation with Emily, "Emily's pony is lame at the moment, so she can't ride. Could she come to the farm with us one day after school and ride Honey out with me?"

Mr Anderson immediately agreed, and it was decided that if it was okay with Emily's parents, she would go with them to Shaw Farm on Wednesday after school.

"See you on Wednesday then," said Amber happily.

"I'll see you at school tomorrow and let you know if it's okay," Emily replied, just as a small blue car pulled into the field, driven by a smiling woman wearing a headscarf with paint all over her nose and forehead. Emily waved as she ran towards the car. "Looks like Mum's been decorating," she called. "See you tomorrow!"

"Bye!" cried Amber, waving madly, pleased to have made a new friend.

- Four -

Honey's Surprise

At quarter past three on Wednesday, Amber went to the music block to meet Emily after her last lesson. She waited a few minutes until the increasing volume of chatter indicated that the Year Eights were on their way out. Emily emerged, talking and laughing with her friends and didn't even see Amber waiting beside the door. She stopped a little way off and continued talking animatedly, her curls bouncing as she threw back her head to laugh at something a tall blond boy had said. He grinned as Emily wiped the tears of laughter away and pushed him jokingly with one hand.

Amber wondered if she'd forgotten about riding and felt nervous about approaching the older group. She sidled over, trying not to look conspicuous, hoping to catch Emily's eye without the others noticing her.

"Amber! Hey!" The plan worked. Emily spotted her, but then waved her over. Everyone turned to look as Amber reluctantly joined them.

"Is this your little pony friend then?" The blond boy asked. Everyone laughed. Amber blushed and looked down uncomfortably.

"Shut up, Paul," Emily chuckled. "Just ignore him." She put her arm around Amber and steered her away, calling back over her shoulder. "He so fancies himself!"

"Not as much as you fancy me," he retorted, blowing a kiss to Emily, who snorted and shook her head.

"Sorry about that," Emily fell into step next to Amber as they walked to the car, "he's okay but sometimes he can be a pain."

"Is he your boyfriend?" Amber asked shyly.

"God *no*," Emily exclaimed, "The only man in my life is my little Fudgey. How could I love anyone else?"

Both girls arrived at the car in fits of giggles and were still spluttering as they fastened their seatbelts. Mrs Anderson raised an eyebrow but decided not to ask as she pulled out of school to head for the farm.

***

"She's lovely," Emily said softly as she ran her fingers through Honey's copper-streaked black mane. "So gentle."

Honey was indeed a gentle pony. Where cheeky Pearl would sometimes give Amber a shove with her head or use her to scratch on when she was itchy, or 'accidentally' stand on Amber's toes when she wasn't looking, Honey was a complete angel. She would lower her head to be bridled, pick up her own feet to be cleaned out and never shoved, pushed or stood on anybody. Her only fault was that she sometimes wouldn't let Mr Anderson catch her, although Amber and her mum never had any trouble.

"Are you sure you don't mind me riding her, Mrs Anderson?" Emily asked politely. "I feel bad that you're going to be sitting around here while I'm riding your pony."

"Oh, don't worry pet. I've brought my book. I'll be quite happy," replied Mrs Anderson, "and I can give Kasper a little walk."

"Ohhhhh," Amber groaned, "I'm surprised she even remembered to come and pick us up if she's reading a book."

Emily's eyebrows rose questioningly. Amber laughed, "The world stops when Mum's reading a book – she doesn't move, she doesn't make tea, she doesn't even go to the loo - she just sits there till she's read it from start to finish. I hope you don't mind sleeping in the stable tonight, as we'll never be able to move her once she's got going. She'll forget we're even here." Amber gave her mother a playful elbow.

Mrs Anderson narrowed her eyes and pursed her lips, though Amber knew she was suppressing a smile. "I'm not *that* bad. I'll definitely get you home…sometime before midnight," she added playfully. They all laughed.

The afternoon was chilly as the girls rode through the silent forestry, the great ominous looking trees sheltering them from the icy gusts of wind that blew through the valley. Amber enjoyed the ride as she and Emily chatted easily about ponies, homework, teachers, music and everything under the sun, until the conversation turned to the show on Monday.

"Natalie's pony seems a bit of a horror, doesn't she?" commented Emily, "I mean, she doesn't want to do anything except argue and fight. I wonder if there's something wrong with Sable or if she really is just bad-tempered and nasty."

"I don't know," Amber replied, picturing Sable's face with ears laid back and teeth bared. "I read somewhere that there are no bad horses, just bad people who ruin them, but Natalie and her dad seem like nice, kind people to me."

"Yeah. Maybe Sable's had a bad experience in the past and it's ruined her, but you'd think Natalie'd have seen her bad temper when they tried her. I don't know why anyone would buy a pony like that, especially when she's so unsuitable for Natalie – 'cause she's inexperienced and a bit nervous. That pony will ruin her confidence and she'll give up before the end of the year I think, if they don't sell it and get her something else."

"You can't just sell a pony and get a new one though!" protested Amber, still shocked at people's ability to regard a pony as just a belonging like an old toy that can be passed on and replaced with a better one without a thought.

"Sometimes it's the best thing to do," Emily replied, looking serious. "If a horse and rider aren't right for each other, they just make each other unhappy, and that's no good for either of them. For the person, keeping a horse you don't like is an expensive way of making yourself miserable, and you could also get hurt." Amber thought back to when she had considered that Pearl was not the pony for her. Emily continued. "Also, it must be stressful for the horse when their owner doesn't understand them – after all, they can't tell us what they want from us to make them happy – their ideas might be different from ours. Sometimes a combination is better off being separated and both find they are much happier with someone else. Natalie would be much happier with another pony, and you never know, Sable might be better tempered with someone else."

"I've never thought of it like that before," said Amber, thinking how sensible Emily's words were. "I suppose it's like people – some you love, some you like, some you can tolerate but there's some you just can't help disliking - sometimes you don't even know why you don't like them. It's weird."

Emily nodded. "That's right, those people who you don't like but don't know why – they haven't done or said anything nasty to you, but still you can't get on – can be because you are just too different. You have different personalities and characters that just don't match. And that can happen with people and horses too. Natalie and Sable obviously can't click together, so why struggle on? I mean, if you started going out with a lad and found you didn't like him, would you carry on or would you find someone you liked who made you happy?"

"Yeah, good point." Amber laughed at Emily's rather grown-up comparison, and thought how she would hate it if she had to go out with someone like Robert from her form group. He picked his nose when he thought no-one was looking, talked with his mouth full, and stared at people in a very unsettling manner. She could understand how she would be very bad-tempered and unhappy if she spent much time in his company.

"Whereas, what would you *give* to have Elisha's new horse? Pfwoar!" Emily said, changing the subject.

"I know what you mean. Her parents must be seriously loaded. She told me his sire's stud fee was nearly half a million dollars!"

"That's unbelievable," Emily scoffed, "I think she's exaggerating there."

"No. I looked him up on the internet – it's true."

"Wow," breathed Emily, awestruck. "Now, I totally adore my Freaky Treacle but what I wouldn't give to have a horse like Thunder Cat. Elisha is *so* lucky."

"*Freaky Treacle?* What's that?" Asked Amber incredulously.

"Oh, that's Fudge's show name," Emily explained, grinning mischievously.

"That's such a cool name!" Amber managed to get out before she exploded with giggles.

The rest of the ride was punctuated with frequent outbursts of laughter, and by the time they got back to the farm track, their sides and faces were aching from laughing so much.

As they rode past Joanne's house, Amber habitually looked over the gate as she rode by and was surprised but pleased to see Joanne coming down the path from the field, leading a pale palomino pony beside her.

"Jo," she called, standing up in her stirrups and waving so she could be seen now that they had ridden alongside the tall hedge that bordered Joanne's house.

Joanne looked up and waved back. "Come in," she called.

Amber hopped off Pearl and opened the gate for Emily and herself to enter the yard. Turning around, she saw that Joanne had tied the pony up and was waiting for them. Amber led Pearl towards the stables and smiled warmly at Joanne, noticing that her blonde bob had grown out to shoulder length. "I'm pleased to see you're out and about again," she said sincerely, "and is this your new pony?"

"Yeah, this is Merry." Joanne stroked the milky coat as she introduced the pony. "She's a Welsh Arab cross, 14.2hh and eight years old, but she hasn't done much except breed a foal. Mum got her quite cheap at an auction – she knew the seller – they told her Merry was really nice, just inexperienced. They were happy to sell her to Mum because they knew her, without Merry even going in the ring. Mum thought she'd make a nice project for me this summer to just bring on and maybe take to a couple of competitions towards the end of the year. She's sweet, isn't she?"

The mare was indeed very pretty. She had the definite Arab dished face with a broad forehead tapering into a small, delicate muzzle. Her coat was a smooth, creamy colour like vanilla ice-cream, lightened further by a long white flowing mane and tail, four white socks and a blaze on her face.

"I was just going to take her in the field and do some little jumps. You two are welcome to come in and jump too if you like."

Amber checked her watch, concerned that her mum would want to get home. Then she remembered she was reading her book and stopped worrying about the time.

"Do you want to do some jumping?" she asked Emily.

"Yeah, great," came the enthusiastic reply.

"Okay, but Honey hasn't done any jumping and she can be a bit of a wimp."

"That's fine, we'll just play."

"Oh, do you two know each other?" gasped Amber, realising that she hadn't introduced Emily and Joanne and the latter was probably wondering who the stranger was.

"Yes, we know each other through the club. We've competed against each other a few times, although Fudge has never managed to beat Flash, obviously," Emily said, turning to face Joanne. "I was sorry to hear about your accident. How is Flash?"

"Well, he doesn't look too bad – he healed up okay, but he still isn't totally sound. I think he's just putting it on so he can carry on enjoying an easy life."

Soon the girls were in the small paddock warming up over trotting poles and small cross poles. Joanne's mum came out to help and watched her daughter anxiously as she popped Merry over the small jumps.

"Okay love?" she asked. Her tone was light, but her furrowed brow betrayed her concern.

"Yes, Mum, stop worrying, I'm fine. She doesn't pull at all and she's enjoying herself," Joanne said, giving her pony a pat on the neck.

Sensing that her daughter didn't want her fussing about her, Mrs Jones turned her attention to Amber and Emily.

"It's nice to see you girls. Jo's only doing little jumps with Merry as she's so green, but we've got some new cross-country jumps in the next field if you want to try them. Peter – my husband - made them, and Matthew's had a go over them. Go through and help yourselves."

Amber had never done any cross-country jumping before and looked with interest at the homemade jumps spread out around the larger field. There was a tyre jump, a hayrack that looked like a crib and was full of straw, a brush fence encased in a wooden support and a box jump. They all looked so solid and strong and intimidating. You couldn't make any mistakes over these jumps as they wouldn't fall like a show jump.

"Cool," said Emily, looking completely confident as she spurred Honey into an active trot and headed for the tyres. Amber decided to follow suit over the smallest and softest of the jumps, and Pearl amiably hopped over it in Honey's wake. Not sure that she was quite ready to tackle the others yet, Amber pulled Pearl up and watched with surprise as Emily got Honey into a canter and rode strongly for the brush fence. Amber couldn't believe how daring Emily was being on a pony she'd never ridden. A pony that wasn't exactly known for her courage and hadn't done any jumping in her life. She almost couldn't bear to look as Honey neared the fence.

Without even a moment's hesitation, the pony picked up her feathery feet and sailed over the imposing brush fence in one fluid motion. Then, without breaking stride, Emily pushed on to the hayrack and finally finished with the box.

"That was *great*," Emily enthused, her cheeks flushed and her eyes wide. "Has she really not jumped before?"

"No, she hasn't," replied Amber, looking at Honey in a new light. She looked… *different*. It was hard to explain but Honey looked more alive somehow; her face looked bold and happy and she seemed to be throbbing with energy. So much different to the quiet, rather nervous and slightly switched off mare she usually was. "She's jumped a couple of tiny logs in the forestry with Dad, but nothing like that. That was amazing!"

"She's a natural." Emily patted Honey's neck vigorously.

They thanked Mrs Jones, and Amber arranged to ride with Joanne on Saturday before they rode the short distance back to the farm, talking all the way about Honey's remarkable jumping.

When they arrived, they rode by Mrs Anderson's car to see her sitting in the front seat, engrossed in her book. She didn't even look up as their shadow blocked the light across the page she was reading.

"See," said Amber, laughing and rolling her eyes. "I hope you're not dying to get home for your tea.

She won't move now until she's finished the chapter."

"Ha, it's just as well I've got two chocolate bars in my bag then isn't it," replied Emily slyly. "Come on, the first person to get untacked gets the one that isn't squashed."

-Five-

🐎

Pony for Sale

Friday night saw the members of Blakefield Pony Club arriving at Mrs Best's house for a stable management rally. Amber hadn't been to a stable rally before, but Emily had told her she would need to learn about the correct care and management of horses and ponies if she wanted to do any Pony Club tests. And Amber, determined to have a circle of coloured felt behind her Pony Club badge like everyone else, had decided to start going to the monthly meetings at the DC's house.

Mrs Best's house was old, and stone built. Fairly large and with an impressive entrance of two imposing stone pillars bearing the name 'Linfield,' it looked like it had, in its time, been a grand residence. But now, wrapped tightly in ivy with paint flaking off the walls to reveal previous colours from its long past, the house was an odd contrast of neglect and disrepair, and much-loved family home. Entering the house gave much the same effect. The rooms were large with original features. Much of the furniture was old and probably valuable, but the chairs were threadbare and covered with an assortment of sleeping dogs and cats. Dusty trophies stood tall and proud on the mantelpiece amongst the colourful rosettes that littered every surface, and the walls were full of pictures of different horses and ponies in action, all apparently ridden by the same girl; the photographs chronicling her equestrian pursuits from toddler to adulthood as she beamed happily from the pictures.

The living room was filling up with people who were chatting with each other whilst standing due to the fact there was a cat or dog lounging on every seat in the room. Amber was looking around for familiar faces amongst the members when Mrs Best suddenly exploded into the room.

"Up, up, up, you old lay-a-bouts!" She bustled in, clapping her hands and shrieking loudly so that furry bodies immediately leapt from the sofa and other chairs and scurried to safety.

"Right, parents, there are refreshments in the second sitting room if you'd like to go through," she said, escorting them briskly from the room and shutting the door on them. "Okay then," she turned to look at the people left in the room, "group one, Jean is waiting for you in the feed room. You're doing feeding and nutrition tonight. Off you go then." She waved her arms and the older members trooped off to the feed store.

"Group two, Rachel is in Woody's stable so you can go and see what she has in store for you."

The two girls in the room with Amber (one of whom was Kate from the mounted rally) left, and Amber thought she'd better check which group she was in to avoid making a mistake like she had at her first ridden rally.

"Er… am I in group two?" she asked tentatively as Mrs Best made for the door to join the parents.

"Oh dear! How silly of me, I'd forgotten this was your first one," she bustled. "Yes, group one is for our members aiming at C+ level and above. Your group covers D to C tests. Run and follow Kate and Chelsea, then you'll know where to go."

Amber ran out into the yard and followed Kate and Chelsea into a small barn that held three internal stables with a hayloft above. Standing outside one of the stables was a young woman of nineteen or twenty, dressed in rather holey jeans, wellies, and an oversized checked shirt. And chatting to her were Natalie and Emily.

"Great, you're all here. Let's get started." Rachel put down the tail bandage she had been rolling and went to collect some other items she needed. Amber slipped in between Emily and Natalie, grateful for the company of friends.

"How's Fudge?" she asked Emily. "Any better?"

"The heat and swelling have gone down but he's still not quite right yet."

"Oh." Amber shook her head sadly in sympathy for Emily before turning to Natalie. "And is Sable okay?"

"Well, no. She's totally in the bad books, actually. I was just telling Emily; my dad went to put her in for the night on Tuesday and didn't come back for two hours. Mum and I just thought he'd got talking to someone but eventually, she phoned him to see where he was. He didn't answer so she went to look for him and found him lying flat on his back in the field. Sable had kicked him right in the chest."

"No!" cried Amber, wide-eyed, unable to believe Sable could be that evil. "Is he alright?"

"He's got a cracked rib and he's really bruised. He's off work. Mum had to bring me here tonight. Although..." her voice dropped sadly, "I think I need more than stable management lessons to cope with Sable. I'd be better off learning self-defence! I know she's awful at shows, but I could put up with that if she could just be friendly at least, but she's always horrible to us."

Emily raised an eyebrow and nodded at Amber with a '*see-I-told-you*' look on her face.

***

An hour later, the girls left Woody's stable and traipsed back to the house. Amber and Natalie were aiming at taking their D and D+ tests and had been looking at a grooming kit, identifying the brushes; their names and correct uses. Then they had tacked up a very patient Woody and discussed how to assess a correctly fitting saddle and bridle. The other girls, who were all thirteen and had already passed their D and D+, were preparing for their C test, so Rachel had quizzed them about what to look for in a newly shod hoof, asked them to identify the farrier's tools and describe their uses, and then they each had to rug Woody and put travel boots on while explaining their use.

Amber had really enjoyed the rally and felt she had learned loads as she'd listened in to Emily, Kate and Chelsea while she was putting together a bridle Rachel had given her and Natalie to take apart, clean and reassemble to make sure they knew how it all fitted together.

Back in the house, the dogs and cats had crept unnoticed back onto the chairs while everyone was in the second sitting room. Rachel gently picked up a tightly curled cat, sat down with the cat on her knee and switched on the TV. Amber was surprised at her making herself so at home, when suddenly the faces looking out of the pictures on the walls became familiar and it dawned on her that the girl in the pictures was Rachel. *She must be Mrs Best's daughter.*

"Are these all *your* trophies and rosettes?" Amber asked while Rachel flicked wearily through the channels looking for something to watch.

"Yep," she replied, giving up on the telly and stroking the cat instead, "although there haven't been any new ones for a while. I got most of them on old Woody and another pony I had called Ghost. She was an amazing show-jumper."

Amber looked wistfully at the silverware, thinking that Rachel must be an excellent rider to have amassed such a collection. Rachel caught her expression. "You'll be winning your own trophies soon," she said, encouragingly.

Amber smiled but shook her head. "No, my pony isn't really into competitions. She doesn't like games at all and she's not too fond of jumping either. She is good at handy pony though," she added, not wanting to sound totally negative.

"That's a shame," said Rachel, "I know of a good competition pony that's coming up for sale if you're looking for one. It's won a lot around here. I could give you the number?"

"Oh, er, thanks but we're not looking for a new pony," Amber replied hurriedly, thinking that although she would love a jumping pony, she was not prepared to sell Pearl to get one.

***

The next morning the Andersons were all sitting at the kitchen table having breakfast. Their cocker spaniel, Kasper begged beseechingly with his brown, sorrowful eyes and Stig the cat sat in the middle of the tabletop, waiting for the milk from their cereal, trying to mesmerise them into eating faster with his supercilious feline gaze.

"I had a good chat with everyone last night," Mr Anderson started talking, "there's more to the Pony Club than we thought. There are proficiency tests, road safety tests, camp and they do team competitions. There's also area competitions, where you go out of the county to compete against clubs from all over the region." He paused before continuing carefully. "The Pony Club isn't for Pearl, Amber. She doesn't enjoy it and she's not really up to it. Mrs Best was telling me about a pony that's going to be for sale soon, so we thought–"

"No!" Amber interrupted sharply, clattering her spoon into her dish, "I don't want to sell Pearl!"

Mr Anderson smiled, "Who said anything about selling Pearl? If we get another pony it will be *as well* as, not instead of Pearl."

Amber was still suspicious. "Sooo… we'd have *three* ponies?"

"Yes, why not? There's three of us so we'd be able to ride out together."

"We just think you're going to need a better pony to do Pony Club activities," added Amber's mum. "We've got a phone number. Do you want to go and see this pony?"

"*Yeah*!" Amber eagerly agreed, as visions of herself surrounded by red rosettes and silver trophies flashed through her mind.

-Six-

Chalk and Cheese

Mrs Anderson spoke to Mrs Dean, the pony's owner, and it was arranged that they would go and see Molly - the pony – the following Sunday as it was a show-free day. Amber could barely contain her excitement through Saturday and became even more restless to see Molly when Joanne said she knew the pony and confirmed that it had won lots of jumping classes.

"Frankie is a really strong rider though, so you might have to work hard, and make sure you ask them about her back."

"Why, what's wrong with her back?" Mrs Anderson's ears pricked up, riding alongside them. Joanne's mum had only allowed her to go out for a hack with Amber because she knew Mrs Anderson was going with them. She was still worried about her daughter riding out on her new, inexperienced pony even though Merry hadn't put a foot wrong since she'd come to live with them.

"She had an accident at Gosforth show. She was wearing bandages instead of boots and one of the front ones unravelled. She stepped on it with her hind foot right in front of the wall jump and went straight through it. We didn't see them again for a while and we heard she'd hurt her back. After she had time off, she came back and has been jumping since so it's probably fine now, but just watch and see if they mention it," Joanne warned.

"Right," said Amber, her enthusiasm temporarily cooled.

***

Sunday dawned bright and breezy and tingles swept through Amber as they travelled to see the pony. The journey wasn't long, but it seemed like an eternity to Amber until Mrs Anderson finally pulled up outside a terraced house and switched off the engine. She frowned as she checked the address.

"I wonder why they wanted us to meet them here instead of where the pony is kept?" she wondered aloud. "Maybe it isn't very far away."

At that moment, the door of the house opened. A tall, lean lady with curly red hair and large square glasses smiled and waved at them from the doorstep.

"Come in, come in!" She ushered them pleasantly from the hall into the living room where Amber saw a collection of trophies and framed photographs to equal Rachel Best's.

"Did Molly win all these trophies?" Amber asked in awe.

"She did indeed. Molly's a very good competition pony. Would you like to see her?"

Mrs Dean smiled down at Amber who nodded distractedly, still taking in the shelves packed with large trophies, shields and smaller silver dishes.

Amber and her mother followed Mrs Dean to the back door, whereupon it was opened to reveal something very unexpected.

"Oh!" gasped Mrs Anderson in surprise.

The back yard of the terraced house was covered in concrete, and on it stood a breezeblock building, a small store and a muckheap. Seemingly unaware of her visitors' surprise at finding out she kept her horses in her back yard, Mrs Dean escorted them into the stone building where they saw two internal stables occupied by horses, and a third that contained mucking out equipment, bales of hay and straw and feed bins. The first stable they came to contained a very large, athletic looking, dark bay thoroughbred.

"That's my endurance horse, Bonfire Bob," explained Mrs Dean. "We've done about ten-thousand miles on endurance rides. He's one tough animal."

They continued to the next stable where a rather stocky girl was grooming a gleaming chestnut pony.

"And this is Molly and my daughter Frankie."

Mrs Dean opened the stable door for Amber to enter. As soon as she was in the stable, the pony turned to look at her. Amber was mesmerised. Her coat was bright chestnut and she had four white socks and a white blaze. She looked like a larger version of Joanne's pony, Flash. Her body was that of an athlete. Long legged, lean and deep chested, Amber knew she would have endless stamina. Strong, bunched muscles showed under the almost metallic coat. This pony was a perfect picture of health and fitness, lightyears away from round, hairy Pearl. They were at different ends of the pony spectrum: like chalk and cheese.

Amber walked nearer to stroke Molly's emblazoned face. The pony regarded her with soft brown eyes, blowing warm air into Amber's hands as she cupped the velvety muzzle and leaned her face against the pony's hard cheek.

"We're very sad to be selling her," Mrs Dean spoke up, "but Fran is too big for her now and she's getting her first horse. She's had a lot of fun with our Molly though, haven't you love?"

Frankie nodded but didn't seem too upset to Amber, who knew that if she had to sell Pearl, she'd be wailing and hanging on to her if anyone came to look at her, to put them off.

"Well, we'd better get her tack on so you can have a try of her then."

Amber went back to the car to get her riding hat, and when she returned, Molly was ready for her. Frankie held her while Amber mounted and adjusted her stirrups. She felt very strange. She hadn't ridden anything but Pearl for such a long time and Molly was a completely different kettle of fish. Pearl was round and short necked with little tiny ears and a thick, bushy mane, whereas Molly was narrow with a long neck lined with a perfectly pulled mane. Her large, pricked ears seemed miles away. Amber felt like she was sitting on a giraffe. Mrs Dean then led Bonfire Bob out and Frankie got on him using the mounting block.

"You can go for a little ride to get used to her first, then you can try her jumping when you get back," Mrs Dean explained. She opened the gate and they walked out into the road, Molly's long walking stride feeling smooth and comfortable.

The ride was all road work so there was nowhere to try a canter, but Molly was very well behaved as she trotted calmly next to the exuberant Bob, who Frankie was having to work very hard to control. Amber found out that the Dean's did not have a field, so the horses were permanently stabled, hence Bob's excitement as he was kept in all day and was so fit, he was ready to burst.

"We have to try and ride him for about three hours a day just to stop him destroying his stable," Frankie told her, "but he's great at endurance. He can do a fifty-mile ride without breaking a sweat. He's like a machine."

Half an hour round the block was obviously not enough to satisfy the big horse, so Frankie guided Amber down a track to where the mothers were waiting and then left again to give him another two hours riding.

At the end of the track was a tiny enclosure of about the size of a twenty-metre circle with a jump made out of a short pole and some crates erected along one side.

"Here we are, dear." Mrs Dean opened the gate for Amber to enter the enclosure. "Have a little pop over that jump and see what you think."

There was no room to trot around first and get settled, so Amber had to go straight for the jump. Molly approached it calmly and hopped over the poles easily.

"Great, hold on!" Mrs Dean tilted the crates which raised the jump to about eighty centimetres. "Try again."

Again, Amber aimed for the jump, in what she now guessed was little more than a chicken enclosure judging by the hen huts beside it, and Molly sailed over it despite the cramped conditions. Amber patted her and rode to the gate.

"So, what do you think?" Mrs Dean asked.

"She's lovely," said Amber, partly because she believed it and partly just to be polite because really, she didn't know what she thought, having only been for a brief ride round the block and tried one jump in such a cramped space.

Mrs Anderson was obviously thinking the same thing as she said, "Thank you for letting us try her but I don't feel we've seen enough to be able to make up our minds. Could we have her on trial for a week to see if they get on?"

Mrs Dean's smile faltered slightly. "Well, I'm afraid that's not possible as somebody else is coming to look at her tomorrow. Molly has a very high reputation around here so I'm sure if you don't want her, they will."

"It's not that we don't want her, and I'm aware she's a very good pony, its just…"

"I'm sorry, Mrs Anderson but if you want her, you'll have to decide today as the people coming tomorrow are from our own Pony Club and know her well. They're very keen to have her."

Mrs Anderson paused for a minute, not knowing what to say. She was not entirely happy with being rushed into a decision, but on the other hand, the pony came highly recommended, and it was probably true that they would miss out on it if she didn't decide today.

"I'll tell you what," she said, "I'll agree to buy Molly if you can cancel tomorrow's viewers so I can have her vetted. I'll give you a deposit now and if she passes the vet, I'll pay the rest. If she fails, you can keep the deposit and you'll still have the pony to sell."

Mrs Dean looked undecided for a moment, but realising she couldn't lose anything out the deal being offered, she agreed.

-Seven-

Just Molly

As Amber stared at the ticking clock at school the following Monday, she realised that time really does go slower when you're waiting for something. She had spent all day impatiently drumming her fingernails against the table, unable to concentrate on any lesson as she daydreamed about show jumping Molly over enormous fences and beating Elisha. Yes, that was what she most hoped to achieve: to put Elisha in her place – *second* place. But Amber was getting ahead of herself. Everything depended on Molly passing the vet's examination that was taking place at 4pm that day. Only if she were given a clean bill of health would she belong to Amber.

The last lesson of the day was geography, a class Amber usually enjoyed as Miss Lewis was her favourite teacher and she was able to sit with her best (although totally un-horsey) friend, Sarah. But today she could hardly keep herself in her seat and was so totally unable to disguise her restlessness that she received some very puzzled looks from Miss Lewis, who was used to Amber being completely attentive in her lessons.

When the bell went to signal the end of the day, it was like the trigger of a rocket launch. Without waiting to walk out with Sarah as she always did, Amber leapt off her chair and ran from the room, calling back to a rather peeved looking Sarah, "Sorry, I've really got to go. See you tomorrow!"

And with that she raced through the corridors, squeezing through gaps between students who were making their way out annoyingly slowly, and across the netball courts to the queue of parents in their cars.

By the time Amber wrenched open her own car door and flung herself into the passenger seat as if she were making a quick getaway from a bank robbery, she was quite out of breath. She sat, puffing and red as a pillar box while Mrs Anderson laughed at her daughter's sudden appearance.

"Look at you, breaking the speed limit! What's the emergency?"

Amber looked crossly at her mother, "You know what. We're going to get Molly vetted, aren't we?"

"Yes, we are, but I don't know why you've rushed down here and left Sarah behind as if your life depended on it. We're going to be sitting in this traffic for at least ten minutes before we can even move."

Sure enough, Mrs Anderson was right as it took precisely twelve minutes (Amber was counting) before the cars and buses started to filter slowly out of the school gates. Much to Amber's embarrassment, Sarah had, just a few minutes after Amber, climbed into her car, which was parked three ahead of Amber's and had left the school first.

***

The vet was already waiting in the Dean's backyard when Amber and her mother arrived. Amber felt a flutter in her stomach when she saw Molly, the light dancing on her perfectly smooth, red coat as Frankie held her for the vet.

"Right, let's take a look," the vet proclaimed, flourishing a stethoscope from his pocket and placing it on Molly's side.

Amber watched anxiously as the vet, a tall man with large, strong hands, examined Molly thoroughly. He listened to her heart and breathing and felt along her limbs, back, neck and pelvis in the yard, then they went out into the alley and Molly was trotted up and down before having various flexion tests performed and finally, her heart and breathing were checked again.

"Well," the vet began, zipping up his bag and slinging it over his shoulder before delivering his verdict, "this is a very fit, healthy pony. She has an excellent heartbeat and her wind is fine. I believe she's had an injury to her back?" he enquired, looking at Mrs Dean.

"Yes, two years ago, but it healed well, and she's had no trouble since."

"Well, it's up to you," he turned to Mrs Anderson. "She's a fit mare and as sound as a pound. I can't detect any problems with her back, but backs are funny things. It could go again in the future, or on the other hand, it might not. It depends whether you want to take the risk."

With that, he shook hands with the two women and left, leaving Mrs Anderson to make up her mind. Thinking it over, she considered that although Molly could have a problem with her back later on, the vet had said it was fine at the moment and that in all other ways she was exceptionally fit and healthy. She also knew that Amber was a small, lightweight rider who wouldn't put undue pressure on Molly's back by being too heavy for her. She looked at Frankie, who was much heavier than Amber and decided that, compared to her, Molly wouldn't even feel her daughter's weight. Plus, there was always the chance that she was completely healed, and the problem would never return.

"What do you want to do then?" Asked Mrs Dean, not unpleasantly.

"Well, I'm satisfied with the vet's verdict, so I think I owe you some more money."

Amber suddenly realised she'd been holding her breath waiting for her mother's decision and gasped loudly when she heard what she'd been desperately hoping for. She felt so happy she could burst.

Everyone was all smiles except for Frankie. Amber noticed the girl's reaction to the news was not as gleeful as everyone else's. Her eyes were flat and expressionless as she raised a hand to stroke Molly's nose. Her face gave nothing away, but Amber could tell from her slumped shoulders and the tender way she stroked the pony that she was not happy.

Seeing Frankie's sadness made Amber's bubbling excitement settle to a simmer, as she knew Molly would soon belong to her, but she could imagine how awful this must feel to the girl who was losing her pony.

Following Frankie when she turned to take Molly back to her stable, she ventured uncertainly, "I know this must be horrible for you, but she'll have a good home. She'll have plenty of company and will be able to go out in the field with our ponies. We'll take good care of her, and you'll probably still see her at shows."

"I know, I'm not upset really," Frankie opened the stable door and led Molly inside, "once she goes, we can bring my new horse home and I'm looking forward to that. It's just that I'll miss her. She's been a good pony."

Amber felt slightly awkward and cast around for something else to say. "So, is there anything else I should know about her?"

They began walking back to the house.

"Only that she doesn't like having rugs put on or having her girth done up. She gnashes but we never tie her up and she's never bitten anyone."

"What do you mean, she gnashes?"

"Oh, she pulls faces and snaps her teeth together, but she doesn't bite. She just likes to let you know she's not impressed!"

"Oh, right!"

The two mothers were both smiling and talking happily, waiting by the front door when Amber and Frankie got back to the house.

"Come on then," Mrs Anderson beckoned to Amber, "let's go and get our tea. Thanks again," she shook Mrs Dean's hand, "and we'll see you at the weekend."

***

Saturday morning was like Christmas to Amber. She was so excited she couldn't sleep, so she got up at 6am and tried to keep busy while she waited for it to be time to go to the farm. Molly was being delivered at 10am.

Eventually, after tidying her room, feeding Stig and Kasper, cleaning out the goldfish, flicking through a magazine and having breakfast, it was finally time to set off. Mr Anderson was as keen to see Molly as Amber, as he'd been at work during the trial and the vetting and so hadn't even seen his daughter's new pony yet. He kept calling her 'Good Golly Miss Molly,' which Amber found irritating. It was a song from the olden days apparently.

They arrived in plenty of time to get Molly's stable ready. Hers was an enormous loose box right next to the farmer's daughter's horse, Oriel. The big bay mare was already looking out of her top door, seemingly aware that something was going on due to all the hustle and bustle going on around her. Honey and Pearl didn't have a clue what was going on, however, as their large shared stable and yard were around the corner and out of sight.

The stable for Molly hadn't had a horse in it for some time and had been used to store old furniture, bits of machinery and so on. But when Mrs Anderson had asked Jerry the farmer if it would be possible to bring another pony, he had been excellent. He and his sons, fifteen-year-old Daniel and eighteen-year-old Jack had cleared the stable of all its contents and cleaned away all the dust and cobwebs, then his daughter, Caroline had whitewashed all the walls until it looked like a brand new stable. And now, with its hay bracket full and deep straw bed neatly arranged, it was ready for its new occupant.

***

On the dot of 10am, the Dean family rolled up the dusty farm track and into the yard. The front ramp of the trailer was lowered, and Molly's striking face poked out, her nostrils dilated and quivering and her eyes wide and worried as she was led down the ramp into the unfamiliar place. Frankie took her straight into her new stable and removed her rug, bandages and head collar.

Molly instantly began exploring the strange new area sniffing and breathing deeply at the fresh new straw, the walls, and the hay. Then, as if she knew what was happening, she ran to the stable door and flung her head out, whinnying loudly to the Deans, who were walking back to the car. Amber's heart went out to her. *She* knew Molly would be getting well looked after and loved here, but to the pony, it must seem like being abandoned to an uncertain future with strange, new people.

"Enjoy her Amber," said Mrs Dean, who looked a bit teary. "Make sure you win everything on her. She's got her reputation to keep up," she joked weakly.

"Does she have a show name?" Asked Amber, knowing that her dad would be itching to call her that annoying song title he kept singing.

"We couldn't think of anything spectacular or imaginative when we got her so she's simply 'Just Molly'. It suits her – she's so good she doesn't need a fancy name."

With that, the Deans climbed back into their car and drove away.

The Andersons stood and looked at each other. Mrs Anderson was the one to break the silence. "Well, we've got a pony, but nothing for her. If you're going to ride her, we'd better sort some tack out."

When they'd bought the Fell ponies, Claire had helpfully included their tack in the sale, but this hadn't been the case with Molly.

"Let's go down and see if Claire has any tack we can borrow until we get sorted," suggested Mr Anderson.

***

Claire had been very helpful and given them a simple snaffle bridle and several saddles to try.

"They might be a bit wide for her," she said, loading the third saddle into the car, as most of Claire's horses and ponies were natives and cobs, "but the last one is probably your best bet. It was Rosie's – a fairly slim pony I used to have. They're all for sale anyway, so if you want any of them just let me know."

The following day, with Caroline's help, they tried the saddles on Molly. Caroline was very quiet and gentle but obviously very knowledgeable as she inserted her fingers between the saddle and Molly's back, peered down the gullet and pulled at the cantle. Just as Claire had predicted, Caroline rejected the first two saddles as they were too wide and would put pressure on Molly's spine and withers, but the third met with her approval.

"This one seems okay," she said quietly as she repeated the assessment methods, "it's a narrower fit so it isn't pressing on her spine and there's plenty of clearance here." She showed them the four-finger gap between the withers and the pommel. "I'll have to see what it's like with you sitting on it," she told Amber.

Mrs Anderson produced one of Honey's girths and fastened it to the saddle. Frankie's warning proved true: as the girth was tightened, Molly put her ears back and started snapping her teeth, but she never turned her head to bite and she was soon tacked up and ready to go.

Amber mounted and Caroline checked the saddle again before watching as they walked and did a little trot around the yard.

"It seems a good fit," she told Amber's parents, "it doesn't restrict Molly's movement and it's the right size for Amber too. A nice quality saddle."

Mr Anderson thanked Caroline, who blushed and muttered that it was nothing, and Amber was left sitting in the yard on Molly.

"Well, I guess we'll go and get Honey and Pearl and ride out with you," said Mr Anderson, "why don't you go down and show Molly to Joanne while you're waiting?"

***

There was no-one around when Amber arrived at Jubilee House, so she dismounted and opened the gate before leading Molly to the front door and ringing the bell. When Joanne opened the door, her eyes nearly popped out of her head as she saw Amber standing there holding Molly.

"Oh wow, you got her!" She came straight out and started looking Molly up and down. "Isn't there a show on at Brantfort Bridge today? I thought you'd have been going."

"We only got her yesterday," Amber explained, "and she didn't have any tack. We've had to borrow some off Claire. We're just letting her settle in first before we go anywhere. And I need to get used to her too. We're all going for a ride now; I'm just waiting for them to come down."

"Oooo, come and do some jumps in the field until they get here," said Joanne excitedly, "let's see what she's like."

***

Amber felt rather nervous about jumping Molly in front of Joanne, who obviously had such high expectations, especially as she'd only jumped her over a small fence in a very enclosed space on her trial. Nerves were soon replaced with elation, however, as Molly cleared the jumps in the paddock effortlessly. There was no pulling or charging, just smooth, controlled jumping from a pony that was completely willing. Amber had never felt anything like it. Jumping on Molly was like floating. Joanne was all for putting the jumps up higher when Amber's parents arrived to meet her.

"Call for me after school next week, I'll ride out with you," called Joanne as Amber rode away with her parents.

"Yeah," she replied distantly, looking down at the unfamiliar chestnut mane in front of her.

Amber was in heaven. Molly was the best pony she could ever have wished for.

- Eight -

Speed Demon

"I hope you don't mind but Matthew's coming with us," said Joanne glumly as Amber arrived at her house with Molly. "Mum says he's got to come because Dad's at work and she needs to go shopping and Matthew whinges something awful if he has to go shopping. Sorry." She rolled her eyes in apology that her little brother would be accompanying them.

Amber laughed at Joanne's exasperation at having to look after her brother and wondered fleetingly what it would be like to have brothers and sisters.

"Don't worry, it's fine if Matthew comes. I don't mind!"

Joanne's younger brother was a quiet boy with dark curly hair and freckles, quite the opposite of Joanne with her pale skin and straight blonde hair. He rode Sam, a lovely hairy bay pony with a bushy black mane and tail and feathery feet. Amber knew Matthew wouldn't trouble them on the ride, he would just plod away at the back in silence thinking about whatever nine-year-old boys think about, while she and his sister rode together at the front chatting non-stop all the way round.

"Isn't your mum or dad coming with us?" Joanne asked, seeing that Amber was on her own.

"Not this time. Dad's brought me today but Honey has lost a shoe so he can't ride: Pearl's too small for him, so it's just me."

"Oh well, we'll be fine. Mum seems to think I need a babysitter. What does she think is going to happen? Merry's an angel compared to Flash and I hardly think Sam is going to have a psychotic moment. We'll just have a nice quiet ride out and she needn't even know we went on our own."

***

Molly and Merry matched each other perfectly, both being the same size and build with the same length of stride. Amber couldn't wait to get back to the forestry hill so they could race up it and see who was the fastest. When she'd ridden with her parents on Sunday, they'd just walked and trotted, so she couldn't wait to have a gallop. Racing would be a whole new experience for Amber as riding with Joanne had always previously meant her getting left behind on Pearl while Flash sped away on his own. Now they had ponies that were much more equally matched, things would be a lot more interesting.

"Do you want to canter here?" Joanne asked as they'd reached the short uphill part of the narrow track they were riding single file on, where they usually cantered. The path didn't last very long before it became rocky and began winding down into the valley, but it was a nice place to have a short, gentle canter before they had to walk to the bottom.

"Yeah great," she replied from her position behind Joanne and Merry and gathered up her reins to set off.

Molly was not used to this sort of riding; her previous outings had either been competing at shows or being ridden on the roads. The feel of soft earth beneath her feet and the sight of Merry cantering away in front of her was just too much excitement for her to bear. The pony couldn't stay calm and controllable when she could feel all her energy bubbling through her body, her rider was so light she could hardly feel her, there were other ponies to race and she had this lovely straight track to run on.

Amber felt the rush of energy surge beneath her as Molly launched into a gallop. She felt no joy or exhilaration from the tremendous speed of her mount as they gained quickly on Merry, only terror as she heaved on the reins to no avail. Instead of slowing down, Molly was pulling against her and her speed was building.

"AAAAAAARGHHHHHHH!" she screamed as they were nearly upon Joanne.

Joanne turned just in time to see Molly drawing up against Merry's quarters and acting instinctively, she pulled Merry back to allow Molly past before she pushed them off the track. The palomino obediently responded and slowed to a trot as Molly streaked past like a thoroughbred racehorse.

"What happened?" demanded Joanne incredulously as Matthew caught up on Sam.

"Dunno, she just went – like Flash, nought to sixty in one second!"

"Oh no," she moaned, "come on. We'll have to try and catch her."

With that, she urged Merry into a trot. Despite the urgency of the situation, there was no way she was risking cantering down the rocky downhill path, never mind galloping.

Meanwhile, a thoroughly terrified Amber was still hurtling along ahead at an unbelievable speed considering the terrain. Tears streamed down her face and blurred her vision and her bare hands were raw from pulling the reins. Wild with fright, she frantically racked her brain for ideas, now having to lean forward to avoid being thrashed by low hanging branches. Feeling her rider leaning higher up her neck, Molly surged forward with even greater speed. Suddenly Amber remembered how Elisha had stopped Rocky from his bolt by turning him in circles.

But the path is too narrow! her brain screamed in despair.

She tried hauling on one rein, then the other rather than pulling both at once. This had the effect of turning Molly's head slightly to the side, but being much stronger than her rider, the pony was easily able to wrench the taut, restricting rein away.

Amber sobbed with fear and frustration. The path had become flat again and Molly levelled out, her long legs stretching ahead of her as she reached blistering speeds. In a few more strides Amber knew they would come to a fork in the path. She needed to take a sharp turn to the right, almost doubling back on herself to get up onto a higher forestry track. The path that went straight ahead led out to the road.

She could see through her tears, not far ahead were the old stone gateposts where the path divided. She began pulling the right rein with all her might to try and get Molly to turn onto the uphill path where she hoped she could stop her. But to make the acute turn, Molly would have to slow down or risk falling, and she had already spied the straight path ahead of her. Deciding she would much rather continue galloping straight on than slow down and make a turn, the pony seized the bit and resisted Amber's concerted efforts to pull her round, charged through the old gate posts and sped along the path ahead.

Amber's brain screamed at her the urgency of the need to stop before they reached the road, but she could fight no longer. The skin on her hands was torn and blistered, her legs had turned to jelly, and her breath came in painful gasps between sobs. She was exhausted. Knowing that she had no chance of stopping Molly before the road, she contemplated throwing herself off into the hedgerow. But even as the thought occurred to her, she knew she couldn't do it – she was too frightened to move – so she sat there feeling the mighty muscles beneath her as Molly powered on, not tiring in the slightest, the fear inside her reaching breaking point.

"HELP!" she screamed in desperation, "HELP, HELP, HELP!"

As if in answer, there was a loud rumble and a tractor pulled out of a field beside the lane, completely blocking the path. Molly saw it and immediately checked her speed, sliding to a bumpy halt in front of the tractor and shooting Amber out of the saddle and up her neck where she remained, slumped and sobbing with relief that the ordeal was finally over. The farmer, now recovered from the temporary shock of seeing an out of control pony hurtling towards his tractor, climbed out and took hold of the reins. Far from being tired from the exertion, Molly was feeling positively invigorated from the experience. Her eyes were shining, and she champed the bit in annoyance at being stopped before she was ready, but she allowed the farmer to hold her and stood still while he turned his attention to the girl who was shaking and crying uncontrollably on its back.

"Now then lass," he spoke kindly, "tis over now. Yer alright. Come on, sit up, I've got yer."

Still trembling, Amber pushed herself back up Molly's neck and sat back in the saddle, wiping her swollen, red eyes. She looked down at her rescuer. Far from being a tall, handsome hero, the farmer looked at least sixty and wasn't an inch over 5ft 3. He was a startling old man to look at, being so small, but with big muscular arms and hands like spades. His face was brown and crinkly with piercing bright blue eyes and his white wispy hair was standing on end as if he had just pulled a hat off his head.

"Tis a fine spirited pony you've got 'ere lass," he remarked, sweeping his eyes over Molly's athletic frame. "A right la'al thoroughbred."

"She's just bolted with me," Amber explained breathlessly as she made to dismount.

"Whoa there, lass!" exclaimed the old man, putting up a hand to signal Amber to stay put. "You don't wanna be gittin off! You git off now, you'll never git back on. You need to master her. Best cure for a bolter is to tek it, get it garn and then, when it wants to stop, keep it garn till it can't ga ne more. That'll make the beast think!" He smiled a toothy grin revealing a large gap in his smile.

"Oh no," replied Amber with a mixture of horror and resignation, "that won't work with her. She doesn't stop – she goes on forever." She thought with a sickening lurch in her stomach of the never-ending gallop through the forest.

"Ah, they can't ga on foriver lass. They's not machines." He shook his head sagely.

Just then there was a clatter on the cobbled path and Joanne and Matthew appeared looking flustered with twigs and pine needles sticking out of their hats and hair. Amber was touched to see that Joanne's face was creased with concern, but on seeing Amber was safe and sound, relief washed away the worry and she seemed to sag as if a weight had been lifted off her.

"Oh, thank God you're okay!" she cried. "We were so worried. Now I know what it must've been like for you last year when Elisha and I disappeared. Oh hi, Mr

Greeves," she addressed the farmer who was still holding Molly.

"Hallo, lass," he replied heartily, then looked up at Amber with his bright blue eyes twinkling out of his nut-brown face. "Remember what I said lass. You'll 'ave to get the better of her or you'll always be afeared. You should turn around and give her a stinkin' good gallop back up the hill till she's on her knees. Cure her for sure."

Amber smiled weakly and gathered up the reins in her raw, tender hands. "Thanks for your help, but I just can't. I'm going to walk back along the road."

Mr Greeves let go of Molly and gave her a vigorous pat before shrugging his shoulders and climbing back into his tractor.

- Nine -

The Good, the Bad
and the Unexpected

Amber was full of trepidation as she sat in the car on the way to her first competition with Molly. After Mr Greeves had driven away in his tractor, the three of them had ridden all the way back along the road at a walk as Amber was so worried Molly would bolt again. Molly, on the other hand, had no intention of galloping off. As soon as she felt the familiar tarmac under her hooves, something in her brain switched off and she ambled home like a perfectly docile donkey.

Later in the week, she'd ridden with her parents – she went back onto Pearl while her mum rode

Molly in case she misbehaved. But, as if she wanted to make a liar of Amber, Molly was perfectly good and even enjoyed a quiet canter. Amber was now sure her parents thought she had exaggerated her recount of the ride with Joanne and Matthew and that she was overreacting – Molly hadn't bolted with her – she was just much faster than Pearl, and Amber would soon get used to her.

Amber wasn't so sure. She'd been so happy when Molly was bought for her but now...

Molly had made her feel fear. Amber had *never* felt afraid riding Pearl or any of the ponies in the riding school, but now she knew what it was like to be scared of an animal's strength. And she hated that feeling. She thought forward to her show jumping later in the afternoon. All images of herself leading the lap of honour, waving her red rosette while Elisha trailed behind her in second place had vanished, to be replaced with pictures of Molly careering wildly around the arena with herself just trying to hang on. She closed her eyes and groaned softly. Molly had such a high reputation in competitions; if Amber didn't do well, she knew what people would say. It would be all her fault. The pressure made Amber's stomach turn over. She wondered if you could be physically sick from worrying.

"Are you okay Amber? You look rather green."

Amber was not alone in the back of the car. Emily sat with her. The vet had proclaimed Fudge was sound again but had advised that he only do gentle work for the next few weeks as Pony Club camp was coming up and light work would ensure he would be okay to go. When Emily had relayed the news to Amber at the last stable management rally and gloomily told her Fudge wasn't allowed to do the fun-jump at the weekend, Amber had asked her dad if they could take Honey for Emily to ride, remembering how well she'd gone for Emily in Joanne's field.

And so, Emily had brought her riding gear and stayed the night. Now they were off to Blakefield's fun-jump with Molly and Honey in the trailer behind.

They arrived early, before any of the classes had even begun, but already the field was filling up with rows of trailers and lorries, their colourful metallic paint gleaming in the sunlight. They unloaded the ponies and Amber noted with interest their different reactions to their new surroundings. Molly surveyed the scene hopefully but seemed to look disappointed and bored as she was tied up. Honey on the other hand, who had never travelled in the trailer or been to a show before, stood at the top of the ramp looking around cautiously, her ears pricked so that they nearly touched – her eyes wide and nostrils flared. She looked like she was having a very serious think about whether she was going to venture out of the trailer or not. Eventually, after being coaxed and cajoled with a large carrot, she allowed herself to be led down the ramp and tied up next to Molly. The girls left Amber's parents with the ponies while they went off to place their entries.

The schedule pinned to the caravan window showed that there were five classes starting at sixty centimetres and ending with a metre. In a change since last year, the classes were no longer linked to the size of the pony. Now, any size of horse or pony could be entered in any height class to make

235

allowances for the different levels of ability and experience.

"What are you going to enter?" Amber asked Emily while nervously deciding what she herself should enter. When she was on Pearl, the decision was made for her as Pearl could only really manage the first two classes, but nobody would be expecting her to enter the little classes with Molly. Her stomach did a backflip and took a bow, celebrating its acrobatic skills.

"Well, it says you can enter two height classes," answered Emily, following the writing with a finger and pursing her lips as she thought. "I think I'll do the first two heights as it's only Honey's first show." And with that, she stepped up into the caravan to place her entries, leaving Amber still fretting outside.

After much deliberation, Amber, at last, decided that she could get away with saying she was still getting used to Molly, it was almost the first time she'd jumped on her, and therefore not feel too much of a wimp for not entering the highest classes. She left the caravan with Emily, both carrying their numbers, having entered the seventy and eighty centimetre classes and feeling slightly happier. Although she still felt as if worms were wriggling and writhing in her stomach, the overpowering urge to be sick had lessened.

***

Emily looked very smart on Honey as they warmed up for the first class. Honey's eyes were still popping as she took in the sights and sounds of the show field, but Emily remained calm – oblivious to Honey's shies and spooks - and soon the pony settled, drawing confidence from her rider as they jumped the practice fence, just as she had when Emily rode her in Joanne's field.

As she was watching Honey canter serenely towards the practice fence, Amber heard a "hi!" behind her. She turned to see Natalie, who had ridden over on Sable to begin warming up.

"Aren't you in this class?" she asked Amber.

"No, I'm in the next two. I've brought my new pony, Molly, today."

"Oh. Can't wait to see her."

"I'm just watching Emily. She's riding our Honey and she's never been to a show before. Fudge is still on light duties until camp so we said Emily could borrow Honey for the fun-jump."

"Ah." Natalie's eyes found the black Fell pony and followed its progress over the practice jump. "Well, I'd better warm-up. I'm in this class and they're ready to start."

"Good luck!" called Amber as Natalie rode away and the first competitor was called to enter the ring.

There were lots of competitors in the class and most people were going clear. Emily was near the end of the class so Amber changed into her riding clothes and rode around on Molly for a while. She was sitting on her, at the ringside, flanked by both parents when Emily was announced.

"Emily Pryde, riding Townend Honeysuckle!" They hadn't had to think of a show name for Honey; as she was a registered Fell pony, she already had a name.

The whistle blew and the speakers crackled. Honey jumped and her ears twitched back. Amber could see Emily's lips moving and knew she was talking gently to reassure the startled pony. Emily nudged Honey into a canter and proceeded smoothly to the first fence.

The round must have only lasted a minute as Honey cantered around, her long, bushy black tail billowing out behind her, happily jumping fences as if she was a pro. They gave a loud cheer as she jumped the last fence to gain a clear round.

"Honey's first ever class and she's in the jump-off," cried Mrs Anderson incredulously. Who would've thought it?"

They watched the remaining three competitors, and saw the first two go clear, only to be followed by another disastrous round from Natalie and Sable. As it was a fun-jump and Natalie was last to go in the class, they were a bit more relaxed with the rules and allowed Natalie to continue after she'd got two refusals by the second fence. However, as Sable continued to stop at every jump and parents waiting for the jump-off started shooting accusatory looks at Mr Best, he had to ask Natalie to leave the arena.

Honey went just as well in the jump-off. Emily didn't push her or make her do tight turns, as she knew the pony had never competed before, but Honey looked as though she was thoroughly enjoying herself.

As there had been so many in the class, Emily and Honey weren't placed but nevertheless, everyone was delighted with their performance – none more so than Honey herself, it seemed. The shy, timid pony Amber knew had disappeared. Her eyes shone and she arched her neck regally, as if inviting people to admire her.

The next class also had a lot of entries and Amber could feel herself getting in a knot as she felt more and more nervous waiting for her turn. Molly had warmed up quietly and was showing no signs of doing anything naughty, but still Amber felt like something large and prickly had got stuck in her throat.

"Next into the arena is Emily Pryde and Townend Honeysuckle. Stand by Amber Anderson and Just Molly," came Mr Best's voice over the tannoy.

Hearing her name called sent Amber into her own little bubble. Sounds became muffled and her vision became hazy as she stared out in front of her but saw nothing. The next thing she knew, her name was being called again over the loudspeaker. Emily had already left the arena and Amber had seen nothing of her round. Feeling a mixture of guilt, nerves and anticipation, she rode into the arena and cantered at the sound of the whistle.

Molly's canter was smooth, balanced and effortless. She approached the first fence and was over it without Amber even feeling anything – it was just like another canter stride. They floated around the rest of the course gliding comfortably over the fences so easily it was like they weren't there. As they cantered out of the arena amidst gentle applause and "*that's a clear round!*" ringing in her ears, Amber's shoulders slumped, and she had to lean her hands on Molly's withers to support her weight; she was weak with relief and happiness. She patted Molly gratefully as Emily and Natalie came to congratulate her; Emily still mounted on Honey, Natalie now on foot.

"Well done Amber! That means we're against each other in the jump-off now," grinned Emily.

"She went lovely didn't she?" Natalie stroked Molly's blaze, a mournful look on her face. "I wish I had a pony like her, one that would just jump without a fuss. Sable totally hates competing."

"Why don't you sell her and get a pony that's more …agreeable?" suggested Emily, choosing her words carefully.

Natalie sighed deeply. "I'd love to, but who'd buy her?"

"Not everybody wants a pony for jumping. Plenty of people just want to hack out. Is she a nice ride?"

"Yeah, she's quite nice but she's so grumpy and bad-tempered, she'd put people off. Who wants a pony that can't even be nice?" Natalie shrugged her shoulders and looked thoroughly fed up. Amber was about to repeat what Emily had once told her, about horses and people either getting on or making each other miserable, but bit her lip and decided to keep it to herself. She didn't think Natalie would be too pleased to hear that it might be her making her pony miserable and that Sable might be much happier and less bad-tempered with someone else.

By this time the remaining competitors had completed their rounds and the order for the jump-off was being called.

Amber didn't have much experience of jump-off technique, not having been in any, but she'd watched enough of them to pick up some tips. She silently memorised the new shortened course and planned her route – where she could save time by cutting corners or going inside fences – and where she could push Molly on.

The first few competitors went quite well, but none of them had taken Amber's planned short cut inside number six; they'd all gone around. When her name was called, Amber entered the arena suddenly unsure of the route she would take – *Should I stick to my plan, or be careful and take the long route*?

Once again Molly loped forward into a smooth canter. They cleared the first and Amber pushed on to the next fence. Molly immediately lengthened her stride and stood off the second jump, but was still perfectly under control. They cleared the wall and Molly was going so well, Amber decided to cut inside fence six as she had planned and jump the double from two strides. Molly responded instantly to her aids and popped over the double easily.

As she brought Molly back to a trot, patting her furiously, she heard her time over the loudspeaker. She was the quickest yet. She was in the lead!

"Well done, that was brilliant! Well ridden!" Emily cheered generously as she rode past Amber into the arena.

"Thanks," gasped Amber. "Good luck."

After Amber, many of the remaining competitors copied her turn inside number six, but one after another, as their times were read out, Amber remained in the lead. Growing more and more excited that she was about to achieve her ambition and win a jumping class, she held her breath as the last rider started his round. Fiercely competitive, he charged over the fences, kicking madly in between the spread-out ones and yanking sharply at his pony's bit on the turns. He too turned inside to the last fence – the double – but pulled his pony around so roughly the poor thing momentarily lost its footing. Gamely, it still tried to jump but the stride wasn't right, and the top pole came down. When the time was announced, he was the fastest and would've won if he hadn't had the double down. Amber felt sorry for the boy's pony as he rode out with a face like thunder – it had tried its best for him, despite his rather rough riding and the boy obviously didn't appreciate it – but soon a great swell of joy was rising in her as the results were called. She was the winner and Honey had come in sixth place after gaining another clear in her jump-off. Amber had never felt so elated as she led the lap of honour around the arena, her red rosette fluttering in the breeze on Molly's bridle. She was dimly aware of people clapping around her, but she couldn't take it in. It was like being back in one of her dreams. She had won her first ever class and it was the best feeling in the world. She never wanted it to end.

Amber had never seen her parents so excited. They were full of congratulations for Amber and gave Molly nearly half a packet of Polo mints, which she crunched up loudly before searching for more. The other half of the packet, unfortunately for Molly, was being fed lovingly to Honey, whom everyone was absolutely delighted with.

"Thanks for letting me ride her," Emily thanked Amber's parents while fondly smoothing Honey's long forelock, "she was great, and I really enjoyed it."

"Oh, no problem," cried Mrs Anderson. "It's been a pleasure and a surprise to see her doing so well. Thank you!"

Amber felt much more confident as she rode into the arena for her next round. She couldn't wait to get started and feel Molly's wonderful jump again. A gate had been added and many of the jumps now had colourful fillers placed under the poles. Amber felt a thrill of excitement as she rode purposefully for the first fence.

As with the first round, Molly jumped carefully and easily, her experience showing as she took the gate and coloured fillers without a second glance. Amber concentrated hard on remembering the course and riding Molly as well as she could. Soon it was all over. Another clear round.

She didn't have as long to wait for the jump-off in this class as fewer people managed to get clear rounds. One of the fillers displaying a vivid orange and black tiger's face was causing problems and several ponies refused to go over. The jump-off course was soon ready, and Amber felt her insides flutter again as she surveyed the jumps, now standing at eighty-five centimetres and looking positively monumental.

"You can do it. Molly can do it. Don't be nervous." she told herself firmly, breathing in deep, calming breaths.

Once again, she watched others tackle the course before her, some attempting the tight turn to the double, others playing safe and going around. By the time it was her turn there hadn't been any fast clears, so Amber resolved to do her best to win again.

Molly responded well to her new, more urgent riding and cleared the fences well until only the double remained. The double was now bigger with fillers under the first part and a back pole added to the second. As Amber steered Molly round to cut inside, she gave her an extra little kick to give her the impulsion she would need to clear the bigger jumps.

It didn't work.

Just as Amber was getting ready to lean forward and move her hands up Molly's neck for the take-off, Molly pulled up and stopped right in front of the fence. Momentarily shocked that Molly had refused, Amber quickly composed herself and brought Molly round for a second and final attempt, giving her plenty of space to approach now that her chance of winning had gone. Amber could feel herself growing hot as she knew many pairs of eyes were watching her, many of whom

248

belonged to people who knew Molly. They would be tutting and shaking their heads.

She rode strongly, determined not to be eliminated. Molly jumped in over the first part unenthusiastically and was backing off the second part as soon as she landed. Amber brandished her whip and smacked Molly on the shoulder, willing her to jump. Much to her surprise, the pony went straight up in the air in an awkward cat jump. She didn't stretch for the spread at all and brought the whole fence crashing down underneath her. The team of helpers rushed to rebuild the fence again while a shamefaced Amber left the arena.

What happened? What caused Molly to go from the winner of one class to almost being eliminated in the next? Was it me? Have I ruined her already, is that possible? What will my parents say? Amber's mind was so full of thoughts, she didn't even notice the blue and yellow horsebox she was riding past or the loud "hello," as she went by.

"Amber!"

Amber's head snapped up and her brain was wrenched away from its thoughts as she heard her name being called. Her mood dropped even further when she saw who it was that had addressed her. Elisha was in the process of putting a saddle on her black horse. She finished pulling the girth up and ducked under his neck, walking directly up to Amber.

Amber leant away from Elisha's approach, like a flower bowing to a storm.

"New pony." It was a statement, not a question. "That's Frankie Dean's' Molly isn't it?" Elisha said, tilting her head slightly.

"Yeah." Then she wished she'd said no, actually, it was *her* Molly.

Elisha's mouth curled into a little smile as she detected the tone in Amber's voice.

"She's a really good jumper – won loads with Frankie. She'll be a big change for you after riding that fat little Fell pony. It's about time you got something decent and started taking competitions seriously."

Amber felt her temper rising but she didn't reply. She didn't want to give Elisha the satisfaction of upsetting her again.

"You'll be going in the big classes today then?" Elisha asked, pushing Amber further.

"No, I've just finished actually," Amber retorted curtly, trying to ride away from Elisha before she said anything else. As she went to steer Molly around her, Elisha caught hold of the pony's reins and began stroking her nose while she looked up at Amber with her hard, blue eyes.

"You've been in the little classes?" she gasped. "What an insult to Molly! You're not riding your no-hope Fell pony anymore. What's the point having a beauty like Molly if you're just going to do the baby classes? She's too good for that."

"I…I'm still getting used to her and I'm not used to big jumps and…and we won our first class so…" Amber flustered until Elisha interrupted.

"Oh, you won a seventy centimetre class? Well done, you'll be at the Olympics next. And how did you do in the other class?"

Amber stared at Elisha, who stared right back, that annoying smirk still playing at the corners of her lips. Amber wilted under the force of Elisha's piercing gaze and broke eye contact.

"Get lost, Elisha!" Amber kicked Molly on so that Elisha had to drop the reins and step aside to avoid being trodden on.

"Ooooh, touchy!" Elisha called to Amber's retreating back. "I was only asking."

By the time she reached the trailer, Amber was shaking with disappointment and rage.

"Never mind pet," her mother consoled her, "I think you were just a bit too ambitious in the jump-off. You're not experienced enough yet to be making tight turns into jumps that size. You can start having your lessons again and you and Molly will be winning all sorts soon."

"Yeah," Emily joined in, holding Molly while Amber removed the saddle, "you did really well. It can take ages to bond with a new pony. Don't worry about it."

But Amber *did* worry. If Molly was supposed to be such a wonderful jumper, surely she should've been able to manage that double? Amber was plagued by the thought that it had been her fault and Molly would have jumped with a better rider. Elisha's words still stung her. The girl had a knack of pinpointing what she was thinking and feeling like a mind reader. Her mood blackened even further when it was announced that Elisha had come first and second in both of the biggest classes on North Quest and Thunder Cat.

"I will beat her one day," Amber vowed to herself, "if it's the last thing I do."

– Jen –

Trojan Horse

"She's certainly a looker." Claire ran her hands over Molly's smooth, hard shoulders that shone like polished wood, before running experienced fingers down Molly's legs. "Plenty of heart room, deep chest, clean legs. Yep, she's a beauty." She stood back to admire the overall picture in front of her. "But you say she's bolted with you and didn't jump too well on Sunday?"

They were standing in the outdoor arena at Pine Tree Stables, ready to start Amber's first lesson with Molly. Gloomily, Amber recounted the terrifying ride through the forest and the abysmal jump-off round at the weekend. Claire listened intently, never taking her eyes off Molly as Amber talked. It was as if she was trying to communicate telepathically with the pony; to see into her mind and read her thoughts.

"And then Elisha Templeton was nasty to me again. I'm sure she saw me jumping but pretended not to just so she could ask how I'd done, to see what I would say. So, I've got to get better so I can beat her," Amber finished, resolutely.

Claire didn't reply immediately. She remained fixed to the spot, scrutinising Molly with a slight frown on her face. "What was her last rider like?"

"Erm, in what way?" Asked Amber, surprised by the question.

"Well, you know: tall, small, light, heavy, timid, bold?"

Amber thought of Frankie. She pictured her astride the mighty Bonfire Bob and remembered what she'd heard people say about her.

"Well, I suppose you'd say Frankie was quite stocky and strong – taller than me. She's pretty confident as she rode her mum's horse when I tried Molly and he was a massive handful. And I suppose she must be quite competitive because she's won loads of rosettes and trophies."

Claire nodded, taking in the information shrewdly. "Did you ever see her ride Molly? Did she show her off before you tried her?"

"No, it was just me. She was brought out of the stable, we rode round the block then I jumped a tiny jump in a really tiny arena – it was a chicken yard really – and that was it."

"Did you ask if you could have her on trial before making a decision?"

"We did ask but they said someone else was interested in her and would definitely have her if we didn't want her, so they said no."

"Hmmm." Claire continued to stand with one hand on her hip, gazing blankly at nothing in particular as if she had forgotten where she was and what she was doing. "Right then," she said briskly, breaking out of her trance. "Let's see her in action."

Amber took Molly through her paces while Claire sat on the fence, watching but offering no comment. This was unusual for her, Amber thought, as she was usually a very attentive instructor who offered a constant stream of advice to help the pupil improve their riding. Still without speaking, Claire climbed down from the fence and erected four small jumps, including a double.

"Shorten your stirrups and try these," she instructed.

Amber pulled her stirrups up two holes and they cantered easily over the small jumps. Silently, Claire put the jumps up so that they were about eighty centimetres and told Amber to come again. Once more Molly cantered smoothly to the jumps and went over them with little effort. Amber patted her gratefully. She was jumping so well, Amber started to think she must've dreamt Sunday's disaster.

"Well done, you're riding really nicely," commented Claire as she jiggled a stiff cup on the fence nearest her. "Now, let's have them up a bit more and see how you manage."

Amber walked Molly around the arena for a few laps as she watched Claire adjust the jumps. She had put them up to about ninety centimetres and fences two and three had been pushed together to make a spread.

"Okay," Claire called to signal the jumps were ready. Just as before, Molly cantered gracefully around the arena, but she went over the first jump rather awkwardly and Amber landed back in the saddle with a bang. Wincing slightly from the jarring landing, Amber rode on towards the spread fence. Molly felt different this time. Instead of moving on and jumping easily, she was backing off and trying to veer off the line Amber was riding. Amber tried to use her legs to keep Molly straight, but she was not strong enough and Molly ran out at the last minute. Claire, who had been watching from the fence, jumped down and waved at Amber to wait.

"You're going to have to be very firm with her," the instructor advised, "her last rider was strong and confident. You are a very gentle rider, which is good, but you do need a bit more drive to persuade her to do these bigger jumps. Start again and really ride her positively."

Amber nodded and gathered her reins up, noticing that they were suddenly slicked with sweat. Looking down at Molly's neck beneath her she could see the pony's coat was dark and wet. *That's funny,* she thought, *she wasn't sweaty at all a minute ago.* Giving it no further thought, she rode Molly strongly onward and slapped her shoulder with the stick as they approached the first fence. Molly jumped but Amber heard the pole fall as they landed. At the spread, Molly attempted to jump but caught the pole heavily with her hind legs and brought it crashing down, and she refused at the double. Amber re-presented her three times, but Molly wouldn't jump and eventually refused to even go near the fence, backing up and shaking her head. Amber's face was burning with frustration and the effort of trying to stop Molly from going backwards. She was getting redder and redder as she tried harder to get Molly moving in the right direction when Claire called to her. "Stop Amber, stop!"

Drained of all energy, Amber gratefully slumped back in the saddle, her head beating and hot inside her hard hat. "What am I–"

"Has this pony ever had an injury to its back?" Claire interrupted.

259

"She jumped through a wall after standing on her bandages a couple of years ago and hurt her back, but we had her vetted and he said her back was okay." Amber puffed.

"I'd get a second opinion if I were you," said Claire, exhaling deeply. "She wasn't happy at all when the jumps went up. She looked uncomfortable once the poles went higher. She might just have some niggling problem that doesn't bother her when the jumps are small, but she can really feel it when she has to stretch more for bigger ones."

Claire saw the dejection in Amber's face and body and knew how she was feeling. No sooner had she got herself a good competition pony after slogging away with reluctant little Pearl than it looked like Molly would be out of action for a while. The instructor patted Amber on the leg. "Don't worry. I've got a number for a very good chiropractor. With a bit of treatment and some rest, I'm sure you'll be jumping brilliantly in no time."

Amber didn't look convinced.

"Think of it like this. A pony trying to jump with a bad back is like you doing PE in trainers a size too small. You could put up with it for a while but eventually, you'd be in agony. If you knew it would be the same every PE lesson, you'd soon start avoiding the class completely. From Molly's point of view, if she feels pain every time she jumps, she'll soon stop jumping altogether, even small ones, because she'll associate pain with jumping. But get her treated now and she'll probably be happy to jump again. Come and get this number."

***

Eddie 'the back man' couldn't come for two weeks, so Molly was allowed to rest while they waited, and Amber went back to riding Pearl in the meantime. As Fudge was now approved for riding by the vet, Emily didn't come back to ride Honey again. The only upside was that Amber could ride out with Joanne again now that she was so much better. Sometimes her mum or dad joined them, other times, one of them took Honey out on her own to get her out of 'riding school mode,' as she was still apt to tuck in behind another pony and hide from any horrors lurking on the way.

261

It seemed strange now to go back to riding Pearl. The difference between her and Molly was huge. Getting back on Pearl was like sitting back in an old comfortable chair, where she could relax with the familiarity of knowing its feel and where the stains were and that she could put her feet up and drop things without worrying about marking it. In comparison, Molly was like a new, tall, hard, straight-backed chair where she had to sit up straight, behave properly, and do everything right. Amber knew that Molly was a classy pony and she needed more time to get used to her, but the bolt and the jumping disaster had unnerved her, and although she didn't want to admit it to herself, Molly had frightened her. Amber was glad for an excuse to not ride her for a couple of weeks.

It was nice to talk to Joanne again after not seeing her for so long, but she was surprised to find that Jo was not having such a good time at her school. She had been off for a couple of months after her accident and had fallen behind in some of her subjects. Amber didn't think it would matter much as Jo was still in Year Six; she was bright and would soon catch up. But the main problem wasn't really the work; it was the other kids.

"Some of them laugh at me and call me thick if I get stuck on work because I've missed what they've done earlier, so I don't know what to do."

"Doesn't your teacher know?" Amber asked, concerned for her friend.

"Not really, they do it when the teacher isn't looking, or they pass me notes. One girl, Megan, is really mean and passes notes either to me or about me saying horrible things."

Amber felt sympathetic towards Joanne as there were kids in her own form at her school who teased her and called her 'swot' or 'goofy' on account of her prominent front teeth. Especially Kieran and Josh, who seemed to think it necessary to say something unpleasant every time they saw her. It didn't bother her too much as they were such ugly boys – Kieran with his small, piggy eyes and Josh with his jug ears - that Amber wasn't much bothered what they thought of her. Especially as she knew her braces would eventually straighten her teeth. Sometimes, when they were taunting her and trying to humiliate her in front of others, she felt like saying something back to them to shut them up, but she never did.

Something always held her back from retaliating, but she didn't know what. She wondered if Joanne stuck up for herself or just let it wash over her.

"Are you going to do anything about it?" she asked.

"Nah, she's stupid. She sends me notes saying how thick I am and nearly every word is spelt wrong. It's like a joke! I think she's just pleased that there's someone in the class doing worse than her, but it won't last long. I'll get my revenge when I start catching up and *she's* still at the bottom."

"I like your style," Amber smiled to herself, impressed at Joanne's positive attitude, "do you want to canter here?"

***

Two weeks sailed by in no time, and soon Eddie was pulling up in his pick-up to examine Molly's back. When Amber saw him lumbering down the yard, built like a rhinoceros, it was clear he had done a lot of hard work in his life. His shoulders were square and solid, his arms heavily muscled and his hands calloused and leathery. He had untidy, greying hair and a crooked nose that looked like it had been broken more than once. But despite his rather untoward appearance, he smiled warmly at the Andersons and softly exchanged the necessary pleasantries before turning his attention to Molly, who was tied up and eating from a haynet outside Honey and Pearl's shared stable. Eddie rolled up his sleeves, revealing his mighty forearms, and after asking what problems they'd been having with Molly, he placed his hands on her back and began his examination. His fingers probed along her spine, along her neck and between her ears, where he lingered a while, rubbing and prodding. Molly, completely unperturbed, carried on sleepily munching her hay. Then Eddie moved to stand directly behind Molly and placed his fingertips on her hip bones. He pressed gently around her pelvis, peered down her spine and lifted her tail to assess the movement of her dock. All this was carried out in silence, with Amber and her parents watching in mute fascination. The only noise was the rhythmical grinding of Molly's teeth on the hay she was eating.

Eventually, the silence was broken as Eddie gave Molly a hearty slap on the rump and turned to face his customers.

"Well, there's nowt wrong wid tha pony's back. She's a la'l bit tight in her poll, but I don't think that would be causing the problems you've described." He wiped his hands on a cloth to remove the grease from them. The Andersons weren't sure whether this was good news or not. They were obviously pleased Molly wasn't in pain, but then if pain wasn't causing her problems, what was the cause?

Eddie ran both hands over his head in a vain attempt to smooth his hair but as soon as he let go, it fell into his eyes again. Amber thought he looked like an Old English Sheepdog.

"But it was her back that was injured a couple of years ago," protested Mrs Anderson, "it must be that. She hasn't had any other injuries."

"You said she stood on an unravelled bandage when she hurt herself, is that right?"

"Yes."

"Well, I'm no vet, but it could be that when she stood on the bandage, it became very tight around the front leg. If it wasn't removed immediately it could've caused some damage to the tissues surrounding the flexor tendon in that leg. A too tight bandage can cut off the blood supply."

Mr Anderson frowned and rubbed his chin, "But if it had been a tendon back then, wouldn't her leg have swelled up and she'd have been lame? They'd have noticed. Like now, if it was a tendon, she'd be lame wouldn't she, and she isn't."

Eddie shrugged, "Like I said, mate, I'm not a vet, but I've been around horses long enough to know their injuries aren't always obvious or straightforward. If there is an old injury, it probably isn't bad enough to make her lame now, but it could be that she didn't get enough time for it fully heal. It could have been very slight and not even showed up, but it might still niggle at her and she'll probably feel it more when she has to jump bigger fences and the landing is more jarring. That could explain her lack of enthusiasm for jumping when they get bigger, but like I said, I'm not a vet. As for the bolting, well, sorry lass," he looked at Amber and smiled apologetically, "that likely has nowt to do with pain and plenty to do with excitement and a light, inexperienced rider she can run off with." He smiled again. "Maybe you should use a stronger bit if you're going out in a group. In the meantime, she needs a few days of just light work to allow those poll muscles to settle down again."

Eddie was thanked for his time and drove away, loudly chased by Kelly and Tess the farm dogs.

"Well, that wasn't what we expected to hear." Mrs Anderson sighed with frustration. "Camp is less than two weeks away and now the pony we've bought for these things might not be fit to go."

Amber led Molly back into the stable – her shoulders slumped – and pulled the door shut behind her. She could still hear her parents' frustrated voices as she gently teased a knot from Molly's silky mane. Amber thought about all the dreams she'd had about winning competitions, beating people like Elisha and riding round in glorious splendour. Those hopes now looked as far away as ever. Molly had seemed like such a prize when she'd arrived, but now Amber wasn't so sure.

***

The evening meal that night was much more subdued than usual, with each person lost in their own private thoughts while Kasper watched each mouthful hopefully, waiting for a tasty scrap and wondering why everyone was so quiet. Eventually, Mr Anderson cleared his throat and spoke. "Did you call the vet?" he asked his wife.

"Yes, someone's coming on Thursday."

"Right."

"God knows what it'll cost."

"Mmm."

Silence ruled over the remainder of the meal, and Kasper slunk off to bed, miserably aware that his legendary begging was not going be rewarded tonight.

-Eleven-

Emily Strikes Back

The bespectacled Irish vet carried out a variety of upper and lower leg flexion tests, which revealed little more than a tiny amount of stiffness in Molly's front left leg after a prolonged period of flexion. He dismissed it as being nothing.

"Seems unlikely she has any tendon problems," he lilted softly, "but we can't x-ray it as that would only show us her bones. If she was lame, we could try nerve blocks, but she's moving fine."

"So, what can we do?" Mrs Anderson asked.

The vet took off his glasses and wiped them on his sleeve. "There's no heat, swelling or lameness, so there isn't really any treatment I can suggest other than to rest her. I'd recommend you don't ride her for a month and after that, light hacking and even showing if she's well-schooled enough, but no jumping for six months. A good rest might be all she needs."

After the vet left, with Kelly and Tess once again noisily escorting his vehicle off the farmyard, Mrs Anderson curled her fists in a Hulk-like frustration.

Amber recognised the rising colour in her mother's face as a sign she was getting stressed and tried to calm her down before she blew up. "It's hard for them to know what's wrong when animals can't tell them what the problem is."

Mrs Anderson was turning puce. "Yes, I know but he was as useful as a…" she clearly couldn't think of anything useless enough to compare the vet to, and left the sentence hanging.

Amber didn't know whether to say that she had a horrible suspicion that the recent gallop over rocky ground on the ride when Molly bolted, followed by the tight turns she'd ridden in the jump-offs at the recent show might have caused an injury to her new pony. She opened her mouth to suggest it, but guilt seemed to block the words, and nothing came out.

Mrs Anderson's slate blue eyes sharpened in her flushed face, her muscles taut and her mouth set in a thin, hard line. Despite knowing her daughter was right, it didn't help her temper to pass. Molly had been recommended to them and they'd had high hopes for her. After watching Amber struggle with Pearl last year, trying to compete against ponies like Rocky and Flash, she and her husband had been looking forward to watching Amber have an easier and more successful season this year. But now they had three ponies to keep and pay for, and not one of them was suitable for competitions. They definitely couldn't manage with four, so it looked like her daughter's hopes were doomed. She sighed heavily, the anger suddenly leaving her like an unwanted evil spirit, leaving her body feeling tired and unfamiliar. "I don't know what you're going to do about camp. Molly can't go so it looks like you'll have to take Pearl."

Amber nodded, accepting the inevitable, until the recent memory of Emily jumping Honey and the

272

pony's joyful performance gave Amber a sudden idea. "I could take Honey to camp!"

"What? Honey?" Mrs Anderson was surprised. "Oh no, I don't think Honey would be very good. You know she's nervous and she's hardly done any jumping. You'd be better off on Pearl."

"She's a lot braver these days, Mum, and anyway, she's only nervous on rides. She was great jumping with Emily. You know I love Pearl, but you can see Honey likes to jump – she enjoys it! Pearl would hate a week of jumping every day. Too much effort! Please, Mum, let me take Honey. She'll be fine."

And so, it was decided. Honey was going to camp.

***

Amber was so excited about her first Pony Club camp, she could barely contain herself as they unloaded Honey from the trailer, her eyes popping as she wondered where on earth she was. Highland Park Equestrian Centre, near Carlisle, was a large, professional establishment. Amber had never been before, but as she stood looking around, she took in the cross-country fences in distant fields, brightly painted show jumps, the two indoor arenas, and the beautiful stable blocks.

The stables were in clusters around the yard. Three to ten boxes were built inside small barns, each containing their own supplies of hay, shavings and mucking out equipment. The centre's own horses had been temporarily moved to the livery quarters or turned out to graze to make room for the Pony Club. Each stable door had the name of a member's pony blu-tacked over the usual occupant's name. Amber found Honey's in a small block of three stables. The stall next to hers belonged to Fudge, and next to that was Breeze, Kate's small bay horse. As she led a very surprised Honey into her stable, Emily's head popped up from the one next door.

The walls between them were thick wooden panels to shoulder height, and on top of them, metal railings extended another three feet so that the occupants of the stables could see into the one beside them.

"Hello neighbour," she greeted Amber with a smile. "It's great our stables are next to each other isn't it? Now Honey and Fudgey can make friends."

"Amber laughed, "How is he now?"

"Oh, fully healed and raring to go, thanks." She planted a big kiss on Fudge's soft muzzle and ruffled his thick blond forelock affectionately, grinning happily at Amber. Amber chuckled again and removed Honey's head collar, allowing the pony to sniff and paw inquisitively at the bed of shavings, which she'd probably never seen before.

"I thought you'd be bringing Molly to camp?" Emily said in a questioning tone.

"Oh, I know," Amber replied with a shrug, "it's a long story..."

There was little time to notice everyone else as members rushed around, unpacking their riding gear, tack, feed buckets, grooming kits and everything else they'd brought for the week. Soon it was time to tack up for the first ride.

"Make sure everything's spotless," Emily advised, "we're judged on turnout every day and the best person out of all the groups gets a trophy at the end."

"Thanks for telling me." Amber hurriedly shoved her long blonde hair into a hairnet and checked her tie was straight in the hazy reflection of the barn window.

"Ah, excellent, you're all here." Mrs Best appeared loudly in the doorway. "Just here to tell you all which ride you're in. Now, we have three groups, based on you and your pony's experience and level of competition." She looked into Breeze's stable, where the small, dark-skinned Kate was tightening the girth. "Kate, I know you were in the top group on the ponies but as your new horse is only a baby, we've put you in the second group. I hope you don't mind that?"

"No, that's fine," the girl replied, "it's what I expected."

"Jolly good. Now, Emily, you'll also be in group two and Amber..." The large, bubbly DC turned to face Amber, "we weren't quite sure where to put you dear as neither you nor your pony have a lot of experience but I think we'll try you in group two as well, although you might need to drop into group three, but we'll wait and see how you get on." She clapped her hands together. "See you all mounted up and ready to go in five minutes."

Soon, the riders of groups two and three were all assembled in the large indoor arena having their tack and turnout inspection. The top group were out of sight in the adjoining smaller arena.

"I thought I saw Natalie earlier," Emily leaned over and whispered to Amber, "but she's not here."

Amber looked up and down the line of riders in her group and also at the other riders who were now occupying the bottom half of the arena.

"No, you're right," she whispered back, "perhaps there's some problem with Sable, so she can't ride?"

Emily shrugged and pulled a quizzical face, ceasing the conversation as the instructor approached for her tack inspection.

***

When the lesson was complete and everyone's tack was cleaned and put away and the ponies were fed and brushed, it was time for the riders to get ready for tea. Amber, Emily, Kate and three other girls were sleeping in an old tack room where odds and ends were stored. They all had camp beds and sleeping bags, and their possessions were already mixed up and strewn around the tiny room.

"Has anyone seen my mug? It's blue." Emily asked.

"And where's my other trainer?" cried Becky, a red-haired girl of about fourteen.

Eventually, everybody found their lost items and crammed all their stuff under their beds before making their way to the large classroom which sat between the two indoor arenas for their meal.

Amber and Emily collected their pizza and oven chips from the mums who were staying to help, and then looked for somewhere to sit.

"Hey, there's Natalie sitting over there with Elisha. Come on." Emily nudged Amber and walked over to join them. Amber grudgingly followed, not relishing the thought of eating with Elisha.

"Hi!" Emily greeted them, plonking herself down opposite them. "So where were you earlier? How come you weren't riding?" she asked Natalie. But before Natalie could get a word out, Elisha answered for her. "She *was* riding."

"Oh, it's just that we didn't see you." Emily frowned.

"No, well she's in the top group, that's why."

Amber and Emily exchanged a disbelieving look. "Oh, right. Well done, Natalie," Emily offered politely.

"Thanks. I'm not on Sable obviously though. If I'd brought her, I'd be in the bottom group."

"No?"

"No, we've decided to sell her... if we can get anyone to buy her, and get a new one. And Elisha is selling her pony, Rocky, so we've arranged for me to try him here all this week and if I like him, we'll buy him."

"You're joking?" Amber blurted out.

"No, why?" Natalie looked crestfallen that her news hadn't received a more exciting response.

"Yeah, Amber," Elisha fixed Amber with her penetrating stare, "have you got a problem with that?"

"No, um, er, nothing, sorry," Amber muttered and looked down.

"So, Nat, is today the first time you've ridden him then?" Emily continued, helpfully removing everyone's attention from Amber.

"I've only ridden him once before at Elisha's – we went for a hack – and today we did flatwork, so I haven't jumped him yet, but I can already tell how much different he is to Sable. He's so forward going. It's great. I'm having to hold him back instead of kicking and pushing all the time. I can't wait till we start jumping tomorrow."

Amber felt her eyebrow raise involuntarily at Natalie's naïve enthusiasm. Sure, it was great to have a livelier pony after the deathly lethargic Sable, but had she forgotten that Rocky had bolted with Elisha and subsequently broke her ankle when he fell on her last year? Or did she even know about it? Amber wondered if Elisha and her father had deliberately failed to mention Rocky's strength and unpredictably, in order to take advantage of the Riley's inexperience, to make a sale. She had no doubt that they were both devious enough. After her own recent, terrifying experience with Molly, she knew she needed to warn Natalie that Rocky was dangerous. She needed to find a way to get Natalie away from Elisha so that she could speak to her privately. But how? Her mind raced as Emily kept talking.

"That's a big step for you then, Nat, 'cause if you're in the top group you compete in the Open at the end of week One Day Event. A one-metre cross-country course will be a challenge on a pony you're not used to," Emily said, her voice heavy with concern.

"Oh, shut up, you're only jealous 'cause you're both stuck in group two on your fat little hair-balls," Elisha spat nastily. "You've been competing for years and still haven't got past ninety centimetres. That's why you're jealous," she said, jabbing a finger at Emily, "because Natalie is getting a brilliant new pony and you're still on Fat Fudge even though you're too big for him. What's up? Can't Mummy and Daddy afford a new one?"

Emily's kind, rosy face drained of colour and hardened like stone. Her soft, gentle eyes narrowed and glinted menacingly as she slowly leaned forward and put her face right up to Elisha's.

"You think you're so wonderful, don't you, looking down your nose at everyone because your dad has loads of money from his dodgy dealings and your ponies are always the best bred and most expensive in the country? *That's* the only reason you've done well in competitions, Elisha, because you're a crap rider. You've had push button ponies that have done it all for you since you started. You couldn't get a thing out of a pony like Fudge or Honey because you only know how to sit there and get carried around. And as for Natalie riding Rocky, no offence Natalie – you and your dad know he's too much for her – she's only eleven and not very experienced, but you don't care so long as you get your money."

Amber and Natalie stared in shocked silence as the normally friendly, easy-going Emily retaliated with force against Elisha. Even Elisha was momentarily taken aback to find Emily's face inches from her own throughout the verbal onslaught. She soon regained her composure and flung back at Emily loudly, "Don't make me laugh! *I* couldn't ride your pathetic second rate ponies? I wouldn't lower myself to their sub-zero standard. I think you'll find it's *you* who couldn't ride *my* ponies, who are *not* push button, they are highly strung, sensitive and so well-schooled they need very precise, skilled riding. And as for our parents, at least *my* dad has money. What does your dad do again? Oh no, I forgot, he doesn't have a job, does he?"

Quick as a flash, Emily lunged forward and dealt Elisha a stinging slap across the face. The loud thwack resounded around the echoey room and all heads turned to stare incredulously just as Elisha grabbed a handful of Emily's curly dark hair and proceeded to twist it until Emily squealed. Amber and Natalie both tried frantically to release Elisha's grip on Emily's hair, but it took the two mothers, who had been filling beakers with orange squash, to leap into action and separate the sparring girls.

As soon as she was free from Elisha's vice-like grip, Emily sprang away from the table, toppling her chair as she pushed it roughly out of her way, and ran headlong out of the building, across the dusty yard and into the small barn where Honey, Fudge and Breeze were stabled. Amber followed immediately before any interrogations began, and found her friend sobbing pitifully on a bale of hay. Her sudden noisy intrusion had startled the ponies and they were all looking at her, wide-eyed over their stable doors.

"Are you okay?" Amber gasped breathlessly, sitting down close to Emily, feeling her icy skin covered in goose bumps as sobs shuddered through her body. "I can't believe you stood up to Elisha! You were so brave. I wish I could be like that. I never know what to say in an argument, I always say something useless and end up looking totally stupid. What you said was absolutely true."

"And look where it got me," Emily snapped. "I hardly won the battle, did I?"

"But…" Amber couldn't think what to say. How could she let Emily know how much she admired her for standing up for herself against a bully like Elisha while she sat there and said nothing? "But you didn't lose anything. You showed her you're not scared of her and she can't just say what she likes to you."

"But she did say what she liked, didn't she? She said I'm too big for Fudge, I still jump at Intermediate level and my dad doesn't have a job at the moment. Everything she said was true too."

Amber put an arm around Emily's shaking shoulders. "Firstly, you're not too big for Fudge – he's stocky and you're not heavy – so he won't even feel you, and so what if you don't jump Opens? You're only thirteen and Fudge is only just over thirteen hands; you've got loads of time to progress. Everyone in the top group, apart from Elisha and Natalie, is at least fourteen and like you said, Elisha only does

Opens because she has great ponies, not because she's a good rider. And so what if your dad has lost his job? He'll get another one."

Emily sniffed and rubbed her eyes, "He's been trying, but nobody seems to be taking anyone new on."

The girls continued talking and gradually Emily calmed down and stopped crying. Presently, Mrs Best found them, still sitting in the barn in semi-darkness, and asked what had happened. To her credit, she listened without interrupting and when she went away, she was shaking her head and muttering to herself.

Emily didn't feel like joining in the evening quiz and having everyone stare at her, so they went to bed early and fell into an exhausted sleep well before the other girls returned and crept into their cramped camp beds.

Trust Elisha to go and spoil things before we've hardly begun, was Amber's last thought before she fell into a deep and dreamless sleep.

-Twelve-

A Whale of a Time

The next morning saw all the riders assembled in their groups for show jumping instruction. Kate, seated on Breeze, yawned and looked at Amber. "Did you know your pony kept everyone awake last night? she asked, stretching.

"What, Honey? No, why, what did she do?"

"Are you kidding? She banged on the stable door all night long. Don't tell me you didn't hear it?"

"No, honestly I didn't. I'm really sorry but she's not used to being kept in a stable and she could be missing our other pony as well."

"Well, you must sleep like the dead. I got up and Chelsea came with me to see what was making the racket. We gave her more hay in case she was banging 'cause she was hungry, but as soon as we came back to bed, she started again. I just hope she's not going to do it every night."

After the tack inspection, group three went to use the outdoor arena, leaving Amber's group with the whole of the large indoor school to themselves.

"Now, as you all know, you will be competing against each other in the One Day Event at the end of the week. This afternoon I will be giving you all a copy of the dressage test you will perform. We will have some time to practise it every day, but in accordance with British Eventing rules, you must memorise the test and perform it accurately with no outside assistance. Any errors in the sequence of the test will incur penalties," Jilly, the instructor, a tweed-jacketed, plain-faced lady, told the group formally. "But as we did flatwork yesterday, our lesson this morning will be show jumping. The show jumps and cross-country fences on Friday will be eighty-five centimetres, so that is the height we will be practising at. Now, I need to get some wings and poles out, so I'd like you all to go and

288

work in, do plenty of transitions and get your ponies relaxed and listening to you. And remember to pass each other left shoulder to left shoulder. Look where you're going, we don't want any crashes."

The six riders began warming up, easily managing to avoid each other in the huge space. Suddenly, as Amber trotted Honey across the centre of the arena, the pony caught sight of herself in the mirror on the wall and uttered a welcoming 'huh huh huh' at her reflection. Amber chuckled. "No girl, that's yourself, it's not Pearl." She caught Emily grinning at her and smiled back. Then, as they trotted around the corner and down the long side, there was another mirror, strategically placed to allow riders to see how straight they were sitting and the position of the horse as it travelled down the line. Honey spied her reflection again and whinnied deeply once more. This time the whole group laughed, and Amber patted the black neck affectionately. "You silly girl."

After that, Honey whinnied at her reflection every time she passed a mirror until the other riders were groaning at her to be quiet. Eventually Amber had to ride so that she was always moving away from the mirrors instead of riding towards them to keep the confused pony quiet.

Fortunately, when the jumping began, Honey was too busy enjoying herself and concentrating on the fences to notice the mirrors. Jilly had put up a short course of a steep-sided cross pole, a gate, a parallel and a double. Each rider had to jump the course shouting out each stride they took in between the fences. Amber found this exercise very useful as she'd never fully understood strides, but counting out loud, 'one – two – three – four -,' in between the jumps helped her to judge her take-off position much better.

"Well done Amber," the instructor patted Honey's already damp neck, "you've got a very game pony there. She's really making an effort for you. Now, at the moment you're getting five strides between fence three and the double, but she's arriving at the double rather flat and's having to make a big effort to clear it. This time, hold her to six strides but still use your legs for impulsion, then she should arrive at the double more in balance and with more bounce so the jumps will be easier for her."

Amber always listened carefully and soon found that the instructor was spot on with her advice. Every time she did what Jilly told her, her performance improved. By the end of the session, both pony and rider were glowing with happiness.

Honey was so willing and easy to ride, and Amber could tell how much she was enjoying this new activity that had crept unexpectedly into her life. It made such a difference to her own enjoyment when riding a pony that was so obviously enthusiastic.

The afternoon's lesson of dressage test practice was harder than Amber thought it would be. Honey's walk and trot were very good, but she ran into canter and was quite unbalanced, especially in the corners. By the end of the session, Amber was dripping with sweat as Jilly had been determined to improve Honey's canter strike off, and had made Amber go over and over it until she was satisfied. In fact, she had spent so much time concentrating on Honey's canter that she hadn't yet practised any of the dressage test.

Amber was sure she wouldn't be able to remember all of the test on Friday. She still couldn't remember all of her seven or eight times tables, and they were just a list of numbers that could be recited in thirty seconds. If she couldn't manage that, how on earth was she going to memorise a four-minute test where she had to remember paces, transitions, circles, changes of rein, letters, halts and salutes? And the descriptions of the movements were so wordy, by the time she'd read the first few movements, she'd forgotten the first one.

"Emily, what does 'change the rein on a long rein H x F' mean?" She waggled the test sheet under her friend's nose later that afternoon and Emily laughed at her panicked expression.

"Come here, I'll show you how to learn a dressage test." Emily drew a rectangle on a piece of paper to represent the arena and quickly labelled the lettered markers around it.

"So, the order of letters is A, K, E, H, C, M, B and F." She pointed them out with her pencil. "The way to remember them is 'All King Edward's Horses Can Move Bloomin' Fast', " she shared. "Right, enter at A in working trot. Proceed down the centre line without halting and track left."

As Emily read each movement, she explained to Amber what it meant and drew a faint dotted line to represent it on the paper. When they came to a part in the test where you had to canter a 20-metre circle, Emily switched to an unbroken line, taking care not to draw over the dotted line. For the few movements in walk, she drew a wiggly line.

"There. That helps you to remember what you're doing where. Now go through it a few times and only look at the instructions if you really need to."

Amber followed Emily's sketch and was surprised to find she remembered quite a lot of it.

"Good, now come on." Emily grabbed Amber's hand and pulled her up off her camp bed.

"Where're we going?"

"To practise!" Emily's eyes twinkled.

Soon Amber found herself in one of the outdoor arenas, minus a pony, trotting and cantering her way through the test on foot.

"This is stupid," she giggled as she cantered past Emily, who was sitting on the gate with the test in her hand. "I hope nobody sees me doing this."

"Don't worry about that. You were supposed to trot *at* F, not after F. You'll lose marks if you're not accurate."

"Oh damn." Amber stopped to catch her breath. "Hang on, I'll do it again in a minute."

That night was the most restless night's sleep Amber had ever had. Unable to switch off from committing the test to memory, she ran through it in her head all night long, seeing herself trotting around the arena in her mind. She probably called out 'between C and M working canter right...' and her legs must have been joining in with her thoughts as her sleeping bag was twisted around her like a boa constrictor when she awoke in the morning. She felt so weary during breakfast that she was sure she would fall asleep during her first cross-country lesson.

***

Wednesday and Thursday flew by with more training in the three disciplines required for the One Day Event. Amber absolutely loved cross-country. They practised over most of the fences that would be part of the course on Friday.

"We'll leave a few out to make the competition a bit more interesting," Jilly said.

They started by tackling one fence at a time, then they linked a few together before Jilly improvised a longer course for them to ride.

"This won't be the course on Friday, so make sure you walk it properly on the day, so you know where you're going."

Jilly set them off one at a time, waiting until the rider on the course had finished before setting the next one off. Amber loved the feeling of being alone, with no-one watching as she rode Honey around the course, feeling the rhythm of her stride and the sound of her hooves striking the earth.

Some of the ponies in the group had refused to jump the ditch in the coffin fence and quite a few didn't want to go through the water jump. Even Fudge had wavered and baulked on his approach, as the water was quite muddy, and the bottom couldn't be seen. Jilly had called on Amber and Honey to give some of the reluctant ponies a lead, to encourage them to follow Honey over the jumps. Amber couldn't keep the smile off her face at being used as the lead rider in the group, and her confidence soared.

Now, as Amber rode the course, over the ditch, up the steps, over the double of logs and through the water, she felt so pleased she'd brought Honey to camp. She thought about what her parents would think when she told them how scaredy cat Honey had been used as a lead to get other ponies to jump.

Honey tired towards the end of the course but gamely jumped the last few fences and returned to a round of applause from the group.

"Clear round! Well done Amber and well done Honey!"

Amber was walking on air for the remaining days as Honey continued to jump well, and she found that she could remember the dressage test every time they practised it. Her mood was further lifted when Emily gleefully pulled her into a corner and whispered that cross-country training hadn't gone so well for Elisha. Thunder Cat had refused to jump the ditch and wouldn't even walk into the water jump, never mind jump into it as the Open class had to. Nor would he jump off the Irish bank. Elisha had sat on top of the bank, kicking and whipping until eventually, the young black horse had reared up. In the end, Elisha had to dismount and help the instructor attach a lunge rein to him. They then managed to coax him down from the ground.

Things had gone just as badly for Natalie, as Rocky had run away with her all over the fields, and when he did go over the fences, he'd jumped so fast and with so much power, he'd thrown Natalie right out of the saddle. When Amber heard this, she felt awful. She'd had every intention of warning Natalie about Rocky but hadn't been able to speak to her without Elisha being around. Unlike Emily, Amber always withered in Elisha's presence, and so Natalie remained unaware of what was in store for her.

The result of this was that both girls had been told they would compete in the Intermediate class on Friday instead of in the Open. Natalie was very happy with this decision but Elisha was apparently fuming and had started her 'do you know how much this horse cost?' speech, only to be told by their instructor that she didn't care how much he had cost, or how he was bred – he was only a five-year-old and didn't need to be frightened while he was still a baby.

"You can't just expect to take an untrained young horse round a metre cross-country course, even if he is show jumping that height. Cross-country training needs to be taken slowly to build his confidence. If you lose his trust now, he'll *never* make an eventer. He's not a ready-made pony like you're used to, Elisha. You're going to have to put a lot of time in to get him to the standard you're hoping to achieve."

"Wow... did her instructor *really* say that to her?" Amber asked Emily.

"That's what Alice, who's in her group, told me. And now she's spat her dummy out and is having a major sulk. She said some nasty things to Natalie too about not being able to ride Rocky properly."

"What a surprise."

"So, you know what that means now?"

Amber's eyebrows knitted together, and she shook her head.

"It means we'll be competing against her. We've got a chance to beat her and her posh horse with our native no-hopers, as she calls them. Oh, wouldn't that be brilliant?" Emily squeezed her eyes tight shut and did a little excited jig.

Amber shook her head. "What do you mean? As if we could beat her. If she's been moved down a group, the dressage and show jumping will be even easier for her. She'll get a huge head start."

"Ah ha, yes, but if she gets eliminated on the cross-country, which she probably will, as our course has ditches and water that her horse doesn't like, her score won't count. She'll be finished. And even if she just gets a few stops on the course, it's twenty penalties for a refusal cross-country. Whatever you get in the dressage, all you have to do is get round the show jumping and cross-country and you'll beat her."

"Really?"

"Yup, really!"

-Thirteen-

A Rider's Responsibility

On Friday morning, Amber was one of the first out of bed. She mucked out the stable quickly then led Honey out and washed her legs and tail before the battle for the hosepipe began. At breakfast she pored over the dressage test again, willing her brain not to forget it. Her stomach began to squirm with anticipation as she thought that this could be the day her dream of beating Elisha came true. She laughed to herself at the thought of potentially achieving what seemed like the impossible on nervous little Honey. If it was ever going to happen, she'd thought it would be on Molly. The very idea of Honey triumphing over the super talented Thunder Cat gave her a slightly hysterical, lightheaded feeling.

Pushing her uneaten breakfast away and pulling herself together, she went back to the barn and cleaned her tack again. Then she rubbed and polished her riding boots until the soft leather gleamed. Next, she brushed her riding jacket and laid it out on her bed with a clean shirt and pair of jodhpurs, her hat, gloves and Pony Club tie. With all the tack and clothing prepared, she went back to the stable with the intention of making Honey look like the best pony there.

An hour later, Honey was immaculate. Her dark coat was lustrous, her heavy wavy tail was soft and sparkled with the baby oil Amber had brushed through it, and her mane was beautifully shown off in a crest plait Amber had recently learned how to do. All that was left was to oil her hooves, but Amber had discovered it was best not to do so in the stable as shavings and dust stuck to the oil.

She looked at her watch. The Open competitors would be doing their tests now. It had been arranged this way so that the Novice group, with the youngest members, would have longer to prepare and so that the older riders from the Open class could help them to get ready. Parents had been invited to watch the competition, and already some mums had arrived to organise their young offspring.

"Michael, where's your clean shirt?" Amber heard a harassed voice shriek. There was a pause followed by another strangled yell. "It's filthy and crumpled! Is it too much to ask for you to fold your clothes up and put them in your bag instead of leaving them on the floor? Look, it's even got a green footprint on this sleeve!"

With a smile and a small chuckle, Amber headed off to get changed herself.

***

Honey warmed up well, although her canter was still a bit rushed and unbalanced. Amber didn't worry about it though as she remembered Emily's advice. She could hear her now in her head saying, *Don't worry about the canter. The majority of the test is in trot, which is Honey's best pace. Just concentrate on being accurate, keep her straight on the long sides and don't let her fall in on the circles.*

Suddenly Emily was beside her on Fudge. He evidently didn't appreciate his bushy mane being forced into golf ball sized plaits and was shaking his head.

"I'm in next," she said.

"Good luck. I hope you do really well." Amber replied sincerely. She didn't know where she'd have been this week without all Emily's help and advice.

In no time Emily had finished her test and it was Amber's turn. The horn pipped and she entered the arena, trotting steadily up the centre line. She circled, changed rein, cantered and walked, all the time trying to execute the movements as accurately as she could. Soon she was trotting back up the centre line to halt and salute the judge. Honey gave her a lovely square halt, right on X. As she left the arena, she patted Honey and felt quite pleased with herself; she'd remembered it all and it seemed to have gone quite well. Her parents appeared and told her they'd seen her test.

"You did well – it was excellent for a first attempt," her dad said.

"I love Honey's mane." Mrs Anderson was stroking the pony's neck and examining the intricate looking plait. "She looks really elegant."

Amber was pleased they were there to watch her as she had a feeling it was going to be a good day.

The results from the dressage phase were pinned up just before the show jumping began. Amber and Emily checked their scores against the rest of the group. Elisha was in the lead with a very low penalty score of 23. A girl called Chelsea who rode a nice grey pony was second with 34. Jake was next with 36, Emily and Natalie both scored 44. Amber had 48. Kate was sixth with 50 and finally Ashley with 54.

Natalie was first to show jump in the Intermediate group and everyone watched with concern as she began her round. She did quite well really and finished with just four faults due to Rocky running straight past one of the fences. Next, Elisha jumped an effortless clear round, no doubt horrified at having to jump such insignificant fences. Kate got round on her young horse with one fence down, and then it was Emily's turn. She'd taken Fudge's plaits out after the dressage and now his thick mane was a mass of curls. He looked so cute with his blond curls bouncing as he jumped round, clearly enjoying himself, to equal Elisha's clear.

When Amber was called, she let out a long, trembling breath and entered the arena to begin her round. Honey felt keen and jumped the first fence enthusiastically. Fence after fence disappeared behind them as they continued to clear them all smoothly. Soon there was only the last left to jump. *We've gone clear*, thought Amber, relaxing as they approached the last fence. Feeling the slight change in her rider, Honey hesitated and put in an extra little shuffle before the fence and got too close to it. She tried to clear the jump, but she couldn't avoid clipping it and Amber heard the pole fall as they landed. *Thud*. Her own heart hit the ground at the same time as the pole as she realised she had cost them a clear round.

"Bad luck."

"What a shame."

Everyone was so disappointed when she re-joined them after her round and took her unhappy expression to be a sign of her own dismay at having a fence down. Amber's real disappointment though was not with Honey, or even about the fence, but the fact that she'd let her pony down, after she'd worked so hard all week, by not riding properly at the end. She'd thought the last fence would take care of itself and now she was kicking herself for denying Honey the clear round she deserved through bad riding.

She put Honey back in the stable and untacked her. After giving her a brush and taking out her plait, she held Honey's face in her hands. She smoothed her forelock, kissed her soft whiskery muzzle and looked firmly into the gentle brown eyes.

"I promise I won't let you down ever again," she told the pony.

"You giving that pony a pep talk?" Emily had suddenly appeared in the doorway and was amused to see Amber holding Honey's face, apparently giving her a good talking to.

"It's me that needs the pep talk," Amber mumbled, leaving the stable and flicking the kick bolt on with her foot, "not Honey."

"Come on then, let's go and walk the cross-country course."

The cross-country phase for all groups was to start after dinner, following the same pattern of Open riders going first. Emily led Amber to the start and showed her the map of the course.

"So, our class follows the blue numbers see, and that's our optimum time: four minutes and twenty seconds. That means you have to try to get round the course within that time. If you go over it, you get time penalties which are added to your score." Then Emily took her to the starting box which was marked out with white painted fencing and looked very professional. "This is where you'll start from. The starter will count you down and tell you to go. There's the first fence."

Amber looked and saw three brush jumps all in a horizontal line. They walked towards them.

"This one's ours." Emily patted the middle brush. "See the blue number? The Open has a red number one and the Novice's is green. And see these flags?" Emily indicated two flags on either side of the largest fence.

"The course is set for the Open as they're first and these flags show them what they have to jump. You must always jump between the flags with the red one on your right. Red and right both start with R so it's easy to remember. For our class, they'll move the red flag out to the end of the middle jump so we can choose to jump either the middle or biggest one, okay?"

Amber nodded and they carried on. Emily was being an excellent course guide, her experience really showing as she explained how Amber should approach some of the fences, where she could save Honey's energy and where she'd need to push her more. They moved out of the field they'd practised in and came to a gate leading into a wooded area. It was flagged.

"You'll have to ride positively here as you're jumping from light into dark and a lot of ponies don't like it. Don't worry about that gate – it's set for the Open; we'll have a smaller one." Amber wondered how much smaller theirs would be as the current gate was enormous.

They continued through the wood where there were a few more scary new jumps and then into an open field that led back to the start. The finish was parallel to the start box. "Make sure you ride through the flags at the finish," Emily warned, "your time doesn't stop until you're through them so don't forget and miss them out."

By the time they got back to the yard and changed into their cross-country gear, Amber's stomach was clenching painfully, and she had forgotten part of the course. She'd been going over the fences in her head and couldn't remember the course from number eight to eleven. Emily tried to describe the fences, but she couldn't picture them properly.

"Don't worry, you'll be able to see the fences and their numbers as you're going round."

"Well, I can't actually," Amber admitted. "I can't see things in the distance very well. The fence numbers will be all blurred from horse height." She knew that she needed glasses as she struggled to see the board at school if she sat near the back, which she often did, but she hadn't got around to telling her parents yet.

Determined not to let Honey down twice in one day by forgetting the course, she knew she couldn't leave it to chance and hope for the best. It was her responsibility to make sure. "Will you put Honey's saddle on for me while I go back and have a quick look at the bit I've forgotten?" she asked Emily.

"Alright, but you haven't got very long. What about getting something to eat?" Emily was sitting on a bale of shavings eating a bacon sandwich. The smell turned Amber's stomach.

"Urgh, no thanks. I'll have something when I've finished. I'll run there and back, won't be long."

"Don't do that, you'll probably pass out or something. I'll tack Honey up for you and bring her out with Fudge. I'll meet you in the warm-up area."

"Oh thanks, you're great!"

Emily smiled. "I know."

With that, she set off to re-inspect the forgotten part of the course. On the way, she bumped into her parents who had been coming to the stable to see if she needed a hand. When she explained what she was doing, her mother offered to go and help Emily with the ponies. Her dad went with Amber to look at the jumps she'd forgotten. She told him all about the numbers and the flags – red to the right – and the time allowed and going through the finish.

"You certainly seem to have learned a lot this week," he said. "Have you enjoyed it?"

"Yeah, it's been great apart from Elisha. And I'll be glad when this is over. I feel sick!"

Mr Anderson laughed. "I bet. Some of these fences are quite difficult. Are you sure Honey can manage them?"

"No. That's *why* I feel sick. But I'm going to do my best to get her over them."

"Good for you. Can you remember it now?"

"Yes, I hope so."

They'd walked through the wooded part again and Amber counted them off: seven – gate into wood; eight – *huge* log pile; nine – tyres; ten – scary trakehner;

eleven – wall out into the field. They'd just got out of the wood when they heard a whistle being blown and a few seconds later the first Open rider came soaring out over the wall. She had let her reins slip and was leaning back. It was then that Amber noticed the ground on the landing side was much lower than the take-off, making quite a substantial drop. She gulped as a wave of doubt crashed over her. She really didn't know if she and Honey could do this. Although cross-country practice had gone well through the week, these extra fences were terrifying.

"They've started. Come on, we'd better get back and get you in the saddle. It won't be long now."

With legs like lead, Amber stumbled back to the warm-up area. She could see her mum holding Honey amidst the circling riders. She swooned as another gut-wrenching wave of anxiety washed over her. What had she been thinking of earlier when she'd felt she might have a chance of beating Elisha? She'd be lucky just to survive this course, never mind be placed. The log pile was huge and really wide, the ditch under the trakehner was black and scary and she'd never jumped an angled rail before, and there was the terrifying drop after the wall.

She barely had the strength to mount, and once seated in the saddle with her shortened stirrups, she felt so precarious and unstable - not at all the easy, comfortable way she usually felt on Honey.

"Good luck! We're going out on the course to watch. See you soon." Mrs Anderson patted Amber's leg and smiled up at her. The smile wavered and faltered as she made eye contact with her daughter and saw the worry on her pallid face.

As they walked away from their daughter, Carol Anderson turned to her husband and whispered fiercely, "She looks terrified, and I don't blame her, having to go round her first cross-country on our Honey, especially when she has an experienced jumping pony back at home. What's the course like? Only small?"

Mr Anderson pressed his lips together and shook his head. "No...I'd say it's a tough course. This place runs a lot of affiliated competitions and the course was professionally built. Some of the jumps are pretty imposing. They're mainly about eighty centimetres but they've put some of the nineties in too. I know she's particularly worried about the jumps in the wood, especially the wall with the big drop on the landing side."

"Oh my God," wailed Mrs Anderson. "I can't watch!"

-Fourteen-

A Ride to Remember

Amber watched as a boy called Ashley was called to the start box. The starter told him he had thirty seconds and then counted him down from five to 'go!' His blue-eyed piebald pony seemed to know what it was all about and leapt out of the start box as soon as the 'g' of 'go' was said. He tore off towards the first jump and flew it eagerly with ears pricked. Amber saw them take the next five fences in the field confidently before they disappeared into the wood. Riders were being started at two-minute intervals and soon the next one was being called to the start.

Amber was busy trying to breathe slowly and convince herself she wasn't going to faint when Natalie rode up alongside her. Rocky's red coat was already damp as he danced and shook his head savagely.

"I don't think he likes this bit," Natalie looked as ill as Amber felt and again, she wished she had made more effort to get Natalie on her own and warn her about Rocky. She was surprised and impressed that Natalie was going ahead with the cross-country phase after her disastrous attempt during the week. She doubted that she would've had the confidence if the same thing had happened to her

"What is it?" Amber didn't know much about bits as her ponies all wore snaffles.

"It's an American gag. He had a kimblewick earlier in the week, but I couldn't hold him, so Elisha's put him in this for the cross-country. She says it'll hold him, but he hates it."

Amber wasn't surprised that he didn't approve of any braking system that would stop him running amok and make him do what the rider wanted instead of having his own way.

"Are you nervous?" Natalie's big round brown eyes looked bigger and darker than ever against her lightly grey skin.

"It's a very real possibility that I'll puke when they call me to the start," Amber admitted.

"Oh, me too!" Natalie looked relieved to find Amber shared her fear. "Elisha said I was stupid to be worried 'cause Rocky's done Opens and he'll find this so easy. I'm terrified I don't go clear in case she thinks I'm useless!"

Amber was just about to tell Natalie that she shouldn't worry about what Elisha said when Natalie's name was called by a steward and she didn't get the chance.

"Natalie Riley. Come to the start please."

"Oh no!" The poor girl looked truly stricken.

"Good luck… and be careful," Amber called as Natalie trotted away. She received a faint nod in reply.

Rocky left the start box like a rocket, just like the piebald pony who had since galloped strongly through the finish and was enveloped in a delighted

318

hug by his red-faced rider. Like the piebald, Rocky cleared the first six fences and was soon out of sight.

Kate was called to the start on Breeze and Amber's stomach twisted painfully as she realised it would soon be her turn. The heavy lump that had been sliding slowly down her throat suddenly seemed to get stuck and threatened to choke her. She knew that she would be sick if she had to wait much longer, so she gave Honey one more jump over the practice fence and headed for the steward to present herself.

"You're keen! Coming without being called. Or is it a case of wanting to get it over with?" The steward was one of the centre's grooms. She was only about twenty and had a very friendly face. She smiled kindly at Amber. "Just go out and enjoy it, that's what you're here for. In five minutes, you'll be back and wondering what all the worry was about."

Amber trembled in response. She just wanted to get started before she lost her nerve, but there seemed to be some hold on the course. Something must have happened to either Natalie or Kate. The wait was torturous as Amber fretted about what was causing the hold up, but eventually the starter beckoned her to come over.

"Good luck!" Amber heard a yell and saw Emily standing in her stirrups on Fudge, waving at her absurdly with both arms above her head like a mayday signal. The sight made her laugh and suddenly she felt slightly more cheerful. She had to pull herself together for Honey's sake. As wonderful as she'd been this week, the little blip in the show jumping had shown she couldn't do it on her own. She needed Amber to be a rider, not a passenger who was a bag of nerves.

"Thirty seconds."

Her insides did a loop-the-loop and the lump in her throat made itself comfortable. She rode into the start box, closed her eyes and inhaled deeply, letting the breath out slowly and shakily as she opened her eyes and gathered up her reins, seeing Honey's pricked black ears ahead of her like the sights of a gun.

"Five…four…three…two…one…go!   Good luck!"

Honey set off and got into canter immediately. She jumped the brush fence happily and took the barrels and tree stumps in her stride. Next was the open ditch, in practice just a gash in the ground, but now it was flanked on either side by a child-sized wooden carving of a bear. Amber felt Honey check and slow down as she spotted the terrible monsters. "Come on girl!" she urged and gave Honey a light tap with the whip. The pony approached hesitantly with popping eyes and twisted her body as she jumped the ditch as if worried one of the bears might take a swipe at her as she passed between them.

"Good lass!" Amber gave her a pat and rode strongly over the Irish bank and double of logs. With adrenaline now coursing through her, Amber's nerves were completely forgotten as she approached the gate into the wood. The large Open gate had been replaced with a lower one, but she remembered the possible problem of jumping from light into the shade of the trees and pushed on. Honey jumped neatly into the leafy cool of the wood and followed the soft, slightly churned path to the log pile. It was the widest jump on the course and Amber knew that jumping width was Honey's biggest weakness. Praying she could make it, Amber kicked on, hoping against hope that with a good run up the momentum would be enough to get them over.

Honey felt her rider's determination and it gave her confidence. She measured the jump up quickly, gathered herself and made a huge effort. Her hind feet just clipped the top as she stretched out to land, but it didn't bother her and they both had a moment to catch their breath over an easy tyre jump.

The next fence was another rider frightener – the trakehner – a wide black ditch with a heavy telegraph pole angled across it. Amber had been very unsure about this fence, but Emily had told her the angle of the pole didn't matter as the pony wouldn't notice it and she should aim for the middle. Amber rode strongly again, but Honey wasn't too sure about this new jump and wanted to get a good look at it.

"*Please* don't stop," Amber pleaded as Honey dropped out of canter into trot. "Go on!"

Honey lowered her head and assessed the jump suspiciously while Amber pushed her on. By the time they reached take-off point, Honey was moving painfully slowly, and Amber was sure she was going to stop. "*Hup,*" she cried sharply, and deciding to do as she was told, Honey jumped awkwardly twisting her body in the air.

Thump. As they landed, Amber missed the middle of the saddle and lost her right stirrup. Clinging on desperately she wriggled back from her lopsided position and frantically searched for her stirrup with her foot. By now the wall fence was right in front of her. If she pulled up now, she knew she would be given a refusal but if she jumped like this, out of balance because of the lost stirrup, with the drop on the other side, she would fall off and get even more penalties.

It was too late to pull out now.

As she felt Honey begin to take off, she kicked her left foot out so that she had no stirrups. It was a risk but at least her balance was equal. She gripped with her legs as tightly as she could. Going over the jump was like a slow-motion replay. As they reached the point just before the descent to landing, Amber looked down. The ground seemed a long way off. As Honey's front end began to tilt forward, Amber felt like she was on a rollercoaster, strapped in looking over the bar just before plummeting, screaming to the ground. Her stomach lurched just as if she *was* on a rollercoaster as they plunged forward. Remembering seeing the girl in the Open class at this fence, she leaned back as far as she could, letting her reins slip so that she didn't jab Honey in the mouth. It seemed to take an age to land but when they did, the impact jolted Amber out of the saddle and she slipped round to the right.

"Aaaarrghh! Honey, wait!" Obediently, the pony slowed while Amber scrambled back into the saddle and pushed her hat up from over her eyes.

"Phew, that was close!" She composed herself, regained her stirrups and patted Honey. They'd cleared the biggest fences on the course, but it wasn't over yet. "Come on lass, let's finish this!"

But Honey was tired now. The big jumps in the wood had taken it out of her and there were still six to go. She kept going but Amber knew she had little left to give and didn't push her. Fortunately, the three steps were jumped downhill and didn't require as much effort as going up them. They trotted through the coffin and the water jump and over the straw bales until there were only two fences left. The penultimate fence was a white house. It had a black door and windows painted on and even had a peaked roof.

"Don't give up, we're nearly home," Amber implored.

Honey's head was low now, but always wanting to please, she cleared the house so that only the last – a chair fence festooned with brightly coloured flowers – stood between them and the finish. Honey saw it and checked. She didn't like the look of those flowers and she was so tired. But Amber was calling to her, willing her to go on. She wasn't going to repeat her mistake from the show jumping of not riding the final fence.

"Please Honey, only one more!"

And so, Honey made one last super effort and somehow got to the other side of the last jump on the course.

Euphoria like she had never known engulfed Amber as they trotted wearily through the finish flags. She jumped straight off Honey and hugged her tightly.

The pony was streaming with sweat and rivulets were running down her face and dripping from her eyelids. She was tired out but as Amber pulled a Polo mint out of her jodhpur pocket and offered it to her, she could see how alive Honey looked. Her eyes were shining, and she looked…what was it?

Proud.

As she stood there crunching her mint, engulfed in a warm cloud of steam, Amber could see she had changed. She wasn't Honey the nervous riding school pony who always went at the back anymore. She was Honey who had just got a clear round! Amber stood and let it sink in. This was real, it had actually happened. She knew she would remember this moment for the rest of her life.

Amber slacked the girth, pulled the reins over Honey's head and began to lead her back to the stables. She was tempted to wait as Emily was out on the course now and would soon be back, but she thought Honey would appreciate getting her tack off and having a nice hose down with cold water to wash away the sweat.

As she walked past the warm-up area, she saw Chelsea on her grey pony heading towards the start. Elisha, at present the top placed competitor, was the only rider left. But if there had been another hundred riders, she would still have been unmissable. Elisha wore white breeches and a white shirt under a banana yellow body protector. Her hat cover was royal blue with yellow stars and pompom. Thunder Cat looked magnificent; his yellow bandages making him look even blacker.

Pulling herself up straight and holding her head high, Amber walked past her, wondering, and hoping, *Will she ask the question*? Sure enough, Elisha trotted up alongside her and called, "She looks tired. Too much for her was it?"

Amber knew that was what Elisha was expecting, since she seemed to believe Fell ponies were completely incapable of anything. She stopped and smiled to herself, savouring the moment, before looking up into Elisha's cold, hard stare. Meeting her gaze unflinchingly, she said, "Yes, she is tired. It wasn't easy for her, only being a Fell pony from a riding school... but we went clear."

327

"Oh." Elisha tried not to let her feelings show but she was too slow to regain her icy smile for Amber to miss her change of expression. "Well…well done." For once, she looked away first.

"Thanks!" Amber said brightly, bursting with joy. She knew it had probably nearly killed Elisha to say that to her, but she'd had to. What else could she have said?

"Good luck for your round!" she called cheerily over her shoulder.

And leaving Elisha frowning behind her, she walked away, leading her pony with the biggest grin on her face and the best feeling she'd ever had in her life. Not only had Honey been fantastic; she was also impressed with her own bravery in tackling such a tough course. And then there was the cherry on the cake, of course; she had finally stood up for herself and left Elisha lost for words. She actually felt *proud* of herself for once and she revelled in the unfamiliar feeling. It was like wearing new clothes …like a new Amber had emerged.

-Fifteen-

Not Second Best

Riders and parents assembled in the classroom. All the action was over, the ponies were relaxing in their stables and everything had been tidied, ready for packing up and going home in the morning. All everyone wanted to know was the result of the One Day Event, although many people already had a good idea of the placings in their class.

The classroom had all the tables and chairs pushed to the edges of the room leaving a large empty floor area in the middle. The tables were piled high with all kinds of delicious party foods and drinks in preparation for the last night of camp.

Mrs Best entered the room carrying a large tray of rosettes. "Okay folks, are we all ready?"

Silence fell and everyone looked eagerly towards the DC in her green wool suit as she beamed happily at everyone.

"Well, here we are! The week is almost over, and it is my pleasure to be here to present the awards tonight. Let's begin with the Novice class."

One by one the riders from the Novice class came out to collect their rosettes while everyone clapped, and they blushed.

"And now we have our Intermediate riders. This was the most exciting class, with the cross-country proving very influential." Mrs Best seemed to be bubbling with excitement. She was like a child surrounded by presents on Christmas morning. "In first place with a score of forty-four, and the only rider to finish on their dressage score is Emily Pryde on Freaky Treacle!" The room erupted with applause as Emily went forward to collect her rosette and trophy. "In second place, with fifty-four after an unfortunate refusal on the cross-country is Chelsea Connor and Skylark." More polite applause. "And in third with a terrific clear in the cross-country, but with eight time penalties is Amber Anderson and Townend Honeysuckle!"

***

The results continued with Ashley moving up to fourth, thanks to his clear round cross-country after having two fences down in the show jumping and being last in the dressage. There were whoops and cheers for Ashley, who rode Bandit, a piebald cob with feathers and a serious moustache that his father also used as a driving pony. He was shocking at the dressage but loved charging round the cross-country and was surprisingly nimble for a part-time carthorse. The final rosette went to Kate who was pleased with her fifth place on the young and inexperienced Breeze.

Natalie had fallen off at the wall that nearly claimed Amber. She hadn't been expecting the drop on the landing side, having not seen it, and wasn't prepared to lean back to help keep her balance. She'd just been tipped off and Rocky had gone for a nice run around the field on his own before someone caught him and reunited him with Natalie. Sadly, because of the fall, she was not allowed to remount and continue but despite this, she'd had a great time as Rocky had flown everything for her and she'd only fallen off because of her own lack of balance.

Amber had sympathy for her; she knew that she too would have ended up on the ground at that fence if Honey hadn't stopped to allow her to get back into the saddle. Natalie's dad had been on the phone with Elisha's dad and agreed that they would be buying Rocky as soon as Sable could be sold.

A boy called Jake had also been eliminated on the cross-country: for missing a fence out. He was gutted as he thought he'd gone clear and would've been well placed otherwise. His misfortune confirmed to Amber that her decision to go back and look at the course again had been the right one.

As for Elisha, who was conspicuous by her absence at the prize giving, she had finished, for the first time in her life, in equal last place after being eliminated on the cross-country. Somehow, she had managed to get Thunder Cat, after more than one attempt, over the first ditch, the trakehner and the coffin, but the water proved to be their undoing again.

Elisha had tried to wear spurs, but the centre's staff had made her take them off as she didn't have a note from the DC giving her permission to wear them. So, when Thunder Cat had skittered and stopped at the water, she'd had a temper tantrum and whipped him fiercely, screaming and lashing hysterically. At that point, the manager of the centre – a tall, serious horseman – had marched angrily across the field, bawled at Elisha until she actually cried, took her whip off her and threw it in the water jump before leading her off the course. She hadn't been seen since.

Natalie confided to Amber and Emily that Elisha had phoned her dad and told him her version of events and that he was coming to take her and the horses away later that night. Although Amber felt no fondness for the girl, she did feel a brief moment of sympathy for her, now sitting alone in her horsebox instead of joining in the party with everyone else.

"Here you go." Emily appeared with a beaker of something fizzy for Amber, with Natalie shyly remaining with them now that Elisha wasn't there.

Emily raised her cup in a toast and Amber playfully joined in, bashing her plastic cup against Emily's.

"Here's to our success." Emily grinned. "And to the best part of the week – beating Elisha!"

Amber sipped her drink thoughtfully. She had, unbelievably, managed to achieve the unreachable dream of defeating Elisha. A sense of peace and contentment hugged her. But was that truly the reason for her happiness? The recent events flashed through her mind like a silent movie. Watching the replay was electrifying and thrilled her each time she re-lived it. She smiled to herself, remembering crossing the finish with a clear round behind her.

"I can see you smiling," Emily teased. "I told you we had a chance to beat Elisha and you didn't believe me. Feels good eh?"

"Yes, but that wasn't why I was smiling."

"No? Then what?"

Slowly, knowing how she felt inside but not knowing how to put it into words, Amber tried to explain. "It's funny, but after all the things Elisha has said to me and all the time I've spent wishing I could beat her, now it's happened I'm not even bothered."

Emily's eyebrows leapt up her forehead as her eyes widened in surprise.

"You're not bothered? What do you mean? Why not?"

"Well, I feel so happy now it's unbelievable, but I would still have felt like this if Elisha had won...although obviously it's much better that you won," she added quickly. "It's just that it doesn't matter to me now about other people. If everyone else had done better and I'd ended up last in our group, I'd still be over the moon because I know I couldn't have done any better, apart from that silly mistake in the show jumping. I was terrified of the cross-country course, but I got round it clear. And what's even better about it is that it wasn't on a ready-made competition pony that I could just point at the fences and know I was getting over them. It was on a pony nobody expected anything of. I brought her here as the second best pony because the trophy winner couldn't come, and despite having no experience, she gave me everything she had. I'll never forget this week. It's let me see that winning isn't everything."

"Wow, well I don't think everyone would agree with you. Elisha for one."

"Well, that's her loss. If you have to win to be happy, it'll probably add up to a pretty disappointing life. You can't win all the time, as she's just discovered."

"Man, that's profound. You've got a wise head on those shoulders for one so young." Emily chuckled and shook her head in wonder, pulling Amber and Natalie into a hug. "But I did win and all I can say is, it made me *very* happy! I may never do it again so let's make the most of it."

Just then, a loud party tune started to play on the centre's loudspeakers.

"Come on girls, let's dance." Emily strutted into the middle of the room, dragging a giggling Amber and a very reluctant Natalie with her.

***

The next morning everybody loaded up their ponies and everything they'd brought, ready to head home. Natalie had gone the previous evening with Elisha when her dad came to get her, since Natalie had been sleeping in the luxurious living quarters of Elisha's horsebox with her all week. Amber waved as first Kate, then Chelsea then Ashley and Jake were driven from the yard by their parents, until there was only Emily left.

"We can wait with you 'til your parents get here," Mrs Anderson said to Emily.

"Oh no, it's fine - you go. Mum's just texted to say they're five minutes away. You'd better go now so you don't bump into them on the lane," Emily answered casually.

Mrs Anderson nodded and went back to the car and got in with her husband who was sitting waiting. Honey was already loaded in the trailer, waiting to begin the journey back to Shaw Farm.

"Well, I'll see you then, probably at school on Monday." Amber gave Emily a shy hug. "Thanks for everything this week. I've had the best time."

337

Emily ruffled her hair in the way adults often do to small boys. "It was great. Our second rate ponies didn't do so bad, did they?" she joked.

"Nothing second rate or second best about them."

"You're right about that," Emily agreed, somewhat solemnly. Amber couldn't understand why Emily didn't look happier when she said this. "So, you'd better get going. Like I said, you don't want to meet my parents on the lane. Two vehicles can't pass on it and it's a long way to reverse with a trailer on." Emily seemed keen to get Amber into her car.

"Okay. See you soon then." Amber opened the car door and got into the back seat.

"Yeah, bye!"

They drove away, leaving Emily waving behind them. Just as they got to the end of the lane, an old battered 4x4 turned in pulling a slightly shabby trailer behind it.

"Emily was right, we've just escaped bumping into her parents," Mrs Anderson said happily.

When Amber looked at the other car, however, there was only one person in it – a woman driver with unruly dark hair like Emily's. Emily had seemed to think both her parents would be coming to pick her up, but it looked like her dad hadn't been able to make it.

Thinking no more of it, Amber settled back into her seat and slipped into a daydream in which she was riding the cross-country course of the previous day again on Honey. She really couldn't think of any experience she'd had that had been as scary, thrilling and wonderful all at the same time. It was, she thought, the best moment of her life so far. *May there be many more,* she hoped as they headed back to the farm and to Molly and Pearl who were there waiting for them.

The Perfect Pony for Me

By Ashtyn Wade

That horse won.
We all knew he would;
The £18,000 imported horse
Who dominated the course.

My tiny Fell pony came in second,
But she's better I reckon.
No, she's not as tall,
But she can still do it all.

You see, my little Fell pony,
She jumped everything, and nothing felt funny.
She was the star,
Flying faster than a car.

She flew higher than a hawk,
And that time she clocked –
I'm proud of my pony,
Way better than any phony.

So, my Fell came in second,
To your expensive Christmas present.
But my Fell pony is first,
In heart, skill, and effort, she means the most.

Author's Note

"There is no secret so close as
between a rider and his horse."
~ R. S. Surtees

Helen and Honey, Greystoke Castle, 1993

Honey was a revelation to me and taught me a lot about underestimation.

When we first got Honey, she was frightened of everything: literally a bag of nerves. I think she was a timid personality, and being a riding school pony, she couldn't get confidence from her riders, who were often novices, so she took it from being part of the herd. She was always part of a large group that went out on rides together, so when we got her, and expected her to go out with just Pearl for company, she couldn't see how she could possibly be expected to manage this dangerous task and tried very hard for a long time to avoid it. The lessons I learned about ponies began right from that first day, when we couldn't even get them to leave the yard of their new home as neither was used to being the lead pony. There began my real-world instruction in patience, perseverance, and trying to see the world through the eyes of a pony.

We did eventually manage to get the pair of them going out almost happily together, though Honey would never take the lead. Beside Pearl instead of behind her was the best she could manage.

So, the thought that this cowardly pony would ever become a Pony Club star never occurred to any of us. How could a pony who couldn't hack out on her own due to all the scary things waiting to kill her (she thought) go around a cross-country course, all alone, jumping solid, imposing fences?

I suppose it was because she, unlike Pearl, absolutely loved jumping, and I hope, because she came to trust me as her rider. Honey was the first pony with whom I shared the fear and exhilaration of riding cross-country. There is nothing like it for creating a bond between pony and rider, and I was hooked.

Jumping was Honey's hidden talent, and it brought out her personality and confidence. She regularly went clear round all the cross-country courses in our local area, back in the days when there was a hunter trials season. When other riders were struggling to get over deep scary ditches or through the brown, muddy water jump, my little scaredy cat jumped everything in sight. It really did seem like a miracle, and every time we came back clear, we all struggled to believe it.

I had thought that because Pearl didn't like jumping, neither would Honey or any other Fell pony, for that matter. But Honey taught us that all ponies are individuals, regardless of their breed.

She wasn't the fastest and her stamina often let her down towards the end of a round, but she gave me *everything* she had and for that, I loved her and could ask no more.

Acknowledgements

My first thanks go to the lovely readers of *Little Pearl* who contacted me directly or left reviews on Amazon to share their reactions to the book. I've had some really positive feedback and it's wonderful to hear from people who have enjoyed it. Particularly thrilling was hearing from World Champion Ros Canter and award-winning author Sheena Wilkinson; I'm grateful to them for taking the time to read the book and contact me about it.

Similarly, thank you to the beta readers of *The Second Best Pony* for your thoughts on the unedited proof version of the story. Your support and comments were positive, constructive and much appreciated.

To those who entered the 'cover star competition' to find a pony model to represent Honey on the cover of this book, I loved seeing all your beautiful ponies. I looked at them all every day for weeks, wondering how they could be narrowed down to one eventual winner, but in the end … Greenholme

Clyde owned by Katie Trotter was voted number one. *Let's Get Booked* then used the image (permission granted by L Meader Photography) to create the book's stunning cover and also helped me to edit and refine the story. Thank you, Amanda, for helping me clarify my intentions for this book.

To the winners of the illustration and poetry competitions linked to this book: thank you for your creativity. The illustration on the dedication page is by 14-year-old Abbie Wilkins, who loves drawing animals and is a talented artist. I'm honoured to have a piece of her art in my book. The poem, *The Perfect Pony for Me,* at the end of the book was written by Ashtyn Wade, also 14 years-old. She wrote the poem without having read *The Second Best Pony* and I thought it was uncanny how her words reflected the sentiment of the story. It was perfect for inclusion in the book. I love working creatively with young people and to have young writers and artists getting involved with my work means a lot.

And finally, thanks again to my husband for being so supportive and for being the final proof reader. There's always something he spots that no-one else has seen!

Trusting Molly

Amber's Pony Tales

Book 3

– One –

The Gate

Amber Anderson lay on the cold, hard ground, listening to the sound of receding hoof beats galloping away. The darkening sky pushed down on her while the damp ground beneath her pushed back, opposing forces squeezing the air from her lungs.

Gasping for breath, she tried to sit up, but a shooting pain stopped her. Flat on her back, she fumbled for her jacket pocket to find her mobile phone, but where was the zip? She couldn't lift her head to look, so she slowly and painfully removed her gloves and tried again, feeling her way.

At last, Amber found the zip, but dismayed, she discovered the pocket was already open. She must've forgotten to pull the zip up and close the pocket when she set off for the ride. Not so long ago, when she'd needed to help two riders involved in a terrible accident, she'd left her phone in the car. And now, here she was, having made sure she brought it with her while riding out alone, only to have left the pocket open and lost the phone in the fall.

She tilted her head carefully and looked around her. Craning her neck as far as she could bear, Amber spied her phone lying in the mud near the forestry gate. It was way out of her reach.

She couldn't move. *What am I going to do?* Moisture from the damp ground underneath her seeped through her jodhpurs. She couldn't stay there. It was going to be dark soon. Amber tried to turn over onto her side, but again the raw pain stilled her.

I've broken my back, shot into her mind and she gasped.

***

It was October and Amber and her dad had come to the stables straight from school. The hardy Fell ponies were turned out, but Molly spent most of her time living inside. Much to everyone's surprise, she seemed to prefer being stabled. She'd had a few months of being turned out and not ridden over the summer, to see if a rest would help her when she'd been reluctant to jump after the Andersons bought her in the spring. They'd thought some rest and relaxation in the field, enjoying the sunshine and plentiful grass might help her to recover from any little niggly injury the pony might have had, and would also be appreciated after years of being permanently stabled. It hadn't gone quite to plan, however, as Molly had spent most of her time hanging around the field gate as if she wanted to come in. She didn't seem to want to have anything to do with Honey and Pearl – the Fell ponies – and appeared to be more stressed in the field than she was in the stable.

Because she was stabled next to Caroline's horse, Oriel, it was suggested that they try turning Molly out with her instead. This had been a terrible idea. The Andersons had come to the farm one Saturday morning to discover the farmer's daughter in a complete panic. Molly and Oriel had gone missing from the small paddock behind the farmhouse. At first, she'd thought they may have been stolen in the night and was ready to ring the police to report it, but then they'd received a phone call from the police to say that a chestnut pony had been caught running along the bypass several miles away. It was Molly.

The Andersons had rushed off with their trailer to bring the pony home. Thankfully, she was completely unhurt and hadn't caused any accidents on the busy road. It was a miracle really and they were extremely relieved.

But there was no sign of Oriel.

The Blakelys and the Andersons, plus many of their friends and local villagers, searched the surrounding area for hours. Dusk was falling when they finally heard the news that Oriel had been found. Everyone was delighted...until they saw the horse. Oriel had been found underneath a bridge. Whether she had jumped over it or fallen, it wasn't clear, but she was a mess; covered in mud, both of her knees skinned and bloody, but worst of all was her face. Caroline had turned as white as a sheet and cried when she saw the broken bone protruding out of her horse's face like a giant white splinter.

Now, months later, Oriel's knees had healed, although the scars were visible if you looked closely. But her face was forever changed, with a long, ugly bump stretching between her muzzle and forehead.

No-one ever discovered how the horses had got out of the field, but there was an unspoken feeling that the escape was down to Molly, and Oriel had probably followed.

Since then, it was decided that for her own safety, Molly would spend most of her time being stabled. That meant that she needed to be ridden daily, so Mrs Anderson had started hacking her out. She'd never repeated anything like the incident where she bolted with Amber soon after coming to live at Shaw Farm, so that was put down to excitability at hacking off-road for the first time.

**

Now that the winter was approaching, and days were getting shorter, either Mrs Anderson rode Molly during the day if she wasn't at work, or Amber rode her quickly after school.

That day, as she mounted Molly in the yard, her dad asked her, as he always did, which route she was taking while he stayed behind and mucked out Molly's stable.

"I think I'll just go round the roads for half an hour tonight," Amber replied, patting her coat pocket to make sure she had her phone.

Her dad frowned. "With it getting darker now, I think you'd be better sticking to the forestry, away from any traffic."

Looking down on him, Amber frowned back, "but there's hardly any traffic on the roads here. It'll be fine."

"I know, but since we've forgotten to bring your fluorescent, I'd be happier if you weren't on the roads. Go into the forestry, it's safer. And make sure you've got your phone with you."

"Yep, I've got it." She huffed, patting her pocket again, reassured to feel that it was definitely there.

Sighing, Amber rode out of the yard, thinking about her day at school. It had been a non-uniform day. Last year, non-uniform day had been a disaster. Excited at having a day free from the school's bottle green and grey attire, Amber had chosen an outfit that seemed like a good idea at the time: a brown crushed velvet skirt and white blouse. But when she arrived at school, she knew immediately she'd got it wrong. No-one said anything to her, but she could feel the eyes following her and sense the smirks behind her back. She had thought that people would want to use a non-uniform day to look their best and wear nice clothes, but everyone else seemed to know that the new uniform for the day was ripped jeans, T-shirts and hoodies.

So, when the day came around this year, Amber took care to choose something that would help her to blend in instead of stick out and wore black skinny jeans and ballerina pumps with a pale grey slouchy sweater. It had been a huge relief to find that no-one had noticed her all day.

As her daydream reached an end, she arrived at the gate into the forestry. It was normally open, held back with a rock so that riders could go straight through, but today it was closed. Frowning, Amber positioned Molly so that she could reach down to try and open the catch. The Fell ponies would have stood quite happily and let her do this, but Molly had never encountered a closed gate on a ride before and did not understand what she was being asked to do. She was being ridden towards it, but she could not go through it. Confused, she backed up, swung her quarters away and refused to stand still. There was no way Amber could remain mounted and get the gate open.

Mistaking Molly's anxiety for awkwardness, Amber flung herself out of the saddle and dragged the pony impatiently towards the gate. She wrestled with the stiff catch but found it rusty from lack of use, so it was unlikely she could have opened it from Molly's back anyway. Remorse for her irritability nudged heat into her cheeks as, eventually, she was able to release the catch and heave the gate back towards the hedgerow. She pushed the large rock in front of it so that it would still be open when she returned, led Molly through into the forestry and went to remount.

No sooner had she placed her left foot in the stirrup and went to pull herself up into the saddle, than Molly abruptly spun around and charged back through the gate. Amber clung to Molly's left side. Her back smashed into the gatepost as Molly hurtled through the narrow space, sending a sharp pain shooting through her body. The agony threatened to engulf her, but Amber knew that she had to hang on. If she didn't, she would hit the ground hard. And, rider-less, Molly would be heading out back towards the road in the failing light at a flat out gallop. Amber couldn't let that happen.

Grimacing, she dragged herself onto Molly's back, but it was a moving target and she didn't land squarely on the saddle. Molly's speed and motion bumped her straight off.

Amber barely registered the sickening feeling of falling before she slammed hard onto the ground beneath her.

- Two -

If Only

Molly was gone. Amber was all alone. She couldn't reach her phone to call for help and she couldn't move. There was nothing she could do but look at the sky above her and try not to concentrate on her discomfort and helplessness.

It would be dark soon. Tears leaked from the corners of her eyes as Amber wondered how long it would be before her dad came looking for her. At least he knew where she was. But what about Molly? The pony was loose on the road. Again. Could she be lucky enough to escape unharmed twice? Amber concentrated on her breathing and tried to quell the rising panic that was growing inside her.

It seemed like hours had passed as she lay on the ground – cold, hurt and alone – before car headlights came bobbing up the pot-holed track. With the beam of the lights blinding her as the car came to a stop, her dad jumped out of the driver's seat and ran to her.

Mr Anderson's face was a map of worry as he crouched beside his daughter. The fact that she had lain there on the cold, wet track without getting up meant something was wrong. Could he risk trying to get her in the car or should he phone for an ambulance? They were in the middle of nowhere. It would be hard to try and explain their location to an operator. It could take ages for them to be found, and all the while Amber would be getting colder. It would soon be pitch black too.

Amber was so relieved to have been found, she let out a mighty sob. The force of it jarred her body and sent a wave of torture through her once more. The cocktail of pain and relief combined rushed to her brain in a dizzying assault. But everything would be alright now that her dad was with her.

"It's okay, I'm here, I'm here, shhhhh." Mr Anderson put his arms around her as best as he could. "Do you think you can sit up?" he asked, wrestling with his instinct to keep her still.

"I've tried," Amber gasped, "but I can't. Maybe you could push me up?"

Still terrified of what injuries she may have sustained, but keeping his fears to himself, he slowly and carefully slid his hands under her shoulder blades and began to inch her into a sitting position. Amber winced and gasped. The pain was blinding, and she tasted vomit in her mouth. Everything spun around her like she had just stepped off a fairground ride and the car headlights continued to bore into her like an unrelenting laser. She took a moment to ease the nausea, taking deep breaths of rapidly cooling autumn air, then with her dad's arms still around her, she managed to roll to the left and onto her knees.

"Okay, well done," Mr Anderson's held breath escaped from him like an air brake. "Now I'll try and get you up. Ready?" Amber nodded. Her dad moved to stand in front of her, slotted his arms under her armpits, and began to gently lift. Amber howled with the flash of intense pain that came immediately from her right side.

"Not the right," she managed to hiss out between clenched teeth.

Mr Anderson repositioned himself on her left side and managed to get her to her feet. The ground beneath her lurched away and Mr Anderson had to practically carry her to the passenger side of the car, where he strapped her in without removing her riding hat or gloves. He then rushed to the driver's seat and reversed all the way back down the track. It only took a couple of minutes, but it felt like hours to Amber as every bump and jolt sent sickening waves of agony through her body.

Soon they were onto the main road and heading for the hospital's A & E, which seemed as if it was the place to be on a Friday evening as it was full of people waiting to be seen. Her mother soon arrived to join them and calmly helped her change into a pair of cosy tracky bottoms in a nearby toilet cubicle. Amber winced as her tight, wet jodhs gripped her legs and refused to slide off, meaning Mrs Anderson had to tug at them. She was as gentle as possible but each pull jarred Amber.

Screwing her face up against the pain, she snapped "be...*careful*."

Surprised by the sharpness in her daughter's tone, Mrs Anderson looked up and wondered whether to scold Amber for her curtness. Deciding against it, she replied, "I am, but I can't get them off unless I pull them I'm afraid." Amber made no further protest as her mother continued to coax the jodhpurs off her until they sat in a defeated soggy pile on the cubicle floor. She was helped into her tracky bottoms and they returned to the waiting room in silence.

While they waited to be called, Amber heard snatches of the conversation between her parents as she concentrated on blocking out the discomfort. The large pink pill given to her by a triage nurse upon her arrival hadn't helped much with the pain.

"...just wheeling the barrow out...Molly flying back into the yard...no Amber!"

"...did you do?"

"…house…only Caroline in…she offered… straight in the car… my fault… I told her to…gate closed… if only…"

At least Molly is alright, Amber thought to herself. It sounded as if Caroline had looked after the pony so that her dad could come to find her straight away. She wanted to tell her dad that it wasn't his fault; he seemed to be blaming himself for telling her to go into the forestry, instead of on the roads as she'd planned, but a weariness had come over her, out of nowhere, and she just slumped against him, the words unspoken.

She must've fallen asleep somehow, for when she awoke, Amber was being wheeled up a squeaky linoleum corridor towards the X-ray department in a hard, uncomfortable wheelchair.

It turned out that she had broken her right collarbone. The doctor showed them a picture of the X-ray and Amber could see the bone was clearly in two halves.

"Not to worry," the doctor said, clipping a pen back into the breast pocket of his white jacket. "Although a broken collarbone can be extremely painful, it should heal well in around six weeks. You must keep it supported at all times with a simple sling and try to avoid moving your arm. If it swells up, use an ice pack, and normal painkillers should be enough to make the discomfort bearable."

Great, thought Amber. *Six weeks? That means no riding for six whole weeks.*

And as well as the riding, there was something else she wasn't going to be able to do now too. Her friend Joanne was *not* going to be happy.

- Three -

A Change of Plan

"You've done *what?*" cried Joanne when she opened her door to see Amber standing with her arm in a sling and an explanation at the ready.

***

When she'd come home from the hospital the previous evening, she'd planned on sending a WhatsApp message to her best friends, Joanne and Emily, to explain what had happened, but by the time she'd struggled out of her clothes and into a bath – it was very hard to get into a bath with only one working arm, she'd discovered – and then into pyjamas and bed, she'd been so exhausted she'd fallen asleep immediately. This morning had been another struggle to do everything without disturbing her arm. Eventually, much later than usual on a Saturday morning, the Andersons were ready to drive to the yard. Although Amber wouldn't be riding for a while, the ponies still needed seeing to and Molly needed to be exercised.

Her dad crawled up the farm track, taking even greater care than usual to avoid the potholes. When they reached Jubilee House, where her friend Joanne lived, Amber asked to be dropped off at the door. She couldn't help with mucking out or be any use at the yard, so she figured she might as well break the news to Jo and get it over with.

"You should go for a ride," she told her parents as she clambered laboriously out of the back seat, "I'll just hang around here for a while."

"You can't invite yourself to stay here for hours," her mother tutted, "they may be busy or going out or something. I'll come and ask Lou if it's okay."

"Oh, you needn't do that," Amber moaned grumpily as her mother went to undo her seatbelt, "I'll find out if it's okay for me to stay and I'll text you if there's any problem."

"Well…alright then," her mother conceded. "But make sure you ask politely."

Amber pulled a sarcastic face. These last couple of months, since she'd started back at school in Year 8 and her 13th birthday approached, she'd found herself getting a bit moody. Although her parents sometimes bore the brunt of her recent mood swings, she always knew to be well-mannered with everyone else.

When the door of Jubilee House opened, it wasn't Lou Jones, Joanne's mum who opened the door, but Joanne herself. Her eyes turned to saucers when she saw Amber and her frown was a question she didn't need to ask out loud.

"I came off Molly last night. Broke my collarbone." She tried to shrug apologetically, forgetting momentarily that she hadn't to move. She grimaced.

"You've done *what?*"

Amber arranged her face into what she hoped resembled a rueful expression. It wasn't like she had done this on purpose, but it was going to ruin Jo's plans.

"How're you going to do the postal shoot now?"

***

Since Amber had discovered that her parents' meek, mild Fell pony, Honey, was a surprise cross-country star at Pony Club camp that summer, she'd spent the rest of the season competing her. Molly, her competition pony, had been side-lined with a suspected injury and given the summer off, so when Honey proved herself to be unexpectedly keen on jumping, she had been taken to all the local Pony Club gymkhanas and autumn hunter trials, and had even gone as far as Hexham for the Fell Pony Performance Trials.

Honey loved to jump, but she wasn't very fast, and however fit she got, her stamina wasn't the best. Amber was amassing quite a collection of green and orange rosettes – the colours given for fourth and fifth place. So, it was a huge shock when they managed to win the junior section of Brantfort Pony Club's hunter trial last month. Honey always went clear everywhere she went, but lost out on the time penalties she picked up. However, there was something about the ditch on this course that was catching even experienced horses and ponies out. Not Honey though; she popped over it in her usual cheerful fashion. Then, near the end was the water jump, sited in a boggy area of the field. The water did look pretty gross – it was brown and murky with green algae snaking across the surface – and lots of riders had to take the alternative to avoid being eliminated at it, as so many ponies refused to enter the swamp. Honey didn't care. Perhaps because she'd spent her early years living wild on the fells of Caldbeck, a bit of bog was nothing out of the ordinary for her and she splashed through the gunge without a care in the world. She still came back with her customary time faults that day…but she was the only clear round. Nobody could believe that a Fell pony who had been a riding school pony all her life could go out and beat combinations who regularly competed at affiliated level.

Amber's confidence had skyrocketed and Honey became a local celebrity. It seemed like everyone knew her, and even when they went, as their last competition of the season, to the Fell Pony

Performance Trials, they found that people there, whom they'd never met, had heard of her too.

Meanwhile, Joanne, who had recovered from a terrible accident just over a year ago, and had been schooling up a new pony, had also begun to compete again. Her pale palomino, Merry, despite being rather careless at show jumping, was a cross-country machine, going fast and clear at every event. This had given Jo an idea that she had put to Amber during a sleepover at Jubilee House a couple of weeks ago.

"A what? A…trackalon?" Amber said when she'd heard the strange term Jo had used.

"No…I've told you before - tetrathlon," Jo had laughed at Amber's mispronunciation. "It's a Pony Club competition that involves riding cross-country, which both our ponies are brilliant at."

"Yes, but what else? You said there were four phases."

"Yeah, there are. You also have to shoot, run and swim. The order is usually shoot first, then swim, then ride and run last."

"Whoa…hang on. Shoot? What do you mean shoot? Shoot what… and with what?"

"At a target with an air pistol," Jo replied casually.

"What? They let children use guns?" Amber couldn't believe what she was hearing.

"Yes, but for minimus and juniors, an adult has to load the gun. Everything is perfectly safe."

"Yeah, but there's one small problem." Amber pointed out. "Where are we going to get a gun from?"

"Oh, we've already got one. Brantfort Pony Club are going to run a tetrathlon for local branches next summer. They used to do it apparently, but haven't for ages. Now they've got a new DC, she's keen to get it going again. When I told my parents I wanted to do it, they were well up for it and my dad found out about postal shoots that run through the winter to let competitors practise their shooting. So he's going to run it for our branch and he bought a gun for me and Matthew to share. You could borrow it too and join in. Then you'll be ready to compete next summer."

Amber went to speak but Joanne, clearly excited with her plan, ploughed on and cut her off.

"And, if we can get two other girls to do it, we could be a team and aim for the Area Qualifier!"

***

A team hadn't yet been sorted out, but the postal shoot was imminent, with the first round due to start in less than a fortnight, during the October half-term. Amber was meant to have been using the time now, before it began, to practise with the gun and get used to it so that her performance in the competition would be helped. But now there was one obvious, major complication: Amber was right-handed…and now she couldn't even move her right arm, let alone grip a gun, lift her arm, hold it steady to aim, and fire.

"I don't think I can," she replied to Jo's question. "Unless I can shoot left-handed!" she added as a joke.

But Jo's head snapped up and she looked fiercely at Amber, determination hardening her pretty face.

"Come with me." She reached forward and took hold of Amber's uninjured left arm, pulling her into the house.

"Ow!" Amber cried, as she lurched forward and jolted her shoulder.

"Oh, sorry, sorry!" Jo hurriedly let go of Amber and closed the door behind her. "But I have a plan. DAAAAAAAAAAAAAAAAAAAAAAAD!"

- Four -

Shoot!

When Amber's parents had come to pick her up to go home after their ride on Molly and Honey, they were chased away by Joanne who had been seized by an ardent fervour and insisted that Amber stayed for a sleepover. Mrs Anderson had fussed for a bit about Amber's arm and her sling and not having a change of clothes or a toothbrush, but Jo had dismissed these concerns, insisting that she would lend Amber whatever she needed and would help her to get dressed. Mrs Jones had been happy for Amber to stay and so she, Jo and Matthew were now standing in Jo's garage. Amber held a gun in her left hand.

Mr Jones had been summoned, following Amber's throwaway comment about shooting left-handed, to see if it would be possible.

The garage had been set up with a bench in the middle, set seven metres away from a row of targets at the far end which were pinned to an old mattress.

"It's to stop the bullets ricocheting back and hitting you," declared Matthew, who was the most animated Amber had ever seen him. "That's what would happen if the targets were against a hard surface."

Amber looked questioningly at Jo and her dad to see if this was true or if Matthew was pulling her leg.

"Yes, it could happen," Mr Jones confirmed, "but 'bullets' is a bit of an exaggeration. They're just pellets, and the pistols are low power so they wouldn't do you much harm. But obviously, there are a lot of safety rules to prevent anyone from being accidentally shot."

Amber watched with interest as Jo and Matthew each took turns to shoot at a target with their gun. Mr Jones loaded the gun for them after each shot; Amber noted that it only held one pellet at a time, and even though it was only an informal practice, he gave commands like 'are you ready?', 'standby' and 'reload' to prepare them for what it would be like in a tetrathlon competition.

Matthew was delighted to be eligible to take part as competitors had to be at least nine-years-old to be allowed to shoot. Although his tenth birthday was coming up in December, he would still be competing in the minimus class next summer. As such, he was allowed to stand square on to the target and hold the gun with both hands, but Jo and herself would compete as juniors which meant they were only allowed to use one hand. Jo was either very well-practised or very strong as Amber noticed that her arm didn't tremble at all when she raised the gun, aimed quickly and fired within the four-second count down provided by Mr Jones.

"In the tetrathlon, juniors have a turning target, which means that when it turns to face you, you've only got four seconds to aim and shoot before it turns away again," Jo explained, "which is why you have to get used to the time allowed. We don't have turning targets here, so for the postal shoot, we'll just be using a static target like the minimus, but you've still only got four seconds to make the shot."

Amber nodded gently, remembering not to make any movement that would jolt her arm. There was a lot to take in.

"Okay then, Amber," Mr Jones pointed to where she should stand, behind the bench. "As you're right-handed, you'd normally stand with your right shoulder towards the target. You'd hold the gun in your right hand, close your left eye and look through the sights with your right, aiming for the bull's eye in the middle, then gently squeeze the trigger. But as your right arm is going to be out of play for a while, you're going to have to at least start the postal shoot using your left. You'll be able to swap back to your right when you're all healed, which will be in plenty of time for the tetrathlon next summer."

Amber stood where she was directed and turned her left shoulder towards the target as Mr

Jones handed her the unloaded gun. She curled her fingers around the handgrip and lifted it tentatively. Mr Jones showed her how to raise the gun and line up the centre of the target with the front and rear sights of the pistol. She practised a few times but found her arm shaking at the weight of the gun. Mr Jones noticed and sent Jo into the house to bring some drinks and biscuits while Amber had a rest.

After a snack of crumbly Hobnobs and some sweet apple juice, it was time for Amber to try a real target. When she saw Mr Jones open the top of the pistol, push the pellet into it and snap it closed, she blinked rapidly and took a deep, steadying breath. She wished that Jo and Matthew hadn't stayed to watch her first attempt – they were both so good. Their targets had been full of neat little holes in the bull's eye, worth ten points, and the next band of eight points. Jo's target had been particularly precise, with a cluster of holes in and around the bull's eye. Amber had a strong suspicion that she would not be a good shot. Her hand-eye coordination wasn't the best and she couldn't catch anything smaller than a netball. She always dreaded any PE at school that involved catching or hitting balls: tennis, rounders, hockey, as she was so bad at them. It didn't help either that her eyesight wasn't brilliant, and it was about time she got herself some glasses. It was going to be a repeat of her first attempt at jumping with Pearl, when Jo and Matthew cleared the fences effortlessly on their ponies while Pearl had embarrassed her by being ridiculously stubborn and refusing tiny cross poles. This was going to be another of those episodes. She just knew it.

"Are you ready?" This was her signal to pick up the gun.

"Standby."

"Fire."

As Mr Jones began to count, Amber raised the gun hurriedly, attempted to line up the sights and pulled the trigger just as "three" was being said.

"Four…stop." Mr Jones finished.

Amber placed the gun back on the bench as Mr Jones looked at the target through his binoculars. "I'm afraid that shot is off-target," he relayed as he scanned the unmarked target ahead of him. "You panicked and rushed. There was still plenty of time. Let's do a few more."

Amber took four more shots, trying hard to block out everything except the gun sights in front of her and the distant target. When she managed to get her fourth and fifth shots into the four and six point bands, Jo whooped and clapped behind her. Feeling slightly more encouraged, she took another rest, this time with some lemonade and a giant bag of marshmallows that Matthew produced with a smirk. Nothing was said, but Amber was sure they weren't his to share.

Of Amber's final five shots, three were on target: two fours and a two. She was disappointed that only half of her ten shots found the target at all, and none were anywhere near the bullseye. But her left arm was trembling and there was an ache developing across her chest as her collarbone throbbed. Even though she'd used her left arm, it felt as if her injured side had also been involved, and it wasn't pleased. It grumbled indignantly, as if reminding Amber that she was supposed to be resting it.

Despite her despondency at her poor performance, Jo was delighted and congratulated Amber at her first attempt.

"That was amazing," she enthused. "I can't do anything with my left hand at all. I'd never have been able to hit the target in a million years with my left. You're so clever!"

Amber blushed at her praise, which she didn't feel was deserved, but it was so like Jo to be encouraging.

Jo was all for Amber continuing and trying some more shots, but when Amber explained that she was starting to feel uncomfortable, she was whisked up to Jo's room and made to lie on her bed with a hot chocolate, topped with some more of the marshmallows.

Amber sighed with contentment as she lay in the comfort of the bedcovers, looking at the horse and pony posters that decorated the walls and the bookshelves filled with Jo's pony books, toys, ornaments, rosettes and framed pictures of her jumping her old pony, Flash, at various competitions.

Just as she wondered wearily what might be for tea and what plans her friend might have in store for them that evening, Jo appeared in the room. She sat on the bed beside Amber and removed the empty mug she was still holding in her left hand, swapping it for something blue and squishy.

"What's this?" Amber asked in surprise, looking down to see a blue-haired ball with two eyes peering up at her.

"It's a stress ball. Mum and the other teachers were given one at work. It's for you to squeeze to build up the muscles in your left hand to improve your grip on the gun. Go on, give him a squeeze."

Amber clenched her palm. It was harder than it looked.

"Harder!" commanded Jo, her face looking at the blue ball keenly.

Amber gave the ball another squeeze, surprised at how little power she had in her left hand. Jo's expectant gaze was replaced with a look of chagrin. She reached out and took the ball from Amber, and with her right hand, squeezed it hard. Amber laughed as the two eyes attached to the ball shot out on stalks, which, combined with the pointy blue hair, gave it a highly startled appearance.

"This is what you're aiming for," Jo instructed. "You've got to get your left hand strong enough to make his eyes pop right out. That's your homework from now on, right?"

Amber could tell from Jo's stern expression that she meant it, so she nodded and took the ball back, giving it the hardest squeeze she could manage. The eyes wobbled slightly but did not leap out.

"Right, athlete in training here. You need building up. Let's go and see what's for tea."

– Five –

Pink

Two weeks later, it was half term. The first Friday evening saw Amber at Mrs Best's house for a stable management rally. Amber had taken and passed her D and D+ tests that summer and was now working towards her C test. This meant that she was still in group 2, which was annoying as her friend Emily had moved into group 1 as she was now aiming for her C+. Emily went to the same school as Amber but as she was in Year 9 – the year above – she hardly got to see her. Although Joanne was now back to full health after her accident, and would be in Amber's group, as she too was aiming for her C test, Amber was desperate to see Emily and speak to her properly. Emily had been a godsend to her earlier in the year at her first Pony Club camp and she'd been delighted for her friend when she'd won the final One Day Event competition at the end of the week, beating their nemesis – the nasty Elisha Templeton. Amber hadn't understood why Emily had seemed so sad at the end of the week when she should have been on cloud nine, but later on, over the summer holidays, she'd found out a bit more.

Emily hadn't been to many competitions over the summer but they'd kept in touch through messages. Amber had learned at camp, through a vicious outburst from Elisha, that Emily's dad had lost his job as the company he worked for as a kitchen fitter had closed down. He'd managed to get a bit of freelance work, but no permanent job. With money uncertain and winter approaching, Emily had been told that her beloved pony, Fudge, might have to be sold. Emily was understandably heart-broken as her 'Freaky Treacle' was the love of her life. On the few occasions when Amber had seen Emily around school before the summer holidays, and since their return in September, she could tell the girl wasn't herself. Instead of being surrounded by a gang of friends, all giggling and relaxed as usual, Emily had looked tired and was more withdrawn from her friends.

But today, at lunchtime, Emily had run up behind Amber and poked her in the ribs, making Amber squeal in shock. When she whipped round to see who her assailant was, Emily's twinkling hazel eyes looked back at her and she registered her friend's huge grin.

"My dad's got a job!" she said, bouncing with excitement. "Oh, bountiful providence!" Emily did a twirl, then closed her hands together in prayer and aimed them at the ceiling as if she was thanking God for this change in circumstances. Amber was pleased to see her return to her usual playful self.

"That's brilliant. So, does that mean you can keep Fudgey?"

"Yes. Fudge is staying, and there's more. I've got a surprise for you." Emily looked as if she could barely contain herself. She was like a fizzy drink that had been shaken and then opened. Emily's bubbling happiness was infectious.

"What is it? What's the surprise?" Amber squeaked in a girly voice, most unlike her.

But just then the end-of-lunch bell clamoured and people started jostling to get to their lessons. Emily was swept up in a wave of moving bodies and carried away like a boat on the tide.

"Fizzlesticks. I'll tell you tonight at the rally," she called, still beaming as she was sucked into the surge of green uniforms and disappeared.

Amber had to endure the rest of the day at school wondering what her news could be, and when she arrived at the rally, desperate to speak to her, she didn't get the chance as Emily was quickly sent outside to join her group who were in the stables looking at first aid and learning how to apply a poultice to a horse's leg. Amber's group had also been scheduled to look at some basic first aid and how to deal with minor wounds, but since Amber could not participate, with her arm still in a sling, they were staying in the house to watch videos and discuss signs of ill health in a pony.

Sitting with Jo and Matthew, who was now aiming for his D and D+ tests, Amber noted the others in their group: Jake, who had been in her group at camp in the summer and a new boy with a happy, friendly face that looked somehow familiar.

Eventually, the videos of ponies with snotty noses, runny eyes, sweet itch and mild colic ended and Amber was finally able to get outside and speak with Emily while they waited for their parents to stop eating the cakes and other goodies provided by Mrs Best. The sweet treats ensured parents brought their children to Friday night stable management rallies, instead of conking out on the sofa in front of Coronation Street.

"Soooo." She grabbed her friend's arm and pulled her away from the rest of the group as Emily left the stable of the horse they'd all been poulticing. "What's your big news then?"

Emily plunged her hand into her hoody pocket and pulled out her phone. A few swipes later, she was holding it out towards Amber and Joanne, who had come out with Amber to hear Emily's news too.

"Boom, shake the room. Meet my new pony!"

Amber swiftly took the phone and held it up for a closer inspection. She nearly bumped heads with Jo as she also crowded in to see the screen. The picture they saw showed a beaming Emily mounted on a spectacular pink pony. Amber knew from her horse books that the colour was strawberry roan: bay with white hairs mixed in to produce what looked like a pink coat. The pony had black legs and a black tail. But the pony's head and neck were what really grabbed Amber's attention. There was a perfectly formed white diamond right in the centre of its forehead and the mane was hogged but growing out so that it resembled a black Mohican. Amber had never seen a more striking pony in all her life.

"This is Pink, AKA Sunset Friday," Emily said, looking over their shoulders at the picture.

"Wha…?" Amber was speechless. A new pony? It had looked like there was going to be no pony and now there were two.

"My dad is now a fitness instructor at the new gym in town and he loves it. He's so happy he's agreed to let me have a new pony as I'm growing out of Fudge. I went to try her last weekend and she's being delivered tomorrow. I can't wait! She's got a good competition record, but she's been a bit of a naughty minx with her current rider. That's how come we can afford her. But I'm sure we'll be a totally amazing team in no time." Emily explained.

"Wow, that's amazing, and not what I was expecting at all." Amber handed the phone back after taking one final look at the pony in the picture, and hugged Emily. She could feel her friend's excitement rippling through her like a mini-earthquake. "I'm so happy for you…but what about Fudge?"

"He's been so good to me, my little angel. He's looked after me for years and taught me everything I know. But it's time for him to teach someone new."

"But…I…I thought you said Fudge was staying?

"He is. Don't worry, I'll never part with my boy and now he's getting a girlfriend to keep him company." The girls turned to face the house just as a man and boy came out of the door and walked towards them.

"Fudge is going to be showing my little brother the ropes."

Then it dawned on Amber. The new boy in her group with the big smile and friendly eyes had seemed familiar because he looked just like Emily. He was her little brother!

"Amber, Jo, meet Harry. And this is my dad."

"Hi," the little boy said, without a hint of shyness.

"Hi," both girls said in unison, smiling back at him. Amber surreptitiously took in Emily's dad, whom she had never seen before. He looked quite intimidating and not like his children at all, who both resembled their mother. He wasn't terribly tall but he had a shaved head, and although he was wearing a baggy sweatshirt and jeans, Amber could tell from the width of his neck and shoulders that he was made of muscle.

"Er...hello, Mr Pryde," she said, her voice faltering slightly.

"Oh, call me Phil," he said, his eyes smiling in the same way that Emily and Harry's did. They lit up his face and suddenly softened his rather fierce first impression.

"Can't wait to see Pink," she told Emily as they parted. "Make sure you put loads of photos and videos on Instagram.

"Course. You'll be sick of the sight of her before Christmas."

As Emily's car pulled out of the yard and they stood shivering as they waited for Amber's dad and Jo's mum to come out of the house with Matthew, Jo turned to Amber. "I wonder if Emily's new pony has done much cross-country?" she wondered aloud.

Amber read her mind. "You're thinking she could be a tetrathlon team member."

"I am. You can compete with a team of three, but it means everyone's score has to count then. It's best if you can have four on a team, then if anyone has a disaster, their score can be dropped as only the best three count."

"So, we just need one more person, as well as Emily."

"Yes, and I think I know who it should be."

- Six -

Jo Takes Charge

Half term flew by and it was soon time to go back to school. Amber had thought she'd be bored stiff with no riding to do over the week off, but she'd gone with her parents to the farm and spent most of her week off with Jo. Mrs Jones hadn't minded as she was a teacher so had the week off too.

Sometimes, she'd sat on an oil drum and watched Jo school Merry over the show jumps or hand-made cross-country fences in their own fields, sometimes they went in the garage and practised aiming the unloaded pistol at targets. Mr Jones was at work and they weren't allowed to shoot the gun without him there. A few times, Amber had managed to cling, one-handed, onto the back of Jo on her bike as she and Matthew rode up to the forestry to build a camp among the trees. Her arm didn't hurt her as much now, though when Jo hit a couple of potholes as she rode up the track, it sent a lightning bolt of agony through her that made her eyes water. She didn't complain and Jo was none the wiser, since Amber was behind her where she couldn't see.

Building a camp had been exciting and she'd done what she could to carry slender branches and moss to the site of a fallen pine tree. They'd used its upturned roots and the mud and stones still attached to them as one wall and then constructed two more using debris they'd found on the forest floor. Because the camp was made entirely from natural resources, and was well away from the forestry tracks, it was impressively camouflaged. But the three of them found it easily every time they returned. They had named it Pine Cone Cottage but the week had run out before they'd had a chance to make a door and a roof. It would have to wait.

During her time spent with Jo, she learned of her plan for the tetrathlon team that did not yet exist but which Jo was already enthusiastically managing.

"So, I thought we could ask Chelsea Connor to be the fourth member," she said one day, while they were in the garage pretending to shoot with the pistol.

Amber knew of Chelsea from camp. She rode a grey mare named Skylark and had come second to Emily in the end-of-camp One Day Event after the pony had initially refused to jump the gate into the dark wooded section of the course. She'd noted that Chelsea seemed like a pretty gutsy rider during the week as her pony wasn't always easy but she always got what she wanted from it in the end.

"Hmm," Amber considered. "Though isn't her pony more of a showjumper than a cross-country-er? I'd thought, maybe Natalie would be good. She seems to be doing really well with Rocky now."

Amber had met Natalie, a new member, earlier that year at the first mounted rally of the season. Natalie's pony, Sable, had been a complete witch and it was clear she was going to destroy Natalie's confidence as she wasn't an experienced rider. So, it had come as a great shock when Natalie had bought Rocky from Elisha Templeton, a pony Amber considered unpredictable and dangerous following

395

his involvement in the accident that could have killed Joanne and her pony, Flash.

But everyone had watched with amazement over the summer as Natalie and Rocky had struck up an immediate bond and in no time were jumping one-metre show jumping tracks with ease. Rocky seemed to have settled and looked much more relaxed when ridden by Natalie than he had when Elisha had been his rider. Amber was both impressed and a little jealous of their swift progress. She knew all about the dangers of envying others and had learned that lesson with Pearl during their first year together. But she couldn't help sometimes letting that little jealous voice in her mind get a few digs in at her. *See*, it would say to her, *there's Natalie doing brilliantly with her new pony, while your competition pony does nothing 'cos you're scared of her*.

"Shut up," Amber would tell the voice and she'd convince herself that she admired the way Natalie adapted to such a high-powered pony so quickly and easily, while she herself struggled to bond with Molly, the trophy-winning pony her parents had bought for her to compete on.

Jo interrupted her thoughts. "I don't really know Natalie so maybe, but Chelsea would be good, I think. Yes, Skye has done more show jumping as she used to be Chelsea's sister's pony and they did BS together but she's given up riding now and Chelsea has taken her on. I think she's always been a bit in Imogen's shadow and is quite determined to be noticed too. Nothing like a bit of sibling rivalry."

Amber didn't know about Chelsea and her sister so she asked, "Why did her sister give up riding if she was so good at it?"

Jo put the gun on the bench and picked up Amber's squeezy blue ball that she was using to strengthen the grip in her left hand. "Catch," she said tossing it to Amber, who reached out her left hand, but missed, and had to bend down to pick it up from the dusty garage floor. "Skye was Imogen's pony. For some reason, they'd gone to some unaffiliated Pony Club event, which wasn't their usual scene. They did British Showjumping, as I said. At the event, there were a few cross-country fences in the field next to where the show jumping was. There was a separate competition to have a go at the six or seven

397

cross-country fences, and the person who could do it fastest in each age group would be the winner. So, Imogen had a go. She was competitive so she was going for the time, but the last fence was a staircase of three steps to be jumped down. Imogen had lost control of Skye and they were flying as they came to the steps. Skye didn't seem to know what she was meant to do with the three steps so she just jumped them all in one go. Imogen flew right out of the saddle and was badly hurt. But more than that, when she was recovered, she refused to get back on. That was it. She just gave up. She does hockey and netball now, I think. Star captain of the teams."

"So, Chelsea took over the ride on Skye?" Amber asked, squeezing the ball absentmindedly.

"Yes, she was also doing a bit of show jumping too, but was never as successful as Imogen so she'd started to get into gymnastics. I think she'd wanted something where they couldn't be compared to each other all the time. But now Imogen has given up, Chelsea has taken over the ride on Skye, though I think she's more interested in eventing than just show jumping so she's introducing Skye to cross-country.

They've been doing quite well I think, and with her background in gymnastics, she's bound to be quite athletic and fit. Perfect for the running and swimming phases."

"So, what are we going to do then?" Amber squeezed the ball in Jo's face. Jo laughed as the white plastic eyes bulged towards her. "There are three potential people for only two places: Emily, Chelsea and Natalie. We can't tell them all and then leave one person out."

"People can compete as individuals too."

"Yes, but it's not nice to think you're going to be on a team and then get left out," Amber pointed out. She suspected Jo had little experience of being left out of sporting teams. She, on the other hand, knew the feeling all too well.

"Yeah, I suppose so. Hmmm, I'll have to think about that one."

While Jo was concentrating, Amber tickled her under the nose with the pointy blue hair of her squeezy ball. "Well don't hurt your brain whatever you do," she teased, boldly.

"Cheeky!"

– Seven –

Team Trainer

As it turned out, Joanne didn't have to worry about who to pick for 'her' team as the matter was taken out of her hands.

Amber's phone buzzed on the Monday evening of the first day back at school. She was lost in reading a book she had to review for English homework. It was one set by the teacher and usually Amber hated reading books she was told to read, instead of ones she could choose herself, but this one was pretty good, despite being a classic, which normally meant difficult and boring in her experience. She ignored her phone until she reached the end of a chapter. When she eventually picked it up, she saw there was a message from Jo.

Have you seen??????? It said, the overuse of question marks implying a sense of urgency.

Seen what? She replied.

The Blakefield Facebook page! There's a post on reminding everyone that the first round of the postal shoot is this weekend and it also asks anyone interested in taking part in Brantfort's branch tetrathlon to message their names to Mrs Best 😲

Okay. What's up with that??

We were going to sort out our own team! Now we won't be able to decide anything as it'll all be run by adults!!!!

Amber wasn't surprised that the club was going to organise everything as it was a Pony Club competition, and couldn't understand why Jo was so upset. She surely couldn't have expected to have been in charge…she was eleven! Amber considered how she could put this tactfully in a message and deleted several attempts before she finally sent off:

Maybe for the best, then the problem of who to pick and who to leave out is for them to worry about not us 😊

Dots appeared showing that Jo was typing a message back but it was several minutes before her reply appeared. Amber guessed she was also struggling to find the right words. In the end, all that came through was a 😕

Instead of going back to her book, Amber opened Instagram and scrolled through various posts to see if Emily had posted anything new. During half term, there had been a daily picture showing what she was getting up to with Pink, but now, with it being term time and the clocks had gone back, there was no possibility of riding after school.

There was nothing new from Emily, but there was a post from Natalie the previous day showing her with Elisha, both holding up rosettes they'd won at an indoor show.

Since her humiliation at camp, when her young event horse had been eliminated on the cross-country course, Elisha had turned her focus away from eventing and back to the world of show jumping. Her horse, Thunder Cat, hadn't been bold with ditches and water fences, but he was a scopey and precise showjumper and she was cleaning up at BS shows around the country. Amber was pleased. Although she couldn't stand Elisha, the fact that she was doing so well at affiliated shows meant that she'd probably stay away from 'poxy' local Pony Club events, which meant that Amber wouldn't have to see her. It was a shame though that Elisha seemed to have adopted Natalie and now took her along with her in her huge horsebox to shows. It looked unlikely that Amber would be seeing much of her either.

Just as she was liking Natalie's post, her phone pinged with a message. It was from Emily. As Amber read it, her left eyebrow arched. This was not good news. Jo would not be happy.

***

The next day at school, Amber forced herself to hang around the Year Nine locker area before the bell went for morning registration, hoping to find Emily. She was nowhere to be seen and Amber found herself receiving some strange looks from the Year Nines, who were clearly wondering why she was there. She returned at break time, much to the delight of her friend Sarah who had wanted an excuse to hang around there to be able to spy on a boy she fancied.

This time Amber was in luck. She stood next to Emily as she opened her locker to put her PE kit in. She was flushed and her hair had frizzed showing she'd had the pleasure of period one PE outside in the drizzle.

"Your dad is going to be coaching the tetrathlon teams?" she asked immediately to confirm that Emily's message last night hadn't been some sort of joke. Emily knew that Amber and Jo were keen to be on a team but she hadn't expressed much interest when the idea of her joining them had been suggested.

"Urgh, yeah," Emily groaned, wrestling with her lumpy kit bag which refused to fit into the narrow locker space.

"Why?" She'd never seen Emily's dad at any events and had assumed he didn't have much interest in her hobby, since his previous job had been Monday to Friday. That meant he wasn't working on Sundays and so *could* have come to watch her.

"Oh, because he's always been a fitness freak, running marathons and going to the gym all weekend…"

Ah, that explains why he never came to any shows then, thought Amber.

"But now he's got this job as a fitness instructor, he's even more obsessed and wants to volunteer his services to Blakefield to help the club." She said this last part sarcastically and Amber wondered what she meant by it. Emily didn't elaborate but Amber could tell she was not at allhappy with the news.

"Are you doing it?" she asked, sensing what the answer would be.

With a mighty heave, Emily finally managed to force her kit bag into the locker and slammed the door. She turned around and leant wearily against the cold metal.

"Well, I wouldn't have been. I HATE running and I mean HATE it. I'm just not built for it with my long body and short legs, but Dad told me I have to. "If I'm the trainer, it wouldn't look very good if my own daughter wasn't involved would it?" Emily mimicked her father's voice with absolute accuracy. "So, my life is going to be hell because I'm not like him, I'm not sporty. But he's really competitive so he'll be pushing me – us – all the time, I know it. He's never bothered about my lack of sporting ability before, as he's had Harry and his cricket and football to concentrate on, but now, with this, I'll be like his advert so he'll be determined for me to be great, and I just won't be."

Amber was shocked to see her friend look so stricken. She was teary, which was so unlike her as she was always positive and upbeat. She cast around for something to say but couldn't think of anything useful. *Why do I never know what to say?* Whether she wanted to offer comfort or a cutting retaliation to wound a bully, Amber could never summon the words she needed until around three hours later when it was too late. Saved by the bell ringing, she gave Emily a quick hug, then dragged Sarah away from where she was gawping at a boy with a crop of curls on his head so long and thick it made him resemble one of those mop-top sheep. She couldn't see the attraction herself.

She didn't see Emily around school for the rest of the week and she was busy with lots of homework. She sent Jo a message to tell her the news about

Emily's dad being the tetrathlon team trainer and was surprised to get no response from her. She'd expected a series of outraged messages with lots of angry emojis, but she got nothing.

What does that mean? she wondered. *Oh well, I'll see her on Saturday for the first round of the postal shoots. Then I'll find out.*

– Eight –

Moody Molly

Amber was sitting on Jo's bed. She'd been dropped off there by her parents before they went on to the farm to see to the ponies. It was the first day of the postal shoot and she'd been expecting to do her first target, but Mr Jones had an idea.

"Everyone has to submit twelve targets – three per month. But rather than do one each week while your right arm is injured, you could just wait another three weeks and do your first three all in one go, once you're healed, rather than having to do it with the handicap of using your left."

She hadn't known what to say as she could see the logic in Mr Jones' suggestion but she was looking forward to shooting her first competitive target.

408

Amber could now squeeze the blue ball hard enough to make his eyes shoot out and she'd even been practising maintaining her grip so that his poppy eyes stayed out on their stalks for as long as possible. She was prepared. It was true, though, that she'd be getting her sling off in a couple of weeks and would be able to use her right hand. Reluctantly, she'd nodded her agreement and gone in the house with Jo to wait for her parents to return and collect her.

"So…you mean you don't want to do it anymore?" asked Amber, incredulously. Jo had just told her that she wasn't bothered about Mr Pryde nominating himself as tetrathlon team trainer, as she wasn't going to be doing any training with him.

"No, I still want to do it," Jo explained, whilst deftly putting her shoulder-length blonde hair into a perfect French plait. "We've put my name forward for the junior girls' team, even though I'm still actually only eleven on the 1st of January, which is when your age is counted from, so, technically I could compete as a minimus. But even if there are more than four junior girls, I'm sure to be picked, as I'm good at all four phases. I live miles away from you and Emily's area though, so I'll just do my own thing. I can already do tumble turns and three minutes of swimming is no problem. The only thing I need to practise is running 1,500 metres, but I can run around our own fields or in the forestry." She quickly secured the end of her plait with a pony's plaiting band and plonked herself on the end of her bed.

"You'll have to teach me how to do that. I can't do a thing with my own hair except put it in a ponytail." She flicked her trademark ponytail to demonstrate.

"Ohh, yeah. You've got such lovely, long, thick hair. It would look great in a French plait."

Jo worked on Amber's hair until a car horn sounded outside and Amber had to rush off. It hadn't taken her parents long as it was a wet day and they'd obviously decided to just do a short ride to let Molly stretch her legs so she wasn't in the stable all day. Not that the pony seemed to mind. Mrs Anderson sometimes joked that Molly was agoraphobic since she never seemed to be pleased to get out of her stable.

As Amber still couldn't lift her right arm, she hadn't been able to try plaiting her own hair, but Jo had shown her how to overlap the strands and Amber climbed into the car sporting a perfect plait.

"How did it go?" her father asked over his shoulder to Amber in the back seat.

"Oh…I didn't shoot today." She explained Mr Jones' idea. Mr Anderson detected the disappointment in his daughter's voice and cast around for an idea to cheer her up.

"I'll tell you what," he said. "Tomorrow is meant to be a nice day. I'm at work but why don't you and Mum try a ride together?"

"Err…'cos of my a…" Amber began in a rather bemused tone.

"Yes, I know, but it's almost healed now. If Mum has you on a lead-rein and you just go for a little walk, I'm sure it'll be fine. Pearlipops will look after you, won't she?"

And so the next day, which was cold but sunny as predicted, Mrs Anderson helped Amber to mount Pearl gingerly from the mounting block in the yard. She adjusted the stirrups, handed Amber the reins,

411

plus an additional lead-rope she'd clipped to Pearl's bit, and made sure Amber was as comfortable as possible before bringing Molly out and mounting herself. Then she took hold of Pearl's leading rein and they walked side by side out of the yard.

Pearl struggled to walk alongside Molly, with her much longer stride, so the leading rein was lengthened to allow Pearl to go at her own pace. There was no wind but the raw air nibbled Amber's cheeks and ears and burrowed under her gloves to stiffen her fingers. It was a joy to be back out riding again and normally she didn't mind the cold too much as a good brisk trot was usually enough to keep warm, but with Amber's arm still in its sling, they had to remain in walk.

"My toes are turning a bit numb, how about you?" her mum shouted over her shoulder as they approached the forestry gate.

"Yeah, me too."

"Shall we turn around here then and go back?"

"Okay."

Molly seemed delighted that her ride had been cut short so early and appeared to remember her recent gallop all the way home from the gate when she left Amber on the ground. She started to jog and snatch the reins from Mrs Anderson's frozen fingers. As she jigged sideways and continued to pull the reins in her attempt to break from walk, Molly managed to cause Mrs Anderson to drop Pearl's lead-rope.

"Oh, damn it! Walk you blasted thing!" Mrs Anderson sat deep in the saddle and hunched her shoulders, doing her 'sack of taties' impression that she knew was often the best way to calm a tense pony down. "I'm sorry Amber, I daren't let go of her to get hold of your lead-rope. Are you okay?"

"I'm fine," Amber assured her. Pearl, as ever, was paying no attention whatsoever to the fine display of impromptu dressage movements being performed in front of her, and continued to amble along peacefully. Amber had managed to pull the lead-rope up so it wasn't dangling down and getting dragged along the ground and had it draped over Pearl's neck. She only had one hand to steer with, but Pearl knew her way home.

As they turned back on to the farm track, Molly seemed to lose interest in all the prancing and piaffe she was performing and went back to a walk. Relieved, Mrs Anderson relaxed and turned around to check on Amber, who at that moment was day-dreaming about being like Jo – having the ability to do tumble turns and beautiful no-bump French plaits. It was also at this moment that Pearl decided she had an itch on the right side of her face. Normally, she'd just fling out a foreleg, come to an abrupt halt, and rub her face on her leg to get rid of the itch, but today, Molly's bottom was conveniently placed just in front of her. Pearl shoved her head against Molly's left hip and rubbed vigorously.

The next moments seemed to happen in slow motion. Molly pinned her ears back in annoyance, Amber tried to pull Pearl away with her left hand and her mother rose higher in the air as Molly's left hind leg shot out like a piston to remove the sudden irritation that had startled her. Her steel-shod shoe missed Pearl and landed squarely against Amber's right knee.

"AAARRRGGHHHH!" she screamed in agony.

"Oh! Oh, are you alright?" Her mother's colourless face now had nothing to do with the cold.

Amber couldn't answer. Her brain throbbed in time with her knee as pain shot through her like a rollercoaster. She squeezed her eyes closed tightly and moaned, trying not to let another scream escape her. When she opened them again and looked at her right knee, she could see it had already begun to swell.

By the time they reached the farmyard, all discomfort from numb fingers and toes had been forgotten and the tears had broken through. Amber's knee was so swollen she couldn't bend her leg, and between that and her arm, it had been almost impossible to get her off Pearl.

Caroline Blakely had been summoned from the farmhouse once more to attend to Molly while Mrs Anderson hurriedly threw Pearl back into the field with Honey and rushed Amber to the hospital.

Again.

- Nine -

New Year's Resolution

The New Year began dismally with rain fattened, bruised clouds glowering in the sky each day. Occasionally, their hostility was softened by a trimming of gold as the sun tried to sneak around their plump outlines, but it was always pushed back and never allowed to break through the oppressive ranks of grey.

There was never anything good about January. Christmas festivities were over, school was beginning again and the days were short and dull, punctuated with regular downpours of rain, hail or sleet. There was Amber's thirteenth birthday on the eighth, which she'd been shocked to discover she shared with Jo, but even this was spoiled by the fact that it fell on a Tuesday that year, meaning she'd spend most of it at school fighting with physics, food tech, history, IT and German.

Amber's hopes for the new year were modest: no more pony disappointments or disasters, and no more injuries. She knew she needed to start riding Molly again to see if the pony had benefited from her six month 'no jumping' period, but the thought filled her with dread. When she'd won a show jumping class with Molly last year, she'd been so full of hope for the fun and success they were going to have. She'd imagined other riders pointing them out and saying, "Oh no, Amber and Molly are in this class. They're the ones to beat."

But then Molly had stopped jumping and the 'back man' and vet hadn't been able to find anything physically wrong with her that could be affecting her performance. The Andersons had been advised to give her a period of rest and relaxation to see if that would help but Amber had an uncomfortable feeling that it could be her own poor riding that had caused Molly's sudden reluctance as she'd been used to a confident, experienced rider before she became Amber's. Added to that was the fact that Molly had also bolted with her, thrown her and broken her collarbone, and kicked her in the knee which had resulted in the most painful procedure of Amber's life involving a huge needle to drain the fluid that enlarged her knee to the size of a football.

With Natalie out show jumping successfully on a pony Amber never thought she'd be able to manage, Amber felt even more pressure to get going with her own *proven show jumper*, knowing that people would be wondering what had happened to the wonderful Just Molly since she'd left the Drake family. But how was she supposed to get over her mistrust of Molly? If just the thought of her made Amber's insides shiver, how was she supposed to get back in the saddle? Molly would feel her fear and that would make both of them nervous and unhappy.

At least there was the tetrathlon to focus on, with the Brantfort branch competition taking place in May.

The postal shoot was nearly over and Amber had ended up shooting all of her targets left-handed after all. She'd waited to get her sling off so she could use her right hand, but her arm felt so weak, she could barely lift it. In contrast, her left side had become much stronger as she'd been forced to do everything with it, and her grip was now fiercely firm from all the frustrated squeezing of the blue stress ball.

When she'd gone for her first competitive round of targets, she'd tried lifting the gun shakily with her right arm and Mr Jones had noticed she was closing her right eye.

"You need to close your left eye and use your right when you're shooting right-handed," he'd instructed her, thinking she'd just got used to looking through the sights with her left eye during her left-handed practice.

"I can't close my left eye."

"What do you mean, you can't close your left eye? Everyone can close both their eyes!" He closed his eyes one by one to demonstrate.

"No," she said, willing her left eye to close but getting no response. "I just can't!"

"Oh. Well…in that case…you'll either have to wear a patch over your left eye or…shoot left-handed."

And so, armed with a new pair of glasses so she could actually see what she was aiming at, she'd shot, left-handed, nine targets out of the twelve required, and was getting better all the time. Her last three had even contained several shots in the bullseye.

Now that Christmas was over, she was due to start training for the running and swimming phases of the tetrathlon with everyone else who had put their names forward to be on a team, in either the minimus, junior or senior age groups. Emily had sensed Amber's reluctance to attend the training after she'd expressed an interest in running the forestry tracks with Jo instead. Her own dad was pretty sporty, playing competitive badminton and having run some half marathons in the past. She was sure he'd be able to help them if needed, but how hard could it be? It was only running after all. There was no skill involved, she just needed to be fitter to cope with the distance. But Emily had pleaded with Amber to come with her for moral support. She seemed pretty convinced she was going to get a hard time from her dad.

The running couldn't start yet as it was still too dark after school and everyone was busy with their ponies at weekends, but the swimming was due to start that month on Friday evenings at the local pool, whenever there wasn't a stable management rally. Amber was determined to try her hardest to match the performance of the other team members; she didn't want to be the weakest link whose score ended up being discounted. *This isn't just a riding competition, she thought to herself, this is so much more. I've got a real chance to be as good as everyone else in the other three phases if I work hard enough.*

Amber looked forward to beginning the training, hoping this might be her chance to shine.

- Jen -

Pride

When Amber entered the changing room, she found Emily and Chelsea already in their swimming costumes waiting for her. *So Chelsea is the fourth member* she thought. *Jo will be pleased.*

The minimus swimmers were about to finish, with the juniors and seniors going next. Amber already had her costume on so she hurriedly peeled off her clothes and rammed them into a locker while sneaking a look at her teammates.

Emily was, as she herself admitted, unusually proportioned with her long back and short, stumpy legs. *But*, thought Amber, *although this might be a disadvantage in the running, it was unlikely to affect her in the swimming*. Chelsea, on the other hand, was built like an athlete. Although she wasn't tall, she was perfectly compact. Her arms and legs were well muscled, giving her a powerful appearance. When Amber compared her own skinny arms and legs to Chelsea's, she doubted she'd match her for athletic ability. Jo had already reported on her own super swimming skills, complete with tumble turns, so Amber's hope that this could be her phase dimmed. It was likely to be between her and Emily as to who was the weakest. She shook her head, seeking to dislodge the thought before it took root. She'd learned her lesson about being jealous of friends some time ago. It was no good and she didn't want to go there again. They were teammates after all. Although they'd be competing against each other for individual placings, they were also working together for the team section of the competition. She had to learn to see their strengths as hers. But there was always that little voice in her head muttering about letting everyone down that nagged at her insistently and made her doubt herself.

The three girls, along with some older members who were in the senior group, made their way to the pool and began warming up. Everyone else stuck to breaststroke but Amber found front crawl easier so pulled her goggles on and did a few leisurely lengths before she had to stop to get her breath back. Just as she was resting in the shallow end, the strident blare of a whistle echoed in her water-filled ears.

"Swimmers, to me!"

Turning around, she saw that Emily's dad was standing behind her. He wore flip-flops, shorts and a vest, which showed off his unusually tanned muscles, considering it was January and everyone else resembled milk bottles. A whistle and stopwatch hung around his bulging neck.

Once all the swimmers had congregated, he addressed them, looking down at their heads bobbing in the water.

"So, both juniors and seniors – you have to swim for three minutes with the distance you cover in that time being measured. You'll score points according to how far you've swum. We're going to cover a range of techniques to build your stamina and increase your speed. To begin with, I want to assess where you are now as a starting point, so…everyone out!"

The girls looked at each other uncertainly. Emily rolled her eyes at Amber.

"Come on! Out you get." He bent down and clapped his hands at them. "I want you to walk up to the deep end and line up. We're going to have a race."

There was a quiet groan as the girls either slithered out of the shallow end on their tummies or swam to the steps and climbed out. They traipsed to the deep end and lined up as instructed, dripping as they curled their toes around the edge of the pool.

"Right ladies. When you hear the whistle, I want you to dive in and swim two lengths as fast as you can. The first to get back here is the winner!" His eyes flashed as he brought the whistle to his lips. The girls pulled their goggles over their eyes and moved into position, ready to dive.

Amber was the last girl to enter the water but she kicked hard and swam as fast as she could, only noticing the other swimmers as she turned her head to breathe. She reached the shallow end and turned, pushing off the wall with force, propelling herself back up her lane. *I'm not last!* She could see she had overtaken some of the other girls. Soon her outstretched hand touched the wall of the deep end, signalling the end of her race. Her heart felt like it was going to jump out of her mouth and her breath exploded from her in a mighty roar; for the last few metres she'd held her breath as she powered towards the finish.

She lifted her left arm and rested her elbow on the edge of the pool, pushing her goggles onto her forehead, just as the last of the girls were finishing.

"Seniors: first – Elise, second – Maia, third – Katie, fourth – Isobel. Juniors: first – Chelsea, second – Amber, third – Emily."

Emily was holding onto the wall, pointedly not looking at her father.

"That was a great swim from Chelsea, who was the overall winner, and Elise, and good competitive spirit was shown by Amber, who, after a bad start, caught up and finished very strongly." Amber was incredulous to receive a compliment and felt a flash of pride crackle through her like electricity. Her eyes flicked to where her dad was sitting in the nearby viewing gallery wondering if he could hear her being praised. "I'll let you get your breaths back and swim some lengths at your own pace, then we'll repeat it at the end."

The hour passed quite quickly, with each girl swimming individually while Mr Pryde shouted encouraging or instructive comments at them like, "nice smooth strokes Katie", "turn your head as your arm is passing under the water Isobel" and "kick faster Emily. Use those legs more!"

At onc point, Emily had tried to have a chat with Amber as they both took a rest in the shallow end, but Mr Pryde was soon there clapping at them and harassing them into getting moving again.

In the second race, Amber was determined not to be left behind at the start. It felt good to have her efforts recognised in the first race and she was keen to give an even better performance. The whistle gave the signal to go and Amber reacted, but somehow, she was still the last one to launch herself into the pool. Again, she fought against the water, pulling herself gracefully along as if her life depended on it. She still didn't beat Chelsea but she came fourth overall, beating two of the senior girls. The praise she'd received seemed to have given her extra power. Poor Emily finished last again.

"That's it, girls. That's the end," Mr Pryde informed them after he'd imparted the results of the race. "See you all next week. Next time you'll be swimming for three minutes to test your stamina. That's what you need – speed and stamina if you're going to be winners!"

Back in the changing room, Amber shyly congratulated Chelsea for winning both of the races.

"Thanks. You seemed to do quite well yourself," she replied, squeezing water out of her stumpy brown ponytail.

"Yeah, when it's only two lengths. The test will be next week when we have to do three minutes."

"I know. It doesn't sound like very long, but I bet it feels like forever when you're doing it."

"Yeah, I bet!"

Amber was about to say more to Chelsea, to try and get to know their final team member better, but Emily had dressed quickly and looked like she was going to leave. Amber turned her attention away from Chelsea and called after her.

"Em, wait! Give me a minute and I'll walk out with you." Amber was struggling with her socks as her feet were still damp. Emily slouched against the lockers as Chelsea gave a cheery, "Bye, see you next week" and left, the door banging loudly as she swung it with more force than was necessary. "Oops," she laughed as the door whacked against the wall.

Reading Emily's slumped shoulders and unsmiling face, Amber knew she was upset about finishing last in both the races. It could be that speed wasn't her friend's forte, but maybe she'd do better with distance. Amber considered saying this in the hope it might cheer her up, but decided to change the subject instead.

"How's Pink?"

It was the right choice. Emily's face lit up. "Oh, she's funny. Some days she seems really pleased to see me, but other days it's all ears back and grumpy faces. Poor Fudgey is terrified of her. She's definitely the boss. I think she's bored and wants to get out of the stable more, but our little field is just a mud bath at the moment so they can't go out. She's bonkers at the weekend when I ride her. I'm supposed to be looking after Harry but he's having to fend for himself. It's okay though 'cos Fudge never puts a foot wrong."

With Emily restored to her usual ebullient self, the girls chatted about their ponies as they walked to the reception area where their dads stood waiting for them, deep in conversation.

"They're probably discussing marathons," Amber joked.

"Wait…is your dad into all that too?" Emily grabbed Amber's arm, making her stop in her tracks.

"Well…sort of. He's quite sporty and he's done marathons in the past."

"Oh! You're in the same boat as me then." Emily chuckled, seeming pleased. "We can weather the storm together."

As Emily bounced merrily towards the two men, Amber followed uneasily. If Emily thought that her dad was going to join in with training or would start getting her up at 5.30am for pre-school runs, she was mistaken. She'd never thought about it before, but her dad was a competitive person, yet he didn't force that part of his personality onto her. She had never been pushed into trying to win anything in her life. She thought about school sports days where some parents had their children in tears because they hadn't done well in their races. Amber herself had always been terrible in any race she was entered for in sports day, but her parents had never failed to congratulate her for her efforts.

Emily seemed to have a premonition that her father was going to be disappointed in her and would push her to be the least disappointing she could be. As Amber got into the car beside her own father, it occurred to her for the first time that maybe *he* was disappointed in *her*…but just didn't show it. She took after her mother and shared many of the same strengths and weaknesses as her, but all the things her dad was good at, like sport, maths and science, she had no affinity with at all.

She looked at him as he was watching for cars at the pool's exit junction and wondered…*what does he really think of me?*

And in that moment, Amber determined, she was going to do everything she could to make him proud of her...in case he wasn't already.

– Eleven –

The Molly Mission

Spring arrived quietly. There was no fanfare or spotlight moment. The sun just gently, gradually nudged the obese clouds aside until there was room for it to stretch and reach out with warm, nurturing fingers to coax buds into flowers and turn the brown fields green again.

The warmer, longer days meant that riding was no longer confined just to weekends. Having spent the winter months watching all of Natalie's posts about her and Elisha's success on the winter show jumping circuit, Amber was determined to conquer her fear of Molly.

She'd started by going out with her parents. The forestry gate had been fitted with a spring-loaded closing mechanism, which meant it was now impossible to negotiate without dismounting and remounting. There was no way she could trust Molly with that yet, so she always had company.

Once she'd built her confidence riding with her parents, she started to venture out with Jo and Matthew. Jo had no problems mounting Merry, who stood like a rock for her rider to climb aboard. Sometimes she and Matthew were asked to trot away so that Merry would follow them, allowing Jo to practise vaulting on. Although Jo had only recently turned twelve, she'd grown again and could vault on the 14.2hh pony easily.

At first, they'd just walked and trotted, with Amber gripping the reins tightly, expecting Molly to launch herself into a flat-out gallop at any moment. But their early rides passed without incident and Amber's iron fists started to soften.

Next, they introduced some canters up the forestry hill. Jo and Matthew stayed well back so that Molly didn't think it was a race, and the incline of the hill was used to tire her out. Once it became apparent that Molly was under control, Amber was able to thrill at the power of her long stride and the ease with which she flew up the hill without breaking a sweat or getting out of breath.

Gradually, canters in other places were introduced. Molly was always allowed to set off first, just in case, but although she clearly enjoyed stretching her legs, she remained calm and showed no signs of bolting. Amber's confidence began to blossom like a trembling flower unfurling its petals and she was able to once again marvel at the gleaming golden neck and long, pricked ears in front of her. As the fragile trust between them began to strengthen, Amber became more daring.

One day, as they prepared for their canter up the hill, an exciting idea crept into Amber's mind and sent a shiver of anticipation coursing through her.

"Jo… can we try something?" she called over her shoulder to her friend who was in her usual position behind Molly.

"Yeah, what?"

"Once we set off, can you let Merry catch up instead of keeping her behind?"

A broad grin lit up Jo's face. "You want to let them gallop?"

"Yeah." Amber couldn't believe she was even suggesting it, never mind looking forward to it.

"Awesome!" Jo clearly approved of the plan.

Molly seemed to understand Amber's words and began to jog on the spot, waiting to be released. The pony's energy infected Amber and she couldn't wait to begin. As she leaned forward and let the reins slip fractionally through her fingers, Molly flowed forward immediately like water bursting from a dam. A thrill of fear electrified Amber, but this time it was good fear, like how it felt to ride cross-country, tackling the imposing, solid fences.

Molly flew like an arrow released from a bow, but Merry's head soon appeared alongside Amber's leg. Jo was crouched over the palomino like a jockey, not letting the pony pick her own pace, but urging her on. *She's trying to race us*, Amber thought. Her brain flicked through images of the last pony race that Jo had been involved in. It had ended in hospitalisation for Jo and horrendous injuries to her pony, Flash, when the race went wrong. Amber instinctively drew back on her reins. Perhaps she was worried for herself, or maybe it was out of concern for Jo, but Molly tugged back, not wanting to be stopped. Amber looked over at Jo, still racing beside her, and a competitive streak suddenly flared within her. At the end of Pony Club camp last summer, she had declared to Emily that winning didn't matter to her so long as she felt she'd done her best, but in that moment, the need to win was fierce. Although Jo had looked after her during their rides, never been impatient, or criticised her lack of confidence, she was always a competitor…and she liked to win. Amber accepted the challenge.

"Go on girl!" she yelled into the wind. If she thought Molly had been going fast before, that was nothing compared to what happened next. Molly shot forward as if she'd been fired out of a catapult, leaving Amber breathless. She saw Jo riding hard to keep up but Molly was not going to be caught. By the time Amber pulled her mount up at the top of the hill, they were well clear of their rivals, and for the first time, Molly's sides were heaving with exertion. Amber patted her ecstatically. After all the times trailing behind Jo on the Fell ponies, she felt so proud of Molly. It was funny; this was no competition really, but Amber felt as if she'd won a gold medal.

"That was amazing!" Jo's face was flushed and her blue eyes seemed electrified as she drew level with Amber. They both brought their ponies to a halt to wait for Matthew to catch up on Sam and let the ponies recover.

"I know! I can't believe we did that."

"You can't? I couldn't believe that you suggested it. We'll be able to have great fun now with these two."

Matthew had appeared on Sam, who was dripping with sweat. He was scowling, no doubt unimpressed with being left so far behind by the bigger ponies. Amber gave him a sympathetic smile – she knew exactly how he felt – but he didn't smile back. They waited a few moments longer for Sam to get his breath back, then they set off for home. Sam trudged along at the back but Molly and Merry appeared to be continuing their race in walk as they matched each other stride for stride back along the lane.

"I'm sorry I beat you," Amber said. She wasn't sorry at all, but it seemed like the best thing to say in case Jo went into a sulk about it. But to Amber's surprise, I-like-to-win-Jo wasn't dismayed.

"Ahh, you won today but there'll be other days and other races. I'm just really pleased that you two are getting on again and you can start to enjoy her now. I don't know if she's done much, or any, cross-country jumping before. The Drake's only did show jumping and gymkhanas as far as I know, but with that speed, she'll be brilliant. When are you going to start jumping her again?"

Amber's joy dampened at the mention of jumping. It was one thing to sit on a pony's back and let it run fast, but jumping required skilled and confident riding. She was still sure, since there seemed to be nothing wrong with Molly physically, that her bad riding must have been the cause of Molly's poor performance last year. She dreaded trying again in case the same thing happened and confirmed that she was a terrible rider who couldn't handle a good pony. *But don't forget*, the voice in her head reminded her, *you've done so well with Honey.*

You can't be that bad a rider to have achieved what you have on a pony like her. But Amber didn't listen. She was so used to the voice in her head telling her things she didn't want to hear; she didn't notice when it was telling her something good for once.

"Erm, I don't know. Soon," she replied, bluntly.

- Twelve -

Candle in the Wind

With two months left until the tetrathlon, it was time for running training to begin. And for pony training.

Although there was no doubt in Amber's mind that she would be riding Honey in the tetrathlon, she knew that she couldn't keep putting off trying to jump with Molly again. All her friends had their own competition ponies, and she needed to get to grips with hers to avoid getting left behind...and to make her parents' investment in her and Molly worth it. Honey was great, but she'd been so good, out of nowhere and with no training, Amber knew that it had nothing to do with her. Honey would be good with anyone...but she was just good. She had limits that Molly didn't have. But Molly was used to skilled riding whereas Honey had had a lifetime of novice riders, so, to her, Amber probably seemed like a blessing.

The Pony Club had shown her that there was far more to riding effectively than she had ever thought possible. In order for a pony to perform well, it needed a driver, not a passenger. Amber had to swallow her pride and accept that she still had a lot to learn if she wanted to develop a partnership with Molly.

Pony Club rallies were great for building trust, but they were not frequent enough. Claire was asked about resuming lessons again, but she was far too busy with her own ponies and the riding school to fit Amber in. Her parents considered asking Rachel Best, their Pony Club DC's daughter if she could offer some private tuition, until Mr Anderson had the brainwave of asking Caroline.

Despite Oriel's lumpy knees and disfigured face, she looked a picture of health. Her muscles were hard and laced with a network of veins, her coat was lustrous and the horse seemed to be bursting with energy. Yet, when Caroline rode her, she was always beautifully well-mannered and appeared to obey every invisible command through telepathy as Caroline's riding was so quiet, her aids were imperceptible. Watching her schooling the big, powerful horse in the paddock one day, while Amber and her mother were out riding, Mr Anderson had a great idea.

As Caroline dismounted and led Oriel towards the paddock gate, Mr Anderson congratulated her on the session. Caroline looked up and blushed, startled by his voice. She hadn't known she was being watched.

"She's going great. It's amazing that such a big horse can move so lightly," he complimented her, pulling the gate open. Caroline looked down, mumbling something that he couldn't make out. "Would you...we're looking for someone to help Amber with Molly," he began. "Her mother and I are fine with the hacking but we've never done any schooling or jumping so we can't be any use with that. Would you be interested in giving her some lessons?"

Caroline looked aghast at the suggestion; her face resembled a mottled plum. "Oh no, I couldn't. I'm not a qualified instructor."

"Pah!" Mr Anderson snorted. "That doesn't matter. You're a brilliant rider. And you do it so quietly, so gently too. You and Oriel work together, you're a team – there's no fighting or force – and that's the way Amber wants to ride."

Caroline looked as if she might cry. "I...I...don't know." Her voice was barely a whisper. "I don't know if I could."

"No pressure. Just think about it. Maybe try one and see how it goes. We could go from there."

The next evening after school, Amber rode Molly into the paddock for her first lesson with Caroline. Her mum had brought her through but tactfully stayed away, knowing that neither Caroline nor Amber would appreciate an audience.

It began with Caroline giving some tentative instructions that Amber could barely hear but she did what she thought she was being asked. Seeing Amber respond to her suggestions, the young woman gradually grew in confidence, and her commands became more audible. After a while, Caroline, watching Molly's movement shrewdly, asked Amber to stop. She walked towards her and reached up to the saddle, feeling around it, sliding her fingers under the seat and the pommel.

"This saddle is feeling a bit tight," she said, so quietly, Amber had to lean forward to hear her. "I think she's put on some weight since you got her, and this could be pinching her. She doesn't look comfortable to me. I'd say this could do with being checked by a saddler before you start doing much more with her. We'll stop there for today."

"Okay, I'll tell Mum and Dad. Thanks for the lesson."

Caroline's gaze slipped away over Molly's shoulder and she smiled.

***

"A saddler now?" her mother exclaimed. "She's had a vet and an osteopath and now she needs a saddler! What next? A dentist? A hairdresser? A therapist? Caroline said that saddle fit her – that's why we bought it."

"She said it fit her a year ago. Molly's put on weight, so it needs checked to see if it still fits. And yes, horses do need dentists too." Amber replied, delivering the news when her mother enquired about the lesson on the drive home.

"Hmph! And where do we find a saddler? Did Caroline tell you that?"

"No." Amber almost wished she hadn't passed Caroline's advice on. Her mother didn't seem pleased, probably because it would be another possibly fruitless expense since the vet and osteopath visits hadn't found anything to explain Molly's behaviour. "I'm sure we could ask around and find out. Maybe her saddle isn't comfortable for her and that's why she's been behaving as she has. It's worth getting it checked out?"

A spark of hope flickered deep within Amber. The saddle could be the true root of the problems which might mean it wasn't *her* the pony objected to, but the discomfort she felt while being ridden. It was like a candle flame at the end of a long, dark tunnel, shivering in a cold wind.

"Yes, well, I suppose we'd better get it checked out and get a dentist out too while we're at it, but don't get your hopes up. It might not be the answer you're hoping for." Her mother seemed to read her mind. Amber didn't reply. The candle flame wavered hesitantly, but it didn't go out.

– Thirteen –

Marlyn

A saddler was soon found through recommendations from Mrs Best, and as she was visiting the area for some other appointments, they didn't have to wait long. She was able to fit them in at 2pm on a Monday, if they could bring Molly to a livery yard near Cockermouth to be seen after the other horses on the yard.

Both of Amber's parents happened to be off work on that day, so they could take her, but Amber wasn't happy that the appointment would take place while she was at school.

"I've only got P.E and chemistry period 4 and 5 on Monday. Couldn't you make up a dentist appointment or something for me so I can be there?" she pleaded.

She could tell her mother wanted to say no, but if she did, how would Amber get home from school? There would be no-one to pick her up if they were both dealing with Molly and who knew where they'd be at 3.15pm?

"I don't think it's a good idea for you to miss chemistry, love. Mr Tippet said at parents evening that you find it quite difficult and…"

"Urgh. God, Mum, I'm only in Year Eight," Amber interrupted. "It's not like I've got my GCSE's this year – they're *three years* away. I can copy Sarah's notes and see if there's any homework in chemistry?" She lightened her voice and put her hands together in prayer, looking at her mother with the same expression Kasper, their cocker spaniel, used for begging.

"Oh, well, alright then!"

And so, at 1.30 pm on Monday, Amber was collected from school for her 'dentist' appointment in the family estate car with a trailer attached, and her pony in tow. If any teachers had witnessed it, they would certainly have been puzzled.

Marlyn, the saddler was a tall wiry woman with a shock of Albert Einstein-esque white hair which framed her smooth, serene face like a dandelion clock. She worked briskly but not unkindly, taking templates of Molly's withers and inspecting her current saddle. She quickly declared it unsuitable for Molly's shape.

"She's a slim pony with a high wither, but she has quite a broad spine and a big shoulder. This saddle doesn't accommodate them," she stated, matter-of-factly, whisking the saddle from Molly's back like it was an irritating fly.

Amber's face was a contradiction of emotions. Her eyes gleamed with the hope that the saddle, not her, could have been the cause of their problems, but her teeth clenched and her jaw hardened at the thought that poor Molly had been suffering for all this time with a pain she couldn't tell them about in any other way than through her behaviour. If only they'd thought to get the saddle checked sooner.

"That's not good news," Mr Anderson said from where he stood in the barn doorway. It was a drizzly day so Molly had been brought inside the large barn for her fitting. Horses and ponies of all sizes and colours reached out over their internal stable doors to inspect the newcomer. Molly's ears flicked and her nostrils quivered in the new surroundings, but she stood very still as Amber held her, out of reach of inquisitive noses. "What does that mean? A new one?"

Amber knew that her father would be worried about the cost. She'd seen some saddles advertised in that month's PONY magazine and noted that they cost thousands of pounds brand new.

"Well, she can't keep wearing the one she's got…" Marlyn replied. "I've got lots of saddles in the van. We can try a few and see what fits, then you can decide what you want to do."

With brisk efficiency, a range of saddles were brought out and tried. Some were immediately discarded; some took a few minutes of examination before also being dismissed until there were just two that were deemed suitable.

451

"I need to have a rider on board now to check the fit again and see how Molly moves in them. And," she added, "it's important that the rider also feels comfortable."

Amber had already changed out of her school uniform into her riding clothes, so she put on her hat and bridled Molly before mounting her to try the first selected saddle. Once Marlyn had approved the fit with a rider on board, Amber was asked to ride Molly around in the yard's outdoor arena.

She could feel the difference immediately. Molly moved forward much more freely and Amber had to check her pace with several half halts to slow her down. She felt so much more secure. This saddle had a smaller, deeper seat with a higher cantle than on the one she had. It held her in place so snugly, she realised how much she'd been slipping around in the old one – an image of a garden pea rolling around in a teaspoon came to mind.

She was grinning when she dismounted to swap the saddles to try Marlyn's second selection. Molly still went well in the second saddle but Amber didn't like it half as much. It didn't give her the feeling of security she'd got from the first one. When asked for her appraisal of the saddles, she chose the first one without hesitation, even though it was black and didn't look as good on Molly as the second one, which was a gleaming conker colour and matched Molly's chestnut coat perfectly.

Marlyn agreed that it was the best choice for both of them and Amber's heart leapt…until Marlyn revealed its price. Two thousand pounds. Mr and Mrs Anderson looked at each other without speaking. Amber knew they were wondering how to tell Marlyn, and her, that it was more than they could afford.

Interpreting the silence, Marlyn said, while putting the cover back on the second saddle, "I know it's a lot of money, but a pony can't do its work in a saddle that doesn't fit."

"Yes, I know, but…" Mrs Anderson started.

"She'll have to make do with something cheaper," Amber blurted out. The disappointment of seeing all her hopes being taken away pulled the trigger and fired the words unchecked.

"Amber!"

The shock in her father's voice made Amber lower her head.

"Sorry," she muttered, embarrassed by her outburst.

"But," Marlyn cut in, "you don't have to have a new one. I've got one just like the one Amber preferred coming in next week in a part exchange. It's brown and a few years old, so it'll be almost half the price of the new one." She slammed the back doors of the van closed and shook the Andersons' hands. "Have a think about it and let me know."

Amber's mother nodded at her father silently and replied with, "No, it's okay. Even we could see the difference in both of them with that saddle, so we'll take it… the second hand one."

A deposit was paid to reserve the saddle and Marlyn even took Molly's current saddle in part exchange there and then, since she advised them not to use it again. Amber was elated and looked forward to a fresh start with Molly. This saddle could be the key to the brilliant future she'd imagined when Molly became hers.

– Fourteen –

Run

Back at the farm, Amber thanked Caroline for her advice and enthusiastically told her all about the 'new' saddle she would be getting next week.

"I can't ride her until the saddle comes but it would be great if you could give me some more lessons when it does." Amber didn't usually like to ask for anything but she admired Caroline's riding and liked her quiet manner. Instructors often had a tendency to roar at riders if they didn't do what they said immediately, but Caroline was patient and didn't have a shout in her. Amber was happy to ask Caroline to explain or repeat her instructions without feeling intimidated.

Not meeting Amber's eyes, Caroline replied, "There are some activities you could do with her from the ground. I could show you if you like? They're good for building your relationship and would give you something to do with her while you can't ride."

Amber was keen to take up Caroline's offer, so on Thursday after school, she chased her parents off on a ride on the Fell ponies while she went to work with Molly in the paddock with Caroline. She felt better with no-one watching.

Caroline explained how to use slight body language signals to get Molly to walk beside her when she asked, stop when Amber stopped, back up and turn. Molly, however, seemed to ignore Amber's signals, leaving her disheartened. Molly clearly didn't understand this silent language that Caroline was talking about.

"She can't do it!" Amber huffed, throwing her whip into the grass at her feet. She'd stepped towards Molly with a whip held out horizontally in front of her. According to Caroline, this was meant to make the pony move away from her, but Molly just looked bored and didn't budge.

Without speaking, Caroline stepped into Amber's place, quietly took the lead-rope and picked the whip up. Standing tall, she locked eyes on Molly and stepped towards her confidently, whip held out in front of her, parallel to the ground. Molly immediately took a calm, unhurried step away. Caroline paused, lowered her eyes, then began again. She and the pony were soon involved in a silent dance that moved forward, back and sideways without a single word uttered. Amber was spellbound. It wasn't Molly who couldn't understand this language – clearly, it was she who couldn't speak it. Unlike Caroline, who was fluent. Amber guessed that Caroline was much happier communicating with horses in their silent language than she was with interacting with people.

Watching Caroline with her pony made her determined to master this secret language, so, instead of sulking, she listened attentively and tried hard to copy what Caroline showed her. Molly didn't react to her as well as she had to Caroline but the young woman assured Amber that progress could be made if she practised, was patient, and kept her signals clear and consistent.

"You could try making an L shape with poles on the ground and get her to go forwards and backwards through it – it's harder than it sounds," Caroline suggested. "Or make a washing line between those two trees, hang some towels or rugs from it and get her to follow you under them. It's good for building her trust in you."

Desperate to impress Caroline, who was becoming her idol, Amber practised some more with Molly back in the stable while she waited to hear the sound of hooves in the yard that signalled her parents' return. She gave Molly her feed, laughing at the way the pony always ate her feed standing on three legs. For some reason, she always bent her left foreleg at the knee and ate the entire contents of her bucket with her left hoof in her armpit. Still chuckling at this odd foible, Amber left Molly's stable and went to help untack and brush the Fell ponies before giving them a hug and kiss on the nose and turning them back out into their field.

458

Over the weekend, Amber was kept busy. As well as riding Honey and Pearl and doing Molly's in-hand groundwork activities, there was also Saturday morning running to do.

Now that days were getting longer, giving everyone more time to fit their busy lives in before darkness fell, Mr Pryde had introduced running training every Saturday. It went straight from Emily's house as a cycle path passed behind their field and could be accessed by hopping over their field fence – after waiting for the electric current to be turned off first so that a nasty shock wasn't received.

The littlies went first – AKA the minimus group – who had to run 1,000 metres. Then the junior and senior groups were together as with swimming, because both age groups had 1,500 metres to run.

At school, Amber was a decent runner at 400 and 800 metres. She wasn't a good sprinter as she wasn't fast enough off the mark, and she wasn't good at distances. Like Honey, she lacked the stamina. But at 400 and 800 metres, Amber could build her speed gradually and hold on at the end where lots of the shorter distance specialists tired and faded away. 1,500 metres was further than she was comfortable with but at least the cycle path was a smooth and mainly flat surface.

Emily was stony-faced as they climbed tentatively over her field fence and did some stretches while they waited for Mr Pryde to appear. There was no Chelsea or Jo but Elise, Maia and Isobel – three of the four senior girls – were all warming up too.

Just as Amber was about to start filling Emily in on her Molly news, Mr Pryde leapt over the fence like a hurdler, wearing a pair of tiny white shorts that did little to cover his bulging thighs, and a loose black t-shirt.

"Right girls!" He hopped on the spot, waggling his arms by his sides, "I've measured out to a point 1,600 metres down the track and marked it with some baling twine tied to a tree on either side so you'll see the end."

"But…we only have to run 1,500 metres, don't we?" asked Maia, looking stricken.

"You do, but you should always train at a level higher than required in competition. If you train over a mile, 1,500 metres on the day will seem easier. Okay then. When I say go, I want you all to set off as fast as you can and sprint for as long as you can. I know you won't be able to keep that pace up 'til the end, but even if you slow down, you'll still be going faster than if you start slow and try to build up as you go."

Amber looked at Emily and pursed her lips. That wasn't how she ran. She was never fast off the mark – her strength was in building up and finishing strongly. She couldn't see this method working for her, but she didn't dare tell Mr Pryde.

And so, the girls formed two starting lines: the three senior girls followed by Amber and Emily.

"On your marks," Mr Pryde called, "get set…go!"

The girls moved off as instructed – fast. Amber struggled immediately as her ankles felt like they'd locked, causing her to hop a few steps to get them working again.

"Come on Amber! Faster," Mr Pryde yelled at her as the others pulled away and left her behind. Afraid to refuse, Amber surged forward and soon caught up with Emily, then Maia, but Elise and Isobel were still well ahead. Elise and Isobel managed to keep going until they collapsed at the marked ending, but the other girls – Amber included – were barely jogging by the time they reached the finishing point.

She folded over like a sapling in a storm, her chest heaving as she clutched her knees and waited for her breathing to return to a steady pace. Beside her, Emily was doing the same, but with one hand pressed against her stomach, fighting the urge to puke.

"Are…you…okay?" Amber panted. Emily didn't acknowledge her, but continued holding her stomach while her breath rasped in and out.

Mr Pryde wasn't remotely out of breath and continued jogging on the spot while he waited for the girls to recover.

"I think we need to work on fitness," he said, stating the obvious. "We'll do some interval training on the way back. Walk 100 metres, jog 100 metres, sprint 100 metres, then repeat. Okay. Come on, let's start walking back."

"How did that go?" Mrs Anderson asked when Amber returned to the house where her mother had been having a coffee with Mrs Pryde.

"Horrendous. Oh sorry!" Amber hadn't noticed Emily's mum in the utility room.

"Don't mind me, love, I know what he's like. He'll train you like Olympians!"

"Let's hope you win the gold then," Mrs Anderson replied, rescuing Amber.

- Fifteen -

A Difficult Choice

Easter holidays were approaching and things were going well for Amber. The new saddle for Molly had arrived and she was going brilliantly in it. She'd had a few flatwork lessons with Caroline, and Molly moved so smoothly it was like gliding on a magic carpet. She'd even been persuaded by Jo to try some of their cross-country jumps with her. Amber had been reluctant at first, but Jo managed to coax her into it.

"Oh, I don't know. I haven't jumped her for ages. I'm not sure if Molly has even done any cross-country before…" Amber's confidence in the pony had been slowing unfolding like a delicate flower, but the flower, afraid of being crushed by a sudden rain shower, hadn't fully bloomed yet.

"I don't think she will have," Jo replied as she saddled Merry. Amber sat mounted on Molly in the yard, waiting for her. "The Drakes just did show jumping – outdoor in summer and indoor during winter. She's probably sick of the sight of show jumps. I bet she'd love cross-country: something new and exciting for her."

"Hmmm, yeah, great. Look what happened last time she did something new and exciting – she bolted." Molly's ears flicked back as Amber's voice rose in pitch.

"Yeah, but…" Jo led Merry out of the stable and vaulted straight on her, wriggling on her belly into the saddle before throwing her long right leg over and sitting upright. "You weren't expecting that then; you'd be ready for her now, and you're a much better rider now too, thanks to all you've done with Honey." Jo rode towards her jumping paddock, meaning that Amber had to follow, abandoning the hack she had planned. "Start with some of the show jumps and then, if you're happy, try some of the cross-country fences. Just see how it goes." Jo took charge, as usual.

Amber tensed and tightened her grip on the reins unconsciously. She wasn't wearing her body protector since she hadn't been expecting to jump, and she'd agreed with her parents that she'd build back up to jumping gradually. But they hadn't factored in the force that was Jo.

Jo shortened her stirrups and started warming up, so Amber felt obliged to do the same. At least no-one else was there watching. If it all went disastrously, no-one would know except Jo.

She started to trot Molly around the perimeter of the paddock but the pony was crab stepping sideways. Amber held her breath and went to tighten her hold on the reins again, until she remembered Caroline telling her that a tense rider makes a pony tense, especially a sensitive one like Molly. So, fighting her instinctive reactions, she let out her breath and her reins and put her leg on. As if to thank her for the freedom, Molly moved forward smoothly. Encouraged, Amber leaned forward fractionally and took her weight in her knees. She gave Molly a tiny signal to canter. Without the slightest fuss, Molly flowed into canter like a feather carried on a breeze. It felt so effortless yet powerful at the same time. Amber let out a small laugh. It was joy escaping from her like bubbles from a bottle of pop.

When she saw Jo starting to jump with Merry, excitement fizzed through her and she couldn't wait to try with Molly, her nerves temporarily held captive by happiness. Taking care to be more mindful of her riding and think about how her actions were interpreted by Molly, she presented her at a low straight-pole. It took all her will power to stop herself from grabbing the reins, but she was rewarded with a lovely jump from Molly. Amber patted her gratefully and continued around the field, taking the planks, parallel, blue barrels and the double with ease.

When she pulled up, patting Molly vigorously with delight, Jo grinned mischievously. "Wow, you could power a small country with that smile! Happy, I take it?"

Amber didn't reply; just carried on stroking Molly's neck lovingly.

"So…cross-country fences?" Jo looked hopeful.

Amber was so full of euphoria; her uncertainty had been squeezed out – there was no longer any room for it.

"Oh, go on then! She feigned reluctance, knowing Jo would be fully aware of her true feelings.

"Whoop whoop! Come on then. You can follow me if you want a lead."

***

That night, Amber could barely sleep. Even after a relaxing bath before bed, she was still alight with elation as she continued to re-live her afternoon. Jumping Jo's cross-country fences with Molly had blown Amber's mind. She already knew that cross-country was her favourite thing since she'd discovered it with Honey, but it felt even better on Molly. It seemed unlikely that Molly had ever done any cross-country before, but she'd loved it and jumped everything boldly. By the time she'd finished riding her, Amber had been filled with overwhelming love for her pony and never wanted to get off her.

Eventually, Jo had decided that the ponies had done enough and they'd ridden back into the yard. While Jo dismounted and led Merry into her stable, she said something that sent Amber into a spin.

She'd once again been patting Molly and convincing herself that what she'd just done was real and not a dream, when Jo's voice reached out of the stable and punctured her reverie.

"…Molly for the tetrathlon instead."

"What?" Amber called towards the stable where Merry's head was leaning over the door, but Jo was nowhere to be seen.

An arm appeared over the stable door and the bolt was slipped back to reveal Jo, laden with Merry's tack. As she flicked the kick bolt on with her foot and dumped the saddle on a stand next to the door, she repeated, "You should ride Molly in the tetrathlon instead of Honey. She'd be brilliant at it and would easily get round inside the time."

The balloon of happiness that enveloped Amber felt like it had been pricked by something sharp and started to deflate.

"Oh…I…" Amber stopped patting and tried to get her thoughts to stop playing leap-frog in her head. *Why do I suddenly feel cold?* she wondered. "Honey's gone clear around Brantfort's course – she even won there at the end of last year. She isn't the fastest but she's reliable. Molly might be awful at ditches or water for all we know."

"She goes through streams on hacks no bother and we could easily find some ditches on the fells to practise over. Brantfort is having a One Day Event on Easter Sunday. Why don't you take Molly? If you do the ninety class, it'll be the same course we'll be doing for the tetrathlon, so it'll be perfect practice."

"I'm already entered for that on Honey though."

"Yeah, but in the eighty, right? For the tetrathlon, our age group have to jump ninety centimetres. Can Honey manage a full course at that height? It'd be no problem to change your entry – just get your mum to ring their DC and ask if you can switch classes. They won't mind."

Amber rode back to the farm with her mind in turmoil. She was bursting to tell her parents about how brilliant Molly had been, but worried how they'd react, since she wasn't even meant to be jumping at all yet. And what would they say about taking Molly to a One Day Event so soon? Did she even want to take her? Yes, today had been brilliant, but was it tempting fate to go to a competition so soon? The course at Brantfort Bridge often caught out even experienced horses and she didn't want to create another disaster with Molly through impatience, just as things were starting to go well. Not to mention that it would feel disloyal to Honey to replace her after all she'd done to rebuild Amber's confidence after Molly demolished it. It would be like she was being relegated to 'second best pony' position again, despite never putting a foot wrong.

But this time, it wasn't just about her – there was the team to consider, and Honey's inevitable time faults could prove costly to her score, and therefore the team's score. Jo's words echoed in her mind, 'can Honey manage a full course at that height?' The truth was, she didn't know.

What should I do?

As she lay in bed that night, trying to get to sleep, a tug of war raged in her mind keeping her awake. Which pony should she choose?

- Sixteen -

Here We Come

As Amber got dressed and put her hair into a lopsided and lumpy French plait – *why can't I get it straight and without bumps like Jo?* – she rehearsed what she would say to her parents over breakfast. She still needed to tell them about jumping Molly yesterday, as she'd chickened out when she got back to the farm and said everything was fine when she was asked how her ride had been. And she also needed to tell them that she wanted to substitute Honey for Molly in the One Day Event. She had made up her mind after a sleepless night.

Her thoughts had gone round and round like a roulette wheel before finally coming to rest on the idea that she had nothing to lose by taking Molly to the One Day Event. If it went badly, then at least she'd know not to take Molly as her mount for the tetrathlon. And if it turned out that Molly didn't like the big ditch or the manky water jump, both of those fences had alternatives she could take. It would mean picking up fifteen penalties but should prevent elimination.

There was also the thought nagging in the back of her mind that all her friends would be on their competition ponies. Jo on the perfect Merry, Chelsea on Skylark – who could be a bit temperamental but was brilliant on a good day. Even Emily on Pink, who she knew through messages with Emily had been a bit difficult since they'd got her. The pony had been reasonably priced because, although she was a capable jumper, she'd terrified her previous child owner by repeatedly taking off with her. Emily said she'd been trying to do it with her too, and their relationship was a battle of wills at the moment. In typical Emily style, though, she wasn't getting stressed over it. She was getting on with it and trying to find the best way to work with the flighty mare.

And then of course, there was Natalie, still tearing around the show jumping circuit with Rocky, picking up prizes wherever they went. Instagram was constantly filled with pictures of her and Elisha Templeton and their stash of red rosettes. Amber didn't want to be left behind or to have people talking about her. She could imagine some of the comments. *'There's that Amber Anderson. She's got Frankie Drake's wonderful pony, Just Molly, but she's always on that Fell pony. Such a waste. Someone else could have had a great pony there.'*

Amber let out a deep breath as she left her bedroom and went downstairs. She would need to be convincing to get her parents on side. If they detected any trace of doubt in her, they'd say she had to stick with Honey and there would be nothing she could do to change their minds. At least, she remembered, her dad was at work today so she only had to deal with one rather than both of them together.

When she arrived in the kitchen, Mrs Anderson was eating toast whilst reading her current book. Stig the cat was trying hard to sit on it to force her to give him some attention, but she gently and repeatedly fended him off. Amber poured herself a bowl of muesli, added some milk and sat down at the table. Stig turned his attention to her and padded over on the table top to stare at her cereal bowl. He knew that when she was finished, he'd be allowed to drink the milk that was left over.

"Mum," Amber started, spooning muesli into her mouth while the cat watched every mouthful.

"Mmmm," she replied, distracted by the events taking place on the page before her.

"Um, well, yesterday when I was at Jo's, we didn't actually go for a ride out." She waited for a response but got none so she carried on. "We did some jumping in her paddock instead and Molly was really good and we even did some cross-country fences and I want to take her to the One Day Event instead of Honey so can you ring up and change the entry?" She blurted it all out in one breath with no full stops, to get it over with, then shoved another mouthful of muesli towards her face while she waited for her mother's reaction.

Mrs Anderson didn't react. She kept reading without looking up and Amber debated whether she should say it all again, wondering if she'd even heard her. She could get so engrossed in books; the rest of the world was blocked out completely. But then her mother closed her book and pushed it slowly away from her, fixing her blue-eyed gaze on Amber.

"What?" she said simply.

Amber tried to read her face to see if she was angry but she couldn't tell. Tentatively, she said it all again.

Mrs Anderson stared at her daughter across the table and Amber stared at her mother's chin, not quite able to hold her eye contact. Stig took advantage of the distraction to start lapping milk from the unfinished bowl of muesli.

Eventually, she spoke. "I don't think that's a good idea, love. I'm glad things are going well but I don't think you should rush it. Work with Molly at home for now and use Honey for competitions. This wasn't Jo's idea, was it?" she asked shrewdly.

"No, it's my idea." Amber knew it would seem better if it was what she wanted.

"Please, Mum, let's just try. If it doesn't go well, *then* I can go back to working her at home, but it might be fine. It probably will be fine."

Again, her mother regarded her. It was unlike Amber not to accept 'no' when she was told. Her daughter seemed different somehow lately. She wasn't a little girl anymore and was starting to come out of her shell. Mrs Anderson sighed as she realised their relationship was changing. They were going to need to compromise more now that she was growing up, rather than just telling her what she had to do. *Why is she so determined to ride Molly in a competition so soon?* Mrs Anderson wondered. The pony had done nothing but terrify her since they'd got her. They'd actually been thinking of selling her now that Amber had Honey to compete and have a good time on. She didn't want to see her daughter get hurt or frightened again, but Amber seemed intent on trying to start afresh with the pony, and she admired her resilience.

"I'll tell you what we'll do." She sighed again. "You're having a lesson with Caroline today. I'll ask her to do some jumping with you instead of flatwork and I'll watch. Then I'll have a chat with Caroline and when your dad comes home from work later, we'll discuss it. It's not a no, it's a maybe."

"Okay," Amber agreed, pushing the cat out of her breakfast and placing him on the floor so that her mum couldn't see her face. She didn't know whether she was pleased or not that it 'wasn't a no' and she worried her indecision would show. Amber wasn't very good at hiding her feelings. She would just have to keep acting like this was what she wanted while she figured it out for herself.

***

Caroline was soon persuaded when Mrs Anderson explained the situation and asked her to give Amber a jumping lesson. Wearing her body protector this time, Amber warmed up and popped a few small fences before they were raised. Molly flowed over everything like silk and Caroline complimented Amber's riding, much to her delight as she so wanted to impress her quiet and patient instructor.

"There's not much we can do to practise cross-country in here, since we've only got show jumps, but I've got an idea. Hang on." She went through the gate and disappeared into the farmyard.

Amber walked Molly around the small paddock on a loose rein until Caroline returned with the black plastic wrapping from a big bale of hay which she had brought to represent a ditch. She laid it on the ground and Mrs Anderson helped her to smooth it out and fold it to a width of around two feet. They then put a couple of poles on the long edges to hold it down and stop it flapping.

"We don't know if she's ever jumped any ditches before, so before she's asked to take on the real thing, let's try this. Get her trotting and ride her positively up to it, see if she'll pop over it. Don't look down, keep your head up and be prepared in case she gives a bigger jump than needed."

Driving Molly into an active trot, Amber turned her towards the improvised ditch. She rode as instructed but as Molly got to the point of take-off, she slammed on the brakes and snorted at the black plastic. She tried to dodge around it but Amber was quick enough to hold her in place and get her to halt. "It's alright, lass, it's just a bit of plastic," she reassured the pony, stroking her neck to soothe her. "Just have a look at it. There's nothing to be scared of."

"Erm, Amber?"

Amber looked up as Caroline stepped shyly forward. She recognised that Caroline was about to 'tell her off' about something. Whereas many instructors would yell at you if you did something wrong, and forcefully tell you what you should be doing, Caroline always delivered criticism flinchingly, as if it hurt her to do so.

"Err, don't stroke or pat her when she's done something wrong. I know you're trying to reassure her, but you're sending mixed messages." Caroline stepped close so that Amber could hear her softly spoken advice. "We pat horses to reward them and tell them when we're happy with them. If you pat her when she's refused to do what you've asked, she will think she was right not to trust you and to stop and look, rather than jumping on the first attempt. If she refuses, you just sit quietly, let her look, then re-present her positively. If she jumps it *then* give her a big pat. She needs to learn to trust you and do what you ask without question. For her to do that, you need to be consistent so that you don't confuse her. Now she's had a look at it, come again and ride positively with lots of leg."

Amber steered Molly away feeling totally stupid. Caroline's words made perfect sense. *Why have I never thought of that?* She'd often seen other riders patting their horses when they were nervous or spooked, but she could see now how that must be confusing for the horse. She'd been so focused on the issue of building *her* trust in Molly, she hadn't even considered that it needed to work both ways: Molly needed to trust her too.

Frustrated with herself, she gave Molly a positive nudge with her legs and urged her towards the ditch. This time Molly tried to veer to the right but Amber quickly straightened her. Molly then tried to go left, but again found that her rider wasn't going to allow that option. "Go on girl!" Amber kicked on and allowed her hands to go forwards in anticipation of the jump. Molly hesitated then made an overly large, rather crooked jump over the scary black bag, but was rewarded with lots of pats and praise. Amber repeated the ditch several more times, including from the other direction, until Molly was jumping it calmly and smoothly.

Caroline gave Molly a gentle pat at the end of the lesson and congratulated Amber. "That was great," she said, pushing her wavy brown hair out of her face. "You're ready to try the real thing now. There are some decent ditches you could try on the fells but take care not to pick one where the take-off and landing are boggy. Make sure you find one in some firm ground."

"Oh, I will, thank you. That was brilliant."

As usual, Caroline blushed at the praise.

On the way home in the car, Amber asked her mother what she thought of her and Molly's jumping.

"Yes, I was pleasantly surprised. You and Molly seem to have gelled much more now, and you're riding with more confidence too. It was good to watch." Mrs Anderson had to keep her eyes on the road, but she flashed a quick smile at her daughter.

"So…can I take her to the One Day Event then?" Amber asked hopefully. She was now feeling more certain that it was what she wanted.

"Hmmm, we'll see. Like I said, I'll discuss it with your dad."

Amber smiled to herself as she slipped into a daydream of riding Molly round a Badminton sized cross-country course while people watched and cheered, gasping in amazement at their bravery and skill. *Watch out everyone, here we come*, she thought.

– Seventeen –

Ready or Not

At last, the Easter holiday came around. Amber spent the first week doing more jumping on Molly so that her dad could observe their progress. He was particularly resistant to the idea of taking Molly to the One Day Event in Honey's place. She had tried to persuade him but he looked uncomfortable whenever it was brought up and said that she'd be better off sticking with Honey. Amber couldn't work out why he was so against the idea until she arrived at the conclusion that he must think she wasn't capable. The thought stung her and strengthened her determination to prove herself. Unusually for her, she'd insisted on him watching her jumping with Molly in Caroline's paddock. He had to admit that he was impressed with their progress but still seemed reluctant.

"It's one thing to jump well in here – it's just a small space – but a wide-open cross-country course is a different thing altogether. I just don't..." he trailed off. Mr Anderson held himself responsible for Amber's recent accidents and he didn't want the responsibility of giving the go-ahead for this latest idea, in case it ended badly. He didn't want to disappoint Amber or burst her bubble of happiness, but he knew he'd feel better if she stuck to safe, reliable Honey and ignored the urge to match her friends and their ponies. It was true that this was part of Amber's drive but he had no idea that a desire to impress him was also fuelling Amber's ambitions with Molly.

"Well...I know!" Amber had declared. "Let's go up on the fells and try some ditch jumping. If we all go, you can see for yourself and if she behaves and jumps the ditches...?"

And so, on the Wednesday before Easter Sunday, the whole Anderson family headed up towards the appropriately named Cold Fell where the winds blew strongly enough to knock you sideways. They had been up there on several rides with the riding school and since buying the Fell ponies, but never with Molly. The Fellies were able to canter along, sure and nimble-footed as they negotiated the undulations of the land they were bred to navigate, but nobody knew how Molly would react to the wildness of a landscape she had never encountered.

They started with a smart trot along the road from the end of the farm track to the gate which took them onto the fell. They then allowed the ponies to walk, three abreast to give Molly time to accustom herself to the springiness of the mossy ground and find her way through the bracken. They steered clear of areas they knew to be full of rabbit holes or ground unsuitable for the ponies, until they came to a stretch that was open and crying out to be cantered upon. The Fell ponies, long used to this being a canter place, started to walk faster and toss their heads, their long black manes rippling in the wind. Even Pearl was keen to get going.

"Okay?" Mr Anderson asked Amber as they prepared to canter. Amber nodded. Knowing what this ride was going to entail, she'd shortened her stirrups from her normal hacking length, as shorter stirrups made her feel stronger and more secure. She prayed that her fragile faith in Molly would pay off.

The three ponies set off together like a cavalry charge, the bright chestnut of Molly's coat flanked by the Fell ponies like two black bookends. Their hooves pounded in rhythmic unison as they matched strides. Molly leaned on her bit; she would have liked to lengthen and increase the pace but she allowed Amber to hold her in a steady canter. Glorying in the power she could feel at her fingertips and the bunched muscles beneath her, Amber loosened her hold on the reins slightly. Molly reacted instantly and her speed increased, but Amber still felt in control. Her eyes blurred with tears from the cold air and the landscape ahead of her became a kaleidoscope of mauve, marmalade and moss colours. By the time she pulled Molly up, her parents were well behind them, trotting to catch up.

"Are you okay?" Her mother's shrill voice reached her faintly as the wind caught it and hurled it into the distance.

"Yes!" Amber laughed, "That was brilliant!" Molly still felt alarming compared to the Fell ponies; there was so much potential for what she *could* do, but now it seemed more exhilarating than frightening.

Before they entered a gate into the forestry to return to the farm, they found a broad ditch and played at jumping it for several minutes. Mr Anderson took the lead on Honey, with Molly happily following. Even Mrs Anderson had a go on Pearl. Amber finished off with a couple of turns without taking a lead from Honey to ensure that Molly would jump the ditch without a pony in front of her to follow, then they headed into the forestry and back to the farm.

"She was so good, wasn't she?" Amber was jubilant for the duration of the ride home and chattered non-stop, reliving the thrilling experience on the fell.

"So, can I take her at the weekend?"

***

On Easter Sunday, the Andersons pulled onto the field at Brantfort Bridge and lowered the front ramp of their trailer to reveal a chestnut face. Mr Anderson had eventually given his blessing for Molly to take Honey's place as a trial and had phoned Brantfort Pony Club's DC to ask for the entry to be changed. Amber had spent the last few days practising her dressage test. At swimming on Friday, she'd found out that Emily and Chelsea were also entered, and she already knew that Jo was going too. It was a strange feeling to know that they'd soon be competing together as a team, but at this event, they were individuals competing against each other.

Amber had been pleased when she'd learned it was all sorted and she could take Molly on Sunday. She'd spent her evenings since then watching her favourite event riders on YouTube. Her special favourite was an Irish rider called Amanda McCarthy who rode a chestnut that looked just like Molly. His name was Zero Fox and he was a gelding rather than a mare, but with his white socks and white blaze, he was like Molly's twin. He was described by one commentator as 'a vibrant ride'. At under 16hh, he was practically a pony competing at 5* level, but he bounced around the enormous courses, making the fences look easy. Amber watched them over and over again imagining that they were her and Molly. She couldn't wait for her chance to emulate them.

But now it was the day of the competition, all her hopes were crushed by nerves which had returned with a vengeance. It hadn't helped that they'd got to the venue early, so she'd have time to walk the cross-country course before she began, to find that the ninety track looked *enormous*, particularly one new, or rather, updated fence. This fence had been an old, ramshackle wall; the remains of a dry-stone wall that had disintegrated over time. But the wall had been repaired and added to, so that there were now three different height options. It was both higher and wider than it had been before – even the lowest element - and was now topped with a railway sleeper. Its square solidity was intimidating. Amber stared incredulously at the fence, trying to ignore the panicked voice in her head telling her that it would be scary enough on Honey, but Molly had had a bad experience with a wall in the past and was likely to take exception to this monstrosity. The ditch also appeared deeper and wider than usual and the water jump looked and smelled like the contents of a witch's cauldron.

By the time she'd got to the end of the cross-country course and started to head back to the parking area, her legs felt like they didn't belong to her and she had to stop and rest against a gnarly old oak tree, taking deep breaths to try and quell the nausea. A knobbly piece of bark dug into her back painfully, and she concentrated on the discomfort as a distraction.

See, you should have brought Honey, her inner voice pointed out unhelpfully. Amber contemplated hiding behind the tree all day. Everyone was here. All her friends, her parents, people who knew Molly. The thought of failing in front of them all was paralysing. She squeezed her eyes tight and fought back an overwhelming urge to cry. She had to pull herself together or she'd have failed before she even tried.

Come on, you need to move, she told herself. The trouble was, her feet wouldn't listen to her brain, and she remained stuck to the tree as if she was its prisoner.

- Eighteen -

Mistake

Amber eventually managed to remove herself from the grip of the oak tree and trudged back to the trailer park. Her stomach, which felt like a nest of snakes, coiled even further the moment she saw her mother. She was holding a tacked-up Molly, craning her neck to scan the area around her like a periscope. Her blue eyes were twin searchlights both ready to lock on to their target when they found it: Amber.

Amber slid behind the nearest trailer to hide and received an inquisitive nudge from a small bay pony who had been tied there without a haynet to occupy him. It hadn't been a particularly strong shove, not like one of Pearl's battering ram head butts, but Amber felt so weak, she staggered and almost fell. Losing the cover of the trailer, she spied her mother again, her face set like a hard, marble statue, her eyebrows a V of annoyance. When her combing eyes found Amber, she experienced the Medusa effect of her mother's anger aimed at her and turned to stone.

"Amber! Where have you been? Get over here *now*."

Molly, looking exactly like a miniature Zero Fox, had been dozing. She'd been to so many competitions in her life, she paid no attention to the frenzied atmosphere of people and horses rushing about her. But Mrs Anderson's screech right in her ear startled and unsettled her. She shook her head roughly in annoyance so that several of her plaits came loose. Amber, with the threatening taste of vomit creeping into the back of her throat, was reeled towards them by the force of her mother's gaze.

"*Where* have you been?" she snapped again, not waiting for an answer. "You've been ages. Your test is in five minutes and you're not even ready to get on! Hurry up."

With fingers that suddenly felt as fat and useless as sausages, Amber fumbled to peel off her hoody and tracky bottoms. Luckily, she already had her jodhs, shirt and tie on underneath so she just needed to change her boots, shrug on her jacket, persuade her uncooperative hair into a hairnet and cram her hat on her head.

Just as her mother was legging her up onto Molly, a flustered Mr Anderson appeared. He had clearly been looking for her as relief smoothed his features when he saw her.

"Ah, phew." He glanced up at Amber's face and noted that it was the same shade of white as her brand-new dressage gloves. "You er, won't have long to warm up but I've asked the steward if you can go at the end of the class and they're happy to move you to the end, since there are other riders there ready to go. Okay?"

Amber nodded silently, not trusting herself to open her mouth. She waited for her mother to wrestle Molly's last loose plait back into its band, "told her she should've stitched these in," being muttered under her breath. Then, without looking at her parents' faces, Amber pointed Molly in the direction of the dressage warm up area. It was on hilly ground, squeezed in beside the dressage arenas and the show jumping course, making it less than ideal for warming up for the test.

The furious whispers of her parents accompanied her as they followed behind. Fragments of their words buzzed around her head like poisonous wasps. "Terrified,"…"mistake,"… "not ready,"… "disaster."

She closed her eyes, breathed deeply and tried to run through the test in her head, but as soon as she recalled, *Enter in working trot and proceed down centre line without halting*, her parents' words started an invasion.

Mistake, terrified, disaster, not ready, terrified, disaster, not ready. Mistake, mistake, MISTAKE.

Molly felt like a plank of wood beneath her. All she'd learned from Caroline about softening her hands, keeping her leg on and allowing Molly to relax and move forward into a receptive contact had been buried by self-doubt. Everyone else warming up around her – the riders in the Open class – looked so professional and polished, she wondered what she was even doing there. *I should've stuck to hacking with Pearl*, she thought. *I can't do this*.

"Amber Anderson? You're next," a steward called and pointed towards the rider currently saluting at the end of their test. It was a sign for Amber to come over and start moving around the outside of the arena until the judge pipped the car horn to signal she should start her test.

"Earth calling Amber!" she heard as she rode towards the dressage arena the steward had pointed at. Somehow, she'd failed to notice that the rider finishing their test was Emily. Her friend was riding out past her, patting Pink. The pony's arched neck, topped with her black Mohican mane, gave her a striking resemblance to the Trojan horse.

"I said good luck, you zombie!"

Still unable to get her brain to formulate a reply, she nodded once more and rode on, frantically trying to recall the movements of the test.

HONK! The car parked at C, containing the dressage judge and her writer, gave a short, sharp signal that she should begin.

Right, come on. We can do this, she told herself firmly. *But not if I ride like a potato.*

As she rounded the turn to enter the arena at A and trot up the centre line, Amber finally forced herself to over-rule her fear and ride as she knew she must. She tried her absolute best to relax, to use her aids softly and to respond quickly to Molly's reactions. The pony was unsettled at first by the sudden change in her rider, who had been as rigid as an iron pole only a moment before, and the first part of the test was jagged and awkward. By the time they'd changed on to the right rein, however, Molly's trot had settled into an even and regular rhythm and her final canter was as silky as ever. She trotted as straight as an arrow up the centre line and her halt was smooth and square. A smile broke through and Amber patted her pony gratefully.

"Good girl." Although the test had started badly, she was sure they'd be awarded some decent scores for the second half. They'd done it. The first phase was complete, she hadn't forgotten the test or made any mistakes and Molly had responded so well when she'd finally started to ride properly. Her grin widened as she reflected on the best parts of the test while riding out of the arena on a long rein towards her parents.

"Well done, that looked great!" Mr Anderson gave her a one-man round of applause.

"Yes, well done love." Her mother patted her on the leg. "You did so well. We could see how nervous you were before you started and we weren't expecting it to go so well. Terrific!"

Amber sat up tall and absorbed the praise until she almost floated out of the saddle. But just as she was beginning to feel as buoyant as a feather, the anchor returned to pin her to the ground when Mr Anderson said, "But you're late for the cross-country now. We'll just have to stick some boots on Molly, you put your cross-country top on over your shirt and throw your body protector on. Let's hope you're in time before they start changing the flags for the Open class."

– Nineteen –

Out of Time

At most One Day Events, the show jumping follows the dressage with the cross-country being the last of the three phases to complete. But, at Brantfort Bridge, with the dressage warmup being right next to the show jumping course, they ran the cross-country second so that those still doing their dressage weren't put off by horses and ponies jumping right beside them.

With three of them involved, it was a quick turnaround to complete the transformation from dressage participants into a cross-country team. Mrs Anderson worked with surprising dexterity to remove Molly's plaits at Amber's insistence.

"We haven't got time to take plaits out. You're already late for the time you were given to ride. Just leave them in," she'd argued.

"No, I want them out. I...I don't feel right when I see all that long neck stretched out in front of me with no mane to grab hold of," Amber replied, thinking of Honey's lovely long mane. "Take them out...please."

And so, while Mrs Anderson raked her fingers through the plaits, pulling out bands and loosening Molly's now curly mane, Mr Anderson quickly secured brushing and over-reach boots to Molly's legs and front feet. Amber did as instructed, and threw her riding jacket hurriedly onto the back seat of the car, replacing it with her green and navy blue quartered rugby top. She didn't have time to change the silk on her riding hat, so the blue velvet cover from the dressage phase remained. She mounted quickly and hiked her stirrups up several holes. Just as she thought she was ready to head down the road to the cross-country start, she realised she'd forgotten to put her number bib back on so she had to dismount and wriggle her way into it.

When she eventually arrived in the collecting ring, the steward checked her over to ensure she was safe and legal, and told her she was next to go. Amber barely had time to notice Emily leaving the starting box on Pink when she was told she had two minutes until her turn.

"But...I've just got here. I haven't jumped a practice fence yet!" Her voice rose in panic.

"Sorry love, but you're the last to go in this class. Got to get it finished for the next lot to start on time. We can't wait for you. Just go and jump a fence now." The steward informed her regretfully.

When her parents arrived to watch her, she'd had just one pop over a practice fence before being called over by the starter.

"Good luck!" Mr Anderson waved, feeling his heart hit the floor. This was the phase he was most worried about. While he knew that he could trust Honey to look after Amber on a cross-country course, this was probably Molly's first attempt. Who knew how she'd handle it? He wanted to tell Amber that they'd be watching from the top of the hill but he didn't get the chance as she was being counted down from ten.

"Four…three…two…one…go, and good luck!" The starter called, pressing the button on his stopwatch.

Amber was scarcely able to register what was happening before they took off. Last summer she'd taken Honey on her first cross-country attempt at Pony Club camp, and she'd felt sick with nerves then too. But this was even worse. It was the biggest course she'd ever tackled, and it was on Molly, who had the potential to completely run away with her if she chose to; she'd done it before. Or perhaps she'd behave herself but get eliminated, something that Honey had never done. The shame of failure on this pony would be a hundred times worse than on Honey as no-one ever expected anything of her since she was 'just a Fell pony'.

As she rode out of the start box, Amber knew it didn't matter what breed of pony Molly was or how good a show jumper she was. She'd never done this before and she needed her rider to give her confidence. Amber had learned to her cost before that there was never any time when you could take a pony for granted and just be a passenger. She needed to ride this course all the way around and leave nothing to chance. She visualised herself as Amanda McCarthy with the pocket rocket, Zero Fox, beneath her and pushed for the first fence.

Fence one was a straightforward brush fence which Molly neatly hopped over, but fence two, named The Monkey Puzzle fence due to the huge monkey puzzle tree that grew beside it, was a solid box with ground that sloped away on the landing side. Amber rode Molly strongly at it and the pony responded, jumping with more vigour than the fence needed. Due to the sloping ground on the landing side, Molly's large jump pitched Amber onto her neck. Sitting up quickly, she steadied the pony and approached fence three – a downhill double – from a trot. Molly jumped this fence more economically, meaning they landed over the second part in good balance. They cantered into the wood to take on the first of two large logs – left over from storm fallen trees – which Molly soared over.

"Okay girl, that's good. Now for the steps." Amber knew it was unlikely that Molly had ever seen a row of steps before, so she collected her into a bouncy canter to ensure she had the necessary energy for the uphill staircase carved into the side of a woodland bank. Molly understood and powered up the three steps enthusiastically. She had never done anything like this before and was electrified with adrenalin. She leaned on the bit as they cantered up the hill, out of the wood, but Amber checked her and she listened, wondering where they were going next.

The first fence out of the wood was a tyre jump which Molly had a look at and jumped cautiously before they took the log pile and chair near the church. Then it was on to the ditch and rails: this course's bogey fence for so many. Amber knew this was where her parents would be to watch as it was the highest point of the course and most of the rest of the fences could be seen from there.

She checked Molly and brought her back to a trot to get her straight for the first set of rails. Then, with a gentle aid, she nudged her into a collected canter. Molly obliged immediately and jumped the first rail sweetly, but when she landed and saw the huge black ditch ahead of her, she baulked and tried to swerve away. Amber was ready for her and kept her straight. Molly slowed almost to a stop, her long neck disappearing in front of Amber as she tried to take in what was ahead of her. Resisting the desire to let her look at the ditch with a pat of reassurance, Amber recalled Caroline's words; *Don't reward her for doing the wrong thing. She needs to trust you and do what you ask. Only pat her when she's done the right thing*, and dug her heels into Molly's sides. "Go on!" she urged.

Molly stopped at the edge of the ditch and teetered there for a moment; her brain filled with indecision. But with Amber's constant urging, she bunched herself up and launched over the ditch from a standstill. The landing jolted Amber and she lost her balance, but somehow they managed to scramble over the second rail and were on their way. Amber took a second to pull Molly back and straighten herself up before they were off again. They were only halfway around the course but Amber was ecstatic.

"Yes! Good girl! Come on!" She clicked her tongue and Molly surged forward. Honey would have been getting tired by now and Amber would need to nurse her home, but Molly was just warming-up. It felt like they already had a clear round. Molly, sensing her rider's new enthusiasm, flew over the ski jump, the skinny log, the palisade, gate, and zigzag fence until they were approaching the dreaded wall.

Amber knew she needed to approach the wide, solid fence with an open, positive stride, but her fear of the wall paralysed her and she felt some other force take over as if she were just a puppet. She felt herself slow Molly down, back to a show jumping canter and screamed at herself, *No, what are you doing? Don't slow down. Push on. She needs more impulsion for this fence*. But the invisible puppet-master continued to steady the pony until Molly reached the point of take-off with no impetus whatsoever. Most ponies, finding themselves with no stride for take-off and no impulsion to carry them over the fence, would have ground to a halt in front of it or ducked out, but Molly was enjoying herself and her blood was up. It wasn't pretty to look at, but somehow the pony managed to tuck her legs up and twist her body, so that, awkward and uncomfortable as it was, they managed to clear the huge wall.

"Yes!" Amber punched the air with her whip and patted Molly wildly. There were only three fences left. Was she actually going to achieve a clear round? She didn't dare believe it.

She turned Molly to head towards fence seventeen, an upright of railway sleepers on a downhill slope, and gasped. As she came over the brow of the hill, Emily was just ahead of her: a vision in pink, wearing hot pink colours on her pink pony. She was approaching the fence Amber was aiming for. How could she have caught Emily up?

As Emily cleared the sleepers and turned left towards the penultimate fence – the water jump – Molly's ears pricked as she noticed the pony in front of her. Her competitive instinct kicked in and she flew down the hill and cleared the sleepers faster than Amber wanted. "Woah, steady girl!" Amber shortened her reins and tried to steady Molly as she lined her up for the water jump. But Molly's attention was focused on the pony ahead of her, not her rider.

Amber tried to hold Molly back to give Emily time to drop into the water, and pass through it to the other side, but Molly did not want to listen. She fought against her rider and snatched the bit in her teeth. Just as Pink was jumping out and heading to the Irish bank, the last fence on the course, Molly hurtled after her.

With all her attention directed at the pony she wanted to catch, Molly ignored Amber's aids to anchor her and misjudged the obstacle in front of her. Instead of slowing to drop down into the sludgy water and crossing through, Molly raced at it and tried to jump the entire thing in one move. Amber gasped as she felt the pony extend, reaching for the other side. There was a moment, like one in a comical cartoon, where they hung, suspended above the gloop beneath them before they were falling, falling.

If Molly had been moving more slowly, she might have been able to keep her feet, but her forward momentum, combined with the thick, gluey contents of the water jump, meant that the outcome was inevitable. She'd cleared well over half the distance of the water crossing, but with a couple of metres between her and dry land, Amber felt Molly's knees buckle under her. Her head went down and her body tipped sideways, spilling Amber into the foul, stinking gunge.

- Twenty -

Grounded

Although Molly had somehow managed to keep herself upright and avoid falling in the water, Amber was not so lucky. After sliding around in the gunge for a minute she was able to get to her feet and stand up, resembling a hippopotamus after a mud bath. She was covered in sludge and slimy pondweed and was soaked through.

The fence judges, having recovered from the shock, and mopped up the tea they'd spilt on themselves, sprung into action. One of them reached tentatively for Molly's dangling reins and coaxed her out onto dry land while the other took charge of Amber.

"There we are dear, reach for me, that's it." Amber managed to take the lady's hand but it looked more likely that she was going to pull her helper into the water as she was literally stuck in the mud.

Her parents soon arrived, having run frantically down the hill when they'd seen their daughter disappear from Molly's back. With each of them taking an arm, they managed to drag Amber onto the bank beside the water. Both were relieved she was unharmed by the experience but neither could help wrinkling their noses. Amber stank as she stood between them, dripping.

"Well, that was exciting," the fence judge holding Molly exclaimed. Mrs Anderson rushed over to take Molly from her. She was one of those pristine women with perfect hair and makeup, manicured nails and an outfit that looked like she'd stepped out of a country life magazine. Mrs Anderson was terrified that the pony might soon shake herself like a dog and spray this perfect woman with all the mud and algae tangled in her tail.

"Yes, it was like being at Burghley when Princess Anne came off at the Trout Hatchery. That was dreadfully muddy too!" The other judge, an older but equally well-dressed woman, was inappropriately delighted at Amber's predicament. Seeming to become aware of this as she watched the young girl begin to shiver in her soaking jodhpurs, the woman added, "I know this wasn't what you'd have been hoping for dear, but it makes you a proper rider now. It even happens to the professionals, so you mustn't worry. At least you're both alright."

Just then, the paramedic pulled up, right in time to cut off any other infuriating remarks. He quickly assessed Amber and passed her fit to ride if she wished to carry on.

"It seems a shame not to when you've only got one fence left, but, well…I think everyone would understand if you decided not to bother." He winked sympathetically.

It was a tough choice. She could either get back on Molly and complete the course but get her lovely new saddle all wet or she could walk all the way back to the trailer in her sodden clothes and boots. Her mind was made up when a man zoomed up on a quad bike to alter the flags on the water jump to make it ready for the final class which was waiting to start.

"You finishing or retiring, love?" he asked, "'cos I've got to get this last fence flagged for the next class."

Quickly making her decision, Amber walked awkwardly over to Molly, her feet squelching in her boots. She gathered up her reins and bent her left leg at the knee to signal that she wanted a leg up. Water trickled out of her boot. Mrs Anderson's eyes widened in surprise but she quickly obliged and hoisted Amber back into the saddle. Squirming at the discomfort of her soggy bottom, she turned Molly in the direction of the finish and was quickly on and off the Irish bank and through the finish flags to complete the course. She found that Emily was still there, waiting for her.

"OMG. You legend! Look at you." She suppressed a smile. "I thought I'd had a bad round but…" she trailed off, shaking her head. The girls set off back up the track towards the trailers, riding side by side. Pink had her top lip curled up revealing her teeth. It looked like she was smiling, but as her mouth was strapped shut by a very tight flash noseband, Amber guessed that she was desperate to be able to open and stretch her mouth and breathe properly.

"Wh…what happened to you?" Amber asked, her teeth starting to chatter.

"Oh, it was fine really, but two stops at the ditch. I could have jumped the alternative but I wanted to make sure she'd jumped the ditch so that she'll hopefully go over it at the tetrathlon. But what about you? How on earth did you end up in the water jump?"

Amber explained how Molly had locked on to Pink and been so determined to catch her, she'd tried to jump over the whole thing.

"You're joking? I'm so sorry. When I realised you'd caught me up, I was chuffed as I knew it meant you must be clear. And I thought it was probably a good thing – if Molly was in any doubt about going into that disgusting water, she'd use Pink as a lead and follow." Emily looked genuinely stricken. "But it's because of me you didn't get a clear!"

"No, it's not your fault. It's this *stupid* pony's."

Emily's head snapped around in shock at Amber's words.

"Stupid? Amber, I know coming off in the water wasn't part of the plan, but surely you're pleased with her? It was her first go at cross-country and if it hadn't been for me, she'd have gone clear." She continued staring at Amber, who had her eyes fixed on the ground. "She jumped the steps and the awful ditch and that new wall – did you see it? It's enormous now!"

Amber didn't reply. She was concentrating on holding in the sob that was threatening to escape, and it was burning her throat.

"Look, I know you're disappointed now but we'll look back at this in the future and laugh our heads off. It'll be a brilliant story to tell people…" Emily trailed off, not knowing what else to say as she saw a tear roll down Amber's cheek and drip off her chin. They rode through the gate into the trailer park in silence.

"Er, I need to get ready for the show jumping. See you later?"

Amber nodded and rode away.

Back at her own trailer, she slithered soggily from the saddle and was immediately enveloped in a fierce hug. Mrs Anderson pulled her close and fought the tears that were stinging her own eyes.

"I'm so sorry, doll. You were fantastic. You didn't deserve to have that happen."

Amber's reply was muffled against her mother's chest.

"Sorry, what?" She released her hold slightly and looked down at her daughter.

"I'm so useless!" Amber sobbed.

"What? Of course you're not useless. What a silly thing to say."

"I am." Amber dragged the back of a wet, muddy glove across her eyes, making her face even wetter. "That was a disaster. I can't ride Molly. I'm not good enough for her. She'd be better off with someone else. Someone who's not crap like me."

Mrs Anderson looked despairingly at her husband, stood holding Molly beside her.

"You are not crap." He said firmly, reaching out and putting a hand on Amber's shoulder. "You're just learning how to do all this and it's not easy. It's been hard for you, getting going with Molly, but she's had problems that have been nothing to do with you and more to do with a huge change in routine and a saddle that clearly didn't fit her. She's frightened you and we thought we'd be better off selling her and letting you stick with Honey, but you've kept on trying. You've listened and learned and worked so hard with her. We're so proud of your determination, Amber. We know you've been terrified, but you haven't given up."

He took his hand off Amber's shoulder and ran it over his greying hair. "But you don't need to be constantly fighting and feeling scared. If you want to sell Molly and go back to Honey, and even go back to just hacking out, that's fine. You don't need to do all this for our benefit. It's supposed to be fun."

Amber let his words sink in. They *were* proud of her. Despite the fact that she was standing there soaking wet and stinking, they were proud of her. She looked at Molly and realised that Emily was right. Just a few months ago, the idea of doing cross-country on Molly had seemed impossible, but now, here they were. And apart from a freak incident, the pony hadn't put a foot wrong. She'd even helped Amber out when she'd ridden badly at the wall. Amber reached out and stroked Molly's blaze. The idea of selling her or giving up was out of the question.

"Amber!" Jo was running towards her, looking odd in her riding jacket, shirt and tie and hat, combined with pyjama bottoms and jodhpur boots. "Emily told me what happened. I've just finished my show jumping, so you can borrow my jodhpurs. They're dry." She held them out, earnestly, waiting for Amber to take them. There was no 'if you're doing the show jumping,' from Jo. Even as Amber paused, Jo continued holding the jodhpurs out to her, fully expecting Amber to carry on and complete the competition.

Slowly, Amber reached out and took Jo's offering. "Thanks." She smiled, then laughed at her friend's appearance and pictured her attending the prize-giving dressed as she was now. She quickly dived into the trailer and changed. It was difficult to get the new jodhs on as her legs were damp and clammy. It was like trying to get changed after swimming, but she managed to wriggle her way into them. They were a bit long but she turned the bottoms up. Her socks were still soaking and she had to put her wet boots back on, but at least she was now partly dry.

Her body protector had kept most of her upper half dry so by the time she got back into her riding jacket, she looked much less like a swamp creature. She pulled her hoody out of the car and used it to wipe her saddle dry.

"Right," she said to Jo and her parents. "I've got a round of show jumping to do. Let's go."

– Twenty-One –

Snakes and Ladders

Now that she had nothing to lose, Amber could relax. The sixty-five penalties she'd picked up from her fall on the cross-country meant she was out of the running for a place and this gave her the freedom to ride like she was in the paddock at home. Gone was the robotic Amber of the morning. She had wet knickers, soggy socks and had made local Pony Club history by being the only rider who had ever landed in the water jump here – the most disgusting water jump anyone had ever seen. She had nothing to lose. And so, when her number was called and she rode into the show jumping arena, she could truly imagine herself as a top eventer, triumphing in the face of adversity. If it was good enough for Princess Anne, it was good enough for her.

She knew that Chelsea and Emily had managed to show jump clear, and even Jo had only picked up four faults on the notoriously careless Merry, but rather than being intimidated by the fact, she was inspired by it. Although the tetrathlon, their team event, didn't feature show jumping, it would still help to make them feel like a united team if they could all do well in one phase today.

The whistle blew and Molly reacted without needing a signal from Amber. She knew what it meant and wanted to get started. The pony had gotten bored with constant show jumping year after year, summer and winter with no rest, but she'd found her recent break from work even duller. Now, combined with a comfortable saddle that didn't nip her when she lifted her shoulders, and the introduction of a new activity into her life, she felt invigorated. The cross-country made her feel alive and free and she was starting to get used to this new rider. This girl was much less decisive and assured than her last rider, which worried her sometimes, but Molly appreciated her gentleness and compassion.

She'd helped the girl out at a fence earlier, despite feeling the lack of commitment and trust, and was rewarded with a glorious glow of gratitude from her. That, combined with the sudden appearance of a pony in front of her, had made her blood surge so much, she'd been unable to listen to her rider's instructions. The result of that had shocked and unsettled her, reminding her that taking matters into her own hooves was not always a good idea. And so, although she reacted instinctively to the whistle, she waited for Amber to direct her.

Their round was smooth, effortless and without a fault. As they cleared the final fence and cantered easily through the finish, the crowd roared. She heard whistles, whoops and wild applause. Still cantering around the arena, stroking Molly's mane lovingly, an array of smiling faces blurred together like melting wax as her eyes misted over. "Good lass," she spoke softly to her pony as they left the arena, applause still ringing in her ears. "I'm sorry I called you stupid.

You're not stupid at all, you're brilliant. I'm the stupid one."

Amber let Jo have her jodhpurs back for the presentation as she wasn't placed so could put her tracky bottoms back on, but Jo had come fourth so couldn't go to the presentation in her pyjamas. First and second place went to members of Brantfort Pony Club. "Their ponies are used to this course. They practise on it all the time," Emily whispered cynically. Chelsea had come third. She'd jumped the alternative at the ditch and rails. Skylark had proved to be unreliable at the ditch here in the past so Chelsea had decided not to risk it. She'd picked up fifteen penalties, but her excellent dressage score helped her to stay ahead of Jo and Merry. They'd only had four jumping faults but their dressage hadn't been as good, dropping Jo into fourth. Finally, a girl and boy Amber had seen before but didn't know, from another club in the county, took fifth and sixth place and got the orange and purple rosettes. Several riders had been eliminated on the cross-country, meaning that Emily and Amber finished in seventh and eighth respectively, though there were no rosettes for them.

They waited for the final presentation of the Open class, but the new DC had an unexpected announcement to make.

"Erm, hem, hem," she began, "ladies and gentlemen, before we go on to the Open class results, there's an additional prize I'd like to present." Riders, mothers, fathers and helpers looked at each other in surprise, wondering what the additional prize would be.

"It isn't one we usually present... in fact, we've just made it up today, in the light of certain...er...events." She chuckled nervously as she turned and picked up a bunch of hastily bought petrol station flowers from the table of trophies and rosettes. "I apologise that it isn't something better but we didn't know we'd be doing this today." Pausing for effect, she looked around at the expectant faces, pleased to see they were hanging on her every word. Blushing slightly, she scanned the audience until her eyes settled on Amber.

"We'd like to present these to… Amber Anderson. Come on Amber!"

Amber spluttered like a fish and turned as pink as a cooked lobster. "Me? Wha…?" Her parents pushed her forward so that everyone could see her. Mrs Winnaker, the DC reached for her hand and pulled her into the middle of the presentation area. "Don't be shy Amber. These are for you." The flowers were handed to her and Mrs Winnaker put her arm around Amber. To everyone else, it looked like a warm embrace. Only the most observant would have seen Mrs Winnaker's grip tighten as she tried to prevent Amber from running away.

Amber felt like a butterfly pinned to a board, with all eyes on her, boring into her. She squirmed under Mrs Winnaker's grip and tried to slide back into the crowd, but Mrs Winnaker held on.

"Hang on, hang on! She's trying to run away!" She said, and the audience tittered. "I just want to say that…well, you've been an inspiration today. To remount and complete the course after taking a ducking in our swamp was impressive enough but to then go on and complete the event with a clear round show jumping…well, just remarkable. And we just wanted to say…well done!"

Amber wished she could teleport right out of there but when Mrs Winnaker released her to use both hands to join with the applause, she made do with sidling back towards her friends and family, grateful when everyone's attention returned to the prize-giving for the final class.

***

For a few days afterwards, Amber was stiff and sore. Considering she'd been wearing a body protector and had a soft landing, she couldn't understand where all the aches and pains came from. She also couldn't work out why she had a large mottled bruise all over her left forearm.

As well as the physical aches and pains, Amber's brain was worn out too as she see-sawed between the dizzying high of Molly's success at jumping, and the sinking low of the disastrous ending to the cross-country. She could accept that it was a mistake and was unlikely to happen again, but that didn't stop her from replaying the memory in her mind.

It bothered Amber that she'd only managed to ride well at the end, in the show jumping, because she knew she was no longer in the competition so her result didn't matter. *I really can't handle pressure*, she thought. She'd decided at Pony Club camp the previous summer that she wasn't interested in chasing trophies and rosettes – so long as she felt pleased with her own performance, she didn't care whether she won or not. She still felt like that, so couldn't work out why she got so nervous. *Is it the fear of falling off and getting hurt, or it all going wrong and making a fool of myself in front of everyone? Is it because I don't want to let Molly down and not be worthy of her?* Amber suspected all the reasons were valid, but with the local inter-branch tetrathlon not far away, she also knew she was terrified of letting the team down. In her sleep, she dreamed of making a series of catastrophic errors in every phase that meant she was by far the discount score. Amber was seriously considering telling her parents that she wanted to pull out.

They were acting very strangely too. Whenever she saw them, they gave her big grins and patted her on the head or shoulder like she was a dog or horse they were pleased with. She pouted, trying to work out whether they were genuine about being proud of her or…if they were trying too hard and pretending.

A ride out with Jo did nothing to allay her fears. Neither of them had attended Blakefield's Easter Monday gymkhana as both girls were giving their mounts a few days' rest, so Amber rode Pearl and Jo came out on her brother's pony, Sam. He hadn't competed yesterday as Matthew refused to learn a dressage test. Jo chattered away as usual, with Amber barely listening.

"Are you listening to me?" Jo asked.

"What Jo? Yes, sorry…?"

"I knew you weren't. I was just saying about calling me JoJo from now on."

"Er, what?" Amber realised she must have been somewhere else entirely. She had no idea what her friend was talking about.

"Well, everyone at school, even the teachers, have started calling me JoJo, 'cos I'm Joanne Jones. And it's cool, so I want you to call me JoJo too."

"Oh, right, yeah," Amber muttered. It was bad enough that Jo actually was cool, now she had a cool name as well. Her only nickname had been Amber Pamber which her parents had called her when she was young. She had banned them from using it when she started school as it was so cringey. If people started using her initials as a nickname, she'd be AA. She didn't know which was worse.

"What's wrong with you?" JoJo interrupted her thoughts. "You seem a bit down. You're not disappointed about the weekend, are you? Things can go wrong on the cross-country – that's what makes it so exciting. But your show jumping was fab. I couldn't believe it was you to be honest, when I think back to that first time in our paddock with Pearl. You'll be brill in the tetrathlon now that Molly has seen the course. You'll go clear for sure."

"Hmmm." Amber appreciated JoJo's encouraging words but wasn't convinced.

"Yeah, it's in the bag. You'll just need to practise opening gates and doing the slip rail so you don't pick up any penalties from those." JoJo kicked her feet out of the stirrups and let her legs dangle by

Sam's side. They were so long now; her feet were level with his knees.

"What?" Amber was suddenly alert. "We have to open a gate? Why?" An image of the last time she'd tried to open a gate on Molly flashed before her eyes: her lying broken on the ground while the pony galloped off and left her there, alone.

"Yeah. Didn't you know?" JoJo's blue eyes were wide. "It's in the rulebook online." Amber shook her head. They'd been told about the rulebook but she hadn't got around to reading it yet. She'd assumed the adults would make sure they knew everything they needed to.

"On the cross-country, riders have to open a gate, mounted. You can't get off to do it. Well, you can, but I think you get two-hundred penalties. You've got to open it, go through and close it again within a minute or it's fifty penalties. And then somewhere else on the course, there'll be a slip rail. For that, you've got to get off, take down the top rail, get yourself and the pony over the bottom rail, put the top one back up and get back on. You've got one minute to get the top rail put back and remount. I'm sure that's right. And it's fifty penalties if you don't get it done in time."

Fear flared in Amber's mind like a peacock's tail at the mention of dismounting and remounting an excited pony that didn't want to stand around waiting for her rider.

"Can you have help? Can someone hold the pony for you?" *So it doesn't take-off while you're trying to get on*, she added to herself.

"Er…no." JoJo sensed Amber's apprehension. "If anyone helps you, you get penalties. Sixty, I think. But you'll be fine. You just need to practise. Maybe you should try learning to vault on like I do. It's way easier, especially as you'll have your stirrups shorter than usual on the cross-country." With that, she slipped off Sam's left side and as soon as her feet touched the ground, she bounced and leapt back on, almost going straight over the other side, as he was much smaller than Merry.

Amber knew the trick was designed to lighten the mood and make her smile, but it didn't work. She completed the ride in near silence, tuning JoJo out as she continued chattering about this and that. By the time they returned to the farm track and she dropped JoJo at her place, Amber realised with a sinking feeling that she had two choices: she could either ride Honey in the tetrathlon as she had always planned to, or she could drop out. That way she could either be replaced or the team could compete without her as a three. But riding Molly was no longer an option. The very idea of having to remount her in an open space where she could see other ponies whizzing around was out of the question. Look at what had just happened when Molly had seen another pony in front of her. Amber's hands trembled at the mere thought of it.

I'm back to square one, she thought miserably as she rode back into the farmyard on Pearl. The first sight that greeted her was Molly's beautiful face looking over her stable door, her white blaze flashing in the sun. A tear rolled down Amber's cheek as the revelation settled on her like a deadly snowstorm and chilled her to the bone.

Molly wasn't the pony for her.

She leaned forward and buried her face in Pearl's mane, the tears falling unchecked into the rough blackness. Pearl remained still, sensing her rider's anguish and feeling the sobs that wracked her body. *I'm still afraid of her*, Amber admitted to herself. I'm such a failure.

Oh, Pearl, what am I going to do?

As if she understood, Pearl snorted. It was like she was trying to answer, but whatever she might have been saying, Amber wasn't listening. The snakes in her stomach had returned, writhing, hissing and slithering up into her throat, choking her. Another sob escaped through her gritted teeth and Molly pricked her ears towards the sound. Through her cloudy eyes, Amber noticed how serene Molly looked, gazing over her door happily. But the warm wave of love that enveloped her was stabbed with a splinter of ice as the memory of lying painfully in the mud while the pony abandoned her jumped back into her mind. She was brilliant, beautiful and talented: all the traits anyone would want in a pony. But the most important thing, the thing she had with both of the Fell ponies, was missing, and without it there could be no future for them: trust.

She didn't trust Molly and without trust…end of story.

Author's Note

When I got Molly, aged thirteen, it was with competitions in mind. I wanted to compete with the riders I saw winning and have a chance against them. In Molly I saw a pony who could get me to where I wanted to be. What I didn't see was that I wasn't ready for her.

It's funny how you can learn lessons in life, but not apply them to other situations. From Pearl, I learned that ponies are all individuals, yet I didn't look for anything in Molly beyond her ability. From Honey I learned that pony and rider need to be a team, but I expected Molly to carry me to victory, despite the fact that I was still quite inexperienced. I wanted her to be the perfect pony. The problem is, there's no such thing.

Molly was as different to the Fell ponies I'd had before her as it was possible to be. We had a lot of problems and it affected my confidence. At the time, I felt that everything was her fault, but now looking back I can see that the problems were due to us being mismatched at the start of our relationship. If we had met several years later, when I had more experience of different ponies under my belt, things could have been a lot different.

I don't want to say too much more as Molly's story isn't over – it will continue in the fourth book – but I do wish I could apologise to her as I must have been a huge cause of frustration to her! Not that she was blameless – she did gallop off with me while I was mounting her and left me with a broken collarbone and she did go for a play on the bypass after somehow escaping from her field.

And, of course, she did dump me in the foulest water jump ever after trying to jump the whole thing. I got back on and finished but I didn't have someone to lend me a nice pair of dry jodhs. I completed my show jumping round that day covered in mud and slime. I thought if I wrote that in the book, readers would think it was too far-fetched, but sometimes the truth is stranger than fiction!

Acknowledgements

I'll start with huge thanks to all the readers and reviewers of the 'Amber's Pony Tales' books. Some have left reviews on Amazon, some have contacted me directly and some have done both! It's always amazing to hear from people of all ages who have enjoyed the books and I really appreciate the time people take to get in touch and share their comments. It means such a lot.

My appreciation also goes out to those who got involved with competitions and activities connected to the books. Marlyn and Isobel have found themselves with characters named after them in this book for entering the 'Little Pearl' writing competition, as have Maia and Elise for being beta readers and providing valuable pre-publication feedback on the unedited version of this story. To everyone who got involved with the cover star competition for this book: thank you. Hundreds of pictures were received but as the series' first two book covers (supplied by Let's Get Booked) are so incredible, the standard was very high so only the very best pictures were accepted. Many people who submitted photographs, but were not successful, still wished me luck in my search for the perfect pony to represent Molly and their positivity was beautiful. As was Strawberry, the eventual winner of the competition, who you can now see on the cover of this book. Big thanks to Myla Postlethwaite-Todd and her mum, Kate, for entering her.

For the cover of this book, I owe lots of Glenfiddich to Neil Routledge for his photography skills and I need to send a box of Galaxy bars over to Amanda Horan in Ireland for her services once again with cover design, editing and preparing this book in every way for publication.

To the teachers who've invited me in to schools to work with their students, I thank you for supporting me as an author and for promoting reading and writing to your students. I love working with children and some that I've met through author visits are definitely potential authors-in-the-making.

And finally, Katy for proof reading and Perrin for helping me to promote the books and reach more people. Thank you.

About the Author

Helen lives in Cumbria with her husband and horses, plus Bella the Dalmatian, Petra the crazy pointer and a variety of hens, ducks and geese.

Helen has been animal mad all her life. Her adventures with ponies began back in 1990 with Pearl and Honey, but they are still continuing now with her three horses, Maddy, Charlie and Holly who are all just as interesting and individual as Pearl and Honey were, and will probably end up in a book in the future too! Watch out for them.

Maddy is the old lady of the herd, and the cheeky one. She's full of personality and mischief. She's got herself into more trouble over the years than all the rest of the horses put together. She's semi-retired now, but still enjoys hacking out.

Then there's Charlie, the opinionated one, who thinks he's a thoroughbred racehorse but was sadly born into the body of a draft horse. He loves jumping, beach rides and charging about on cross-country courses.

Finally, there's Holly, who's a sensitive girl but with plenty of sass too!

When Helen isn't busy writing books or playing with horses, she can be found being a libress (something a student once called her – perhaps an appropriate title for a librarian who has been known to roar on occasion) and English teacher at a secondary school in the Lake District. She also writes books with children through her Writers & Illustrators club. They write as a team under the pseudonym K.S. Aitken.

For free bonus material linked to these books, plus news, competitions, and exclusive opportunities connected to the author's other books, sign up to the mailing list at www.helenharaldsen.co.uk

Did you enjoy this book? The author would love to see your reviews on Amazon. Please feel free to post your comments and let others know about Amber's Pony Tales.

Follow Amber's Pony Tales on Facebook.

Look out for the next books in the

Amber's Pony Tales series.

For more information go to:

www.helenharaldsen.co.uk

Printed in Great Britain
by Amazon